CHAPTER 1

JASON

WE'RE LED DOWN A LONG, brightly lit hallway, the walls littered with artwork. Not Picassos, Rembrandts, and Monets. The artists are patients of the institution. Our escort, Kristen, a sprightly, young woman in nurse's garb, plays tour guide on our journey to Matthew's room.

"This is our recreation area," she points out as we approach a large, window-lined room at the end of the corridor.

A ping pong and pool table occupy the center of the deserted room, surrounded by tables. A bookcase, adjacent to the sliding glass door leading outside, houses board games and coloring supplies.

Beyond the game room lies a grassy yard, bordered by shady oak trees. A couple of folks play badminton, a few seem engrossed in a game of croquet, with a handful of others scattered across the grounds. With one of the hottest summers on record for Vermont behind us, it's a good time to be outdoors.

Despite limited exposure to mental instability, I'm surprised by the lack of people in straitjackets, muttering to themselves.

"Activities are optional but encouraged," Kristen explains. "Many patients suffer from boredom, a lack of motivation, and depression. We promote getting them up and about, being engaged, and purposeful. We only administer medication after exhausting alternatives."

My girlfriend, Tess, and I nod our approval, with Tess saying,

"That's great." Stealing a last glimpse of the grounds before rounding the corner to another hallway, she adds, "It's beautiful here."

"There are various meetings, ranging from support groups to addiction therapy. There's a medical staff presence at these sessions, but a great deal of latitude is granted. We foster patient interaction and the sharing of feelings and experiences. Patients often feel alone. Listening to others in similar circumstances can be cathartic."

I'm sure she has delivered this spiel a thousand times, but her pride in the facility laces her words. Finally arriving at Matthew's room, we thank Kristen as she heads back toward the lobby.

A distinct body odor aroma invades my senses as Tess and I walk past Matthew's sleeping roommate. Cleansing, like participation in activities, must be optional. Matthew, my kid brother, has the window bunk. His bed is partially reclined, his TV on, volume muted, his face expressionless. A barely perceptible body movement is the only indication he knows we're here.

"Hey bro." I pull up a cushiony chair to within inches of Matthew's bed. Tess grabs a twin chair, joining me in the front row.

Matthew appears haggard, his good looks obscured by unruly facial hair and dark circles below his eyes.

"Hi Jason. Hi Tess."

His voice lacks inflection. Lacks enthusiasm. His body language reads listless. He turns his head in our direction, but he's more looking through us than at us.

"So, how are they treating you here?" I ask.

"All right."

I strain to hear his softly spoken words. "This place isn't bad. You check out the game room yet? Wanna shoot some pool?"

"Nah. I'm kind of tired."

I interpret tired as depressed. Unless you're an insomniac, there's no reason to be tired here. No responsibilities, and a bed as home base, add up to plenty of opportunities for sleep. His head vacillates back in the direction of the TV. He stares into space.

Matthew has become a shell of his former self, unrecognizable. His zest for life a memory.

Tess leans forward, elbows on knees, willing Matthew to snap out of it. She pleads with him, without uttering a word. A smart tactic, given the results of my verbal approach.

During a minute or so of awkward silence, I divert my eyes to the ceiling tiles in an attempt to maintain composure. Then I wrap an arm around my brother's neck.

"Everything's gonna be okay, Matthew." I find myself fighting off tears.

I'm reassuring myself as much as him. I want to shake him, to awaken the real Matthew. We separate, and he pats my back.

"Thanks, bro. You too, Tess. Thanks for coming by. I'll be fine. Really."

This is our signal to leave. Tess stands, bends over Matthew, and kisses him on the cheek. "Take care, Matthew. We love you."

She's crying as she rests her head on his chest.

"Hang in there, bro." I extend my hand for a fist bump. "I'll be back. And next time I'm dragging your ass to the pool room."

A small smile escapes Matthew's lips. Our fists collide as he responds, "Bye, guys."

Tess and I return to our apartment, following a quiet forty-five minute drive back from the Dover Psychiatric Institute. The sadness I've been feeling since seeing Matthew today has turned to anger. This is nothing new. Since Matthew's release from prison ten days ago, my emotions have been oscillating between the two states. Tess calls me into the kitchen, where she deposits two plates of tuna salad with potato chips on the table.

"Babe, you've got to stop torturing yourself," Tess says. "The doctors say he'll be fine. We just have to give him some time." She adds, optimistically.

I circle the table a couple of times before taking a seat. "How much time? He'll never be the carefree, outgoing, enthusiastic, innocent kid he was. Getting violated in a jail cell isn't something you recover from."

Tess slides her chair closer to mine, and puts a soothing hand on my knee as I continue.

"This isn't right. Matthew takes a few sips of alcohol and winds up in the slammer, where life as he knows it goes *poof.* How can a nineteen-year-old kid be old enough to get prosecuted as an adult, yet too young to drink? And Chang, the man responsible for all this, the asshole who calls the cops, gets portrayed as a good guy, a guy doing his part to clean up the streets. He doesn't care what happens to Matthew, what the consequences of his actions are."

I pause, to take a couple of bites of my sandwich. Tess allows me to vent without interruption.

"And this is justice? Our legal system in action? A snitch and an inept defense lawyer add up to a kindhearted kid getting thrown to the wolves."

Tess busies herself pouring iced tea into glasses. "I know. I know," she says softly, her gaze drifting away, her mind likely wandering to memories of our joint family outings.

I've known Tess since I was eight, when a friendship between our moms led to barbecues and backyard playdates. Matthew and I hit it off right away with Tess and her sister, Tina. Matthew and Tina are the same age, four years younger than Tess and me.

There must be retribution. With Matthew too weak for vengeance, I need to even the score. I casually finish off the remainder of my lunch, as my inner thoughts flow and crystalize into the beginning of a plan. Aware that my attention has wandered, Tess asks what I'm thinking. I tell her.

Slamming down the pitcher of tea, Tess's voice turns stern. "What are you talking about, Jason? Even the score how?"

"I'm going to disrupt Chang's life."

The color fades in Tess's face. "Disrupt?" she asks cautiously.

"Yeah. Scare him a little. Make him feel pain. Let him know he can't play God without repercussions."

Tess is the one pacing now, while I'm at ease, having verbalized thoughts running through my mind all week. She appeals to logic.

"This isn't a good idea. It's not gonna help Matthew. It might make you feel better about yourself, but it won't change Matthew's situation. And it could land you in trouble with the law. Wouldn't your energies be better served concentrating on rehabilitation rather than retaliation?"

Tess has ethics. Her resistance doesn't surprise me. I stand, responding calmly.

"I'm responsible for Matthew. You know we didn't have a father around. It's just me, my mom, and Matthew. I'm supposed to be his protector. I can't stand by idly. What kind of man would that make me?"

Tess seizes my hands and speaks in a whisper.

"I know you've had to assume a protective fatherly role, but Matthew wouldn't approve of this. Neither would your mom. Isn't there another way for you to get peace of mind?"

"There isn't. And yes, I have been thinking a lot about this. I'm working on a plan. You're a part of the plan."

"I don't want to end up in jail."

"I need to do this so I can carry on with my life. So we can carry on with our lives together. If I don't do this, if I don't stand up for my brother, I'll never forgive myself."

We embrace, my head resting on her shoulder, both of us exhausted. After a while, I break the silence, talking into her ear.

"Will you help me if I take the rap?"

CHAPTER 2
JASON

One month later...

I'M AT THE PEKING DRAGON, enjoying a nice meal. It's the height of the lunch hour. Patrons and workers mill about, a buzz of chatter fills the room. The dimly lit atmosphere works in my favor. The back corner booth affords me a strategic view.

My face is covered with eye black, the charcoal-like stuff football players apply under their eyes to reduce glare from sunlight and stadium lighting. A costume-store-purchased fat belt transforms my physique from lean to pillow soft. Three-inch heeled hiking boots, hidden beneath my jeans, deceive my actual height. My chestnut brown hair, dyed black, along with blue contact lenses masking my brown eyes, complete the disguise. I barely recognize myself.

Pushing aside a bowl of wonton soup, I place my elbows on the table as my eyes follow Tess's movements. Even with an auburn wig concealing her long, silky, jet black hair, she is beautiful. Olive skinned, full lipped, and shapely, she stands out in a crowd, despite an affinity for blending in. Posing as a waitress, she hangs around the swinging double doors leading to the kitchen, a popular spot for servers waiting for their orders to be up. Dressed like the real waitresses, holding the requisite prop, a serving tray, she's playing her part to perfection.

While projecting a calm exterior, I'm consumed with nervous

energy. I'm running on adrenaline, pushing aside the second thoughts creeping into my psyche. Despite all the planning and anticipation, sitting here now, with it all on the precipice of coming to fruition, the finality of the situation is overwhelming.

Tess makes brief eye contact with me, before returning her gaze to the front entrance. I turn around to glance out the window, relieved at the sight of my scam in action. Moments later, the mark, as in gullible sucker, waltzes in, gift in hand. Tess walks toward him, simplifying his search, as the two of them nearly collide. Following a brief interaction, the guy heads for the exit.

I inconspicuously rise from my booth, wipe my mouth clean of Mongolian beef remnants, and saunter towards the restroom. En route, I brush past Tess. The gift—a sterling silver letter opener with a Bowie knife-like serrated edge—smoothly passes from one set of gloved hands to another. Tess strolls to the rear exit, a mere ten minutes since her arrival.

Without breaking stride, I proceed to the proprietor's office, away from the commotion of the dining area, where Michael Chang, adhering to routine, takes refuge. I enter the room, closing and locking the door behind me.

This guy lives too well. The office is huge. The asshole grins smugly, leaned back in his tan, leather recliner, his feet up on his mahogany desk. A renewed anger floods over me. The walls are cluttered with ugly, and no doubt expensive, paintings. And he has a mini refrigerator. *Really?* He must make Tess's co-workers deliver him meals from the kitchen.

I pull my iPod out of my pocket, bring up the rock playlist, hit play, and crank the volume way up. AC/DC riffs fill the room and will drown out the imminent screaming. I figure I have two minutes max before someone tires of that blaring rock 'n roll crap.

"May I help you? What the hell? Who are you?" Chang's rapid fire questions, each with increased urgency, go unanswered. He has his desk phone pressed to his ear, his fingers primed to press buttons, as I get to him.

Taking the shortest route by lunging over his desk, I swat away the phone with my left forearm, swiftly followed by a right cross to his face. Grabbing him by his dress shirt collar, I hoist him onto the desk, banging the back of his head against the timber surface.

Chang, being small in stature, facilitates my ability to manhandle him. I'm six feet even, about 180 after a double cheesecake. Am I Rocky Balboa? No. Am I stronger than I look? Absolutely. Pit me against the average guy on the street and I like my chances.

He kicks his legs into my lower body, while swinging his arms and contorting his body wildly, all to no avail.

"What do you want? I have money in my wallet. Take it."

Ignoring his plea, I stab him in the chest with the letter opener.

"Matthew Rincon. Remember him?" I wind up for another strike.

"No! No! I don't know him. You've... got... the wrong... guy." His response is interrupted by another penetrating blow, this time right of center, a full-force stab, puncturing a lung.

"Wrong answer, fucker!" My infuriation level rises with the knowledge Matthew was merely a fly to Chang. An annoyance he had swatted away.

I continue dispersing blows of excruciating pain, moving down from the heart and lung region, to the stomach area, inflicting damage to more vital organs, targeting the spleen, liver, and kidneys. Each successive thrust brings more blood, and less resistance.

Chang's movement has ceased. He's silent and appears unconscious. For good measure, I administer several more stabs into his chest cavity. My desire for Michael Chang to experience a slow and torturous death is realized, my weapon of choice being well suited for the occasion.

Convinced the bastard is history, I leave the corpse spread eagle on the desk, soaked in blood. Droplets drip off the desk's edge onto the floor, as I turn off the music and hurry to the door, closing it behind me. I race to the restaurant's rear exit, toss the letter opener in a dumpster just beyond the back door, where it will undoubtedly get discovered, dash to my car, and am off in a flash.

CHAPTER 3
PETER

I'M SCARFING A SLICE OF homemade pumpkin pie, washing it down with coffee, when a promo for the eleven o'clock evening news airs. The anchorman teases with a murder at the Peking Dragon restaurant.

Whoa. I was at the Peking Dragon today. I sit up straighter on the couch. The anchor says to stay tuned for details following regularly scheduled programming. My curiosity piqued, I scrap web-surfing plans in favor of the local news, coming up in five minutes.

They lead off with the murder. Michael Chang, the restaurant's owner, was pronounced dead at the scene. His picture fills the screen. I've never seen the guy. He's Asian, with a full head of jet black hair and a distinguished, if not handsome, face. His life has been cut short at the age of forty-four. I'm stunned by this report. I feel a connection to him, due to my presence there. How could this happen in a nice neighborhood? The estimated time of death is three pm.

My palms are moist, and I'm shaking. The time aligns with when I was there. The camera switches to a cop who says there are no suspects yet. I'm about to turn off the tube, thinking the story is over, when the anchor adds a detail. Multiple stabs wounds caused Chang's death.

My heart thunders. This can't be. I advance toward the TV, my face inches away. I'm hoping to see a picture of the murder weapon, but as is typical of police holding back information early in an investigation, none is forthcoming.

———————⟡———————

I'm sitting motionless at my kitchen table, staring out the large bay window overlooking my apartment building's parking lot. I'm not looking at anything in particular. My vision blurs to the point where focusing on a given object, even one a few feet in front of me, is a daunting task. I've been in this catatonic-like state for the past hour. Or has it been longer? My typically acute perception of time is way off. Everything about me is way off.

It's dark outside, the sun's appearance still an hour or so away. The lights are off, but I haven't slept. Reality presses down on me, stealing my breath. I can trace my predicament to one word. *Sure*, uttered in response to a friend's request, shortly before Chang took his last breath. A solitary word. *Sure*. If only I had replied *no* instead. Or asked for time to think it over.

Time to consider the possible consequences.

———————⟡———————

Rap! Rap! Rap! It takes a moment to register that the source of the annoying noise is a pounding at my door. The sun has just risen over the horizon. I check my peephole. Two men in off-the-rack suits. My heartbeat races. My hope for Jehovah's Witnesses ends with the synchronized yell of "Homicide, open the door!" Sensing impatience, and figuring the suits are armed, I do as I'm told.

"You Peter Garrison?" barks the taller, meaner one.

Before I can respond, the shorter cop, who looks like a kid out of high school, cuffs me. Meanwhile, the barker reads me my rights.

I'm being arrested for the murder of Michael Chang. The kid spits in my face as he tells me I'd better get myself a damn good lawyer. Once I'm cuffed, the barker throws me against the wall for good measure—not hard enough to leave a mark, but hard enough so I'll feel it afterward.

These guys must have ditched the police brutality seminar. They seem convinced they have their killer. They don't.

"Look, I didn't do it, I'm a lawyer. I believe in upholding the law. I'm not the type of guy to kill someone," I plead.

"Save it for the judge," snaps the barker.

I've just been photographed, fingerprinted, and stripped of my clothes in favor of an orange jumpsuit. I'm sitting in a holding cell at the county jail, along with about twenty other misfits in matching outfits. I can't be certain, but am guessing I'm the only lawyer of the bunch. Not that I consider myself above anyone.

A prison guard enters the bullpen, seizes my arm, and says I may now make the phone call I requested three hours ago. I look up from my overpriced shoes, which I've stared at since my unceremonious deposit into the new digs, and the guard leads me on a journey to a telephone. I should clarify: the back of the line for the telephone.

Twenty minutes later, I'm dialing Hank's number. My back-stabbing friend Hank. The guy who got me into this nightmare. I haven't been able to reach him since he framed me for murder, so I'm not optimistic that he'll answer this time. I'm greeted by a recording informing me the number has been disconnected. Sweat pours off my forehead. My fingers tremble as I try his workplace. A co-worker says Hank resigned this morning.

Wonderful. Looks like my *buddy* has bolted town.

CHAPTER 4
JASON

I'M DRIVING DUE WEST, STRAIGHT through the night again, putting as much distance as I can between myself and Quincy, Vermont. The first twenty plus hours on the road had me traveling south, to Georgia. The open windows and blasting radio in my sky blue '64 Ford Mustang keep me awake. That and the lingering rush of adrenaline coursing through my veins.

I'm the reason they hung a *Closed* sign on the front door at Peking Dragon. With the deed now done, my feelings are mixed. I'm surprised how easy it was for me to kill Chang. I had worried about hesitating or changing my mind, but anger carried me through. Even though the guy who sent Matthew to prison is dead, my brother is still a mess. And now I have to deal with my actions. I'm consoled by the notion that Chang's death will ultimately help Matthew get better faster.

I'm cruise controlled in at eighty-four, nine miles over the posted seventy-five mph speed limit. Most pigs will give you ten miles. I balance the probability of an unwanted encounter with the cops against my desire for a fast getaway.

My mind turns to memories of Matthew. The two of us were inseparable as kids. Racing through our neighborhood on bikes, climbing trees, wrestling. Teaming up to take on the Grimly brothers in backyard snowball fights.

On the last night of Matthew's prison stint, Bruno, his six-foot-four, two-hundred-fifty-plus-pound bunkmate, decided my brother wasn't going to leave hell without a parting remembrance. He ripped off a section of his prison-issued shirt, using it to gag Matthew. The full weight of one arm strategically pressed against the back of Matthew's neck was all Bruno needed to combat resistance. Matthew's flailing leg kicks offered no defense against the onslaught. It was fast. It was rough. It was disgusting. By the time Matthew's muzzled screams resonated in the ears of a guard, my kid brother's clothes were torn and littered on the cell floor. He had been penetrated from behind, violated, and brought to tears.

All because Matthew, leaned up against his car in Chang's parking lot waiting for friends, had a can of beer in his hand. Chang could have simply given my little bro a stern lecture, telling him to get lost. Instead, he opted for punishment.

From there, Matthew's overpriced lawyer did him in. He works for a reputable law firm, and certainly not a cheap one. My mom picked it out, sparing no expense. When my mom and Matthew first met with him, he assured them it would be an open-and-shut case. The worst-case scenario would be performing community service. I hate people who make promises they don't keep. It's like when you ask someone a question. I'd rather be told *I don't know* than be fed a load of crap. The lawyer took it for granted he'd get Matthew off and didn't try hard enough. If my mom had any inkling the guy was incompetent, she would have hired a different attorney. Matthew had himself a real winner in his corner. Clearly, the moron lawyer had to pay. He's bunking with some new buddies these days. I hope he receives the same hospitality my brother did.

The judge bears responsibility as well. He's not exempt from payback, but this requires careful consideration. I need to wait, even a year, so as not to risk anyone seeing a connection.

It's almost four in the afternoon the following day, Saturday. My thoughts wander. Despite never applying myself in high school, as teachers and guidance counselors repeatedly told me, I managed to get decent grades. College wasn't for me, but three years ago, I found my niche, completing an electrician apprenticeship program. I have worked at the same lighting installation company since then. While I didn't love the job and it didn't pay particularly well, the work was meditative and stress free. Dispatched to people's homes, I liked that nobody watched over me, and I didn't really answer to anyone. I turned in my resignation last week. It feels strange not going to work.

Having grown tired of truck stops, yet needing to stretch my limbs and escape the whiz of oncoming traffic, I exit the interstate in search of a more serene setting. A large, green sign informs me I'm entering Salin City Park.

Scenic is the way I'd describe this place, loaded with big shady oak trees. I wander over to one such tree and lean up against its trunk. In a nearby grassy area, a guy wields a baseball bat, a woman lobs in pitches, and their dog plays outfield. In a more distant section of the park, small kids play soccer.

Trapped with only my thoughts for the past twenty hours, watching the mindless activity in the park is therapeutic. I turn my attention back to the baseball game. The guy takes several pathetic-looking swings, before finally sending the ball flying halfway to the pitcher. The canine lies down and starts licking his balls. I yell, "Let the girl hit!" My wisecrack goes unanswered.

Break over. Kicking my mind back into gear, I replay the events of the past twenty-four hours for the umpteenth time. The media calls it the *Quincy tragedy.* Is that the best they can come up with?

Tess: Likely enjoying an in-flight alcoholic beverage about now; her magic carpet ride from JFK to the Cayman Islands took off half an hour ago. She'll arrive a few days before me. My route is less direct.

Hank: Peter's not-so-loyal friend chose the Virgin Islands for his all-expense-paid destination. Has enough cash now to buy a nice-sized boat and start that fishing-expedition chartering business he blabbed incessantly about when we met.

Garrison: He has no clue what hit him. He knows he has been set up, but hasn't put together the *by who* or *why*. He'll still be in the slammer while I'm guzzling Red Stripe beers, dancing on the beach with Tess.

Mom and Matthew: After some time passes, and once Matthew gets released into my mom's custody, the two of them will embark on a one-way trip to the Cayman Islands. Neither my mom nor Matthew know about this part of the plan. My mom thinks I'm taking a little vacation to clear my head. As news of Chang's murder breaks, and as my excursion extends, she'll put two and two together. She'll be angry and will have some strong words for me, but I know I can count on her loyalty.

I rise, taking a couple of long, deep breaths of fresh air, before returning to my 'Stang. Next stop – Dallas/Fort Worth International Airport.

The ringing of my phone disrupts my meditative state.

"What the hell, Jason?"

It's Tess. She's angry. I've anticipated this moment. Simply a matter of when.

"You've heard the news, I take it."

"You killed him? You killed him! What were you thinking? This wasn't the plan."

I've prepared for this conversation, but words elude me.

"Jason? Hello? Are you there? Do you have anything to say?"

Tess is a woman of patience by nature. Now is an exception.

"I'm here, babe. I've been trying to come up with the words to tell you. I wanted to tell you in person. Once we're together in the Cayman Islands. I thought you'd be on the plane by now."

"My plane is delayed, so I gave my mom a call. She mentioned off-handedly how this restaurant owner in Quincy was killed. Wouldn't you know it, the guy is Michael Chang. Please talk to me.

15

And fast. You know, I'm kinda wondering whether hopping on a plane to meet you is the wisest move right now."

My heart races. It's funny because I was calm as a cucumber slicing up Chang. Having deceived Tess bothers me.

"I purposely didn't tell you about the last part of the plan." I'm pacing, circling my car.

I question whether telling her I would merely intimidate and scare Chang was the right thing to do. Neither of us speak for a beat.

"This is unreal. What have you gotten us into?"

Her voice is tranquil now. She's processing, trying to play it out in her mind. How this will end.

"Look, I know this isn't what you bargained for. If you want to bail out, I won't blame you. I love you, and I don't want to be without you, but I'll understand if you're overwhelmed. Think about this though. You did nothing wrong. All you did was hand me a letter opener. Nobody saw you do this. I'm sure of that. You had no knowledge of my intentions to kill."

"And what about you?"

"Me? It's something I'll have to live with. As for getting caught, it's not going to happen. My prints aren't on the murder weapon. There are no witnesses. And I'll be out of the country."

"So you're fine with the lawyer guy taking the rap? It's one thing when the offense was roughing up Chang a little. Can you live with another man serving a life sentence for what you did?"

Her ethical side again. On the plus side, it distracts her from the me-in-jail scenario.

"He'll get off. The evidence against him is circumstantial. He will only be inconvenienced a little. A small price to pay for not getting Matthew off."

"I should have seen this coming. I must be pretty stupid."

"No, I'm the stupid one. Stupid and passionate."

These words linger as we remain silent for a while. Uncertainty momentarily creeps into my mind. Did I do the right thing? I convince myself that I did, but am no longer sure I'll go after the judge in a year. Finally, Tess speaks, in an exhausted tone, saying she needs to let it all sink in. In the meantime, she will take her flight, as planned, and be with me.

"Thanks, babe. We'll talk this whole thing out and proceed however you want. You're the smart one and I trust your judgement."

I'm relieved things are back on track. Everything is going according to plan.

CHAPTER 5
PETER

I'M PUNCHY AND IRRITABLE AS I'm led in handcuffs by a CO—prison speak for Correctional Officer—to meet my counsel. I've just spent the longest two nights of my life. I've learned I wasn't carrying any four-leaf clovers the day of my arrest. Getting booked on a Friday means you aren't getting out until at least Monday. No judge will interrupt a boating expedition or round of golf on account of an inmate not thrilled with his accommodations.

You would think, as a former defense attorney, I'd be capable of retaining counsel for myself. You would be wrong. And, oh yes, I tried. I've seen firsthand the difference a big-shot lawyer makes. I nearly got a bite from an old NYU law school buddy who enjoys bar exams so much he took it three times. Alas, having depleted my savings by paying off student loans, I failed to meet his not-so-modest retainer demand. Guess money trumps old friendships.

Three years into my career, all at the firm of Henderson & Gates, I found my disenchantment with the judicial system reach a breaking point. The politics, the inequities, the manipulation, the grandstanding. I can't reconcile the reality that guilty clients sometimes get off, while innocent ones get put away. High-priced lawyers and technicalities too often play a role in acquitting bad people. The innocent often face the uphill climb associated with the presumption of guilt for getting this far in the process. Feeling like

I wasn't making a difference, and lacking the control and influence I naïvely imagined I'd possess, I quit last month.

In the interim, while deciding upon my next move, I accepted a position for a firm specializing in Probate. What the job—basically distributing a deceased person's property under a will—lacks in excitement, it makes up for in its lack of stress. I'm halfway through my sixty day probationary period. Benefits don't kick in until I'm off probation, nor does my promised salary bump. I'm paying big bucks for health insurance and don't go to the dentist. I quicken my pace to keep up with my escort, who seems to be in a hurry.

The long weekend provided me with plenty of idle time. Time to think things over. I hadn't given much thought to the strange disappearance of Hank after I delivered the letter opener for him the previous afternoon. He had told me the gift was something special for her to open his love letters. He has always been something of a flake, and he did leave me a voicemail explaining how something unexpected had come up. He went on to say he was anxious to hear all the details of my interaction with his future bride. So it wasn't until the evening news broadcast that I knew I was screwed. His lovesick routine with the waitress he recently met, an obvious sham.

But why? Who harbored such hatred for me? Hank? I've known him for almost a year and not once have we even argued. I met him on a basketball court, and on occasion we would grab a bite to eat after our pickup games. I have no connection to the victim and, as far as I know, neither does Hank. Could he be an innocent pawn in this deadly game as well?

No. I've convinced myself his involvement was premeditated, perhaps criminal. He had to be in on some elaborate ruse to set me up. If it wasn't him, then who? Could I have been randomly targeted? My spider sense says no. Killers generally plan in excruciating detail, leaving nothing to chance. If I rule out Hank, where does that leave things? Why aren't the cops looking for answers to these questions? Oh yeah, they think *I'm* the killer.

I'm uncuffed before pulling up a seat across from my court-appointed attorney. The plexiglass separating us is three inches thick. We each have a telephone headset pressed to our ear. I'm positioned in the middle of a long row of booths, where a few other inmates speak to their visitors. A CO paces behind us, ready to jump into action should the need arise.

"Hello Pete. Dan Cortaro. It'll be my pleasure to represent you." *Sure Dan. You don't give a shit about me, just your bank account balance.*

Dan, a balding, middle-aged guy, has questionable style. He's dressed in standard lawyer attire, but the stripes on his tie clash with the pattern on his shirt.

"I've been leafing through your file and there seems to be some holes. I need for you to fill them in."

Gotcha. You want me to do your job for you.

"Take it from the top and don't leave anything out," Dan continues.

He removes a yellow legal pad from his briefcase and pats his pocket, searching for a pen. He doesn't seem to notice my haggard appearance nor does he ask how I'm holding up. He looks at his watch.

Are you here with me or on planet Pluto?

I ask when he can get me out of here.

"Oh yeah. Sorry. I'll be requesting bail at your arraignment hearing, which is the day after tomorrow."

I'm furious at the notion of spending another two days in this hole. Arraignments usually take place within forty-eight hours from the time of your arrest, seventy-two if you're unlucky enough to get arrested on a Friday. There must have been a flurry of Friday and weekend arrests, resulting in a full Monday docket. My Tuesday hearing date must mean the guilty receive preference over the falsely accused. He reminds me of the charges, and says the District Attorney will be trying the case himself. Homicides aren't all that common in Quincy. The DA must figure it's a slam-dunk case and will secure his re-election. I ask what they've got on me.

They have placed me at the scene of the crime, and my prints are all over the murder weapon. I inquire about motive. He glances at his watch again. *Sorry if my unjust incarceration bores you.* I interpret his lack of interest as an indication he thinks I've got no chance, and this case won't be worth his time.

"They're working on that, but figure they have enough to hold you over for trial without it. They're investigating a murder-for-hire angle as well."

I grin, picturing myself as a hit man, before anger washes over me. I proclaim my complete and utter innocence and demand my return to society. I don't expect this to elicit much of a reaction, and it doesn't. In my time at Henderson & Gates, I never ran across a guilty client. Even convicted felons think they are wrongly imprisoned. My cellmate, caught red-handed on videotape robbing a convenience store, claims he was framed.

Pluto Dan takes me through some standard rhetoric.

"Don't say a word about your case to anyone. This includes your fellow inmates, guards, cops, representatives from the DA's office, anyone. You talk to an inmate and they'll be on the horn with their lawyer looking for some kind of plea bargain."

How my proclamation of innocence can lead to another's sentence reduction is beyond me, but I know the drill and let him finish.

"From this point forward I am the only person you trust. I'm your only friend. Got that?" He glances around as he concludes the spiel.

After confirming I understand him, and that, yes, I was properly Mirandized, Dan is ready to hear my story.

⸺⊸०੦⟡०੦⊷⸺

I'm back in my cell now. Pluto Dan rushed me through my side of the story, jotting down a few notes along the way, all the while doing a poor job of masking his apathy. I couldn't discern whether he had something more pressing on his mind—other cases, happy hour with colleagues, getting laid tonight—or if he just doesn't like me. Maybe he dug into my financial situation, deciding to provide representation at a *you get what you pay for* level.

During the escort back to my cell, the CO informs me my convenience-store-looter cellmate has been transferred. My private residence doesn't last long as couple of COs lead a huge, chiseled, bad-ass dude in my direction. They deposit Rambo in my cell without introduction, and the bars clang shut. I turn over on my hard cot, instinctively drawing up my paper-thin blanket. His look is hardened, intensified by a scar below his left eye, which runs halfway down his cheek. Rambo deposits a duffle bag containing his belongings on the floor and plops down on his cot, which responds with a *squeak*.

Several hours of awkward—for me anyway—silence later, Rambo grunts something resembling small-talk, and my heartbeat stops racing a bit. Paranoia had set in as I was certain a trip to the infirmary was in my immediate future.

"What're ya in for?" Rambo asks.

We're sitting on our cots, on opposite sides of the cell, facing each other.

"Murder."

I keep my reply short, holding off on elaboration. If my answer surprises him, his facial expression doesn't show it.

"Who'd ya kill?"

"Nobody. I was framed. Really."

I'm not sure why I threw in the *really*. He shows no sign of doubt. I want to explain, to spill the whole story. Instead I wait for a prompt.

"You don't look like no killa. But never can tell what a man capable of. Don't matter to me either way."

He's not asking for my story, so I change gears. After weighing the prudence of an inquiry, I go for it.

"What're you in for?"

"Me? I'm small time. Nutin like murder."

This is all I'm going to get. For now, anyway. He turns away and stretches out on his cot, indicating our soul-baring session has ended.

I think about how if we were regular folks meeting on the outside, introductions would have been made by now.

I force down dinner, unsure of what's on my plate. Some kind of overcooked meat mixed with soggy noodles and a bean-like vegetable is my best guess. Forget the Atkins diet, the Paleo diet, or any of the others—three days on the Prison diet and I'm ten pounds lighter. Of course, I came into this establishment underweight to begin with, so forgive my lack of excitement.

Nine p.m. Lockdown time. Evening roll call is next. Inmates in each prison block get counted twice a day to make sure nobody has acted on their fantasy of breaking out. It's unnerving how I'm already entrenched in the routine. Funny how quickly perspective can change. Just last week I was wallowing in self-pity over my pathetic existence. Now, I'd give anything for a glimpse of that life. Yes, I'm grateful things are cool with Rambo. I overheard a few guys calling him *Guts* in the chow line. Is this because he's capable of ripping someone's guts out? And yes, I'm glad nobody has taken special notice of me. I keep my head down, remain quiet unless spoken to, and am respectful, polite, and courteous. All of which seem to be working for me.

But I can't keep up this imprisonment thing much longer. The lifestyle is beyond demeaning. Being told when to eat and shower. Being marched around in formation, our every movement scrutinized. No personal space. No privacy. Not even while taking a dump. Simple things you take for granted, like grabbing a Starbucks or going on a bike ride, are no longer options. Forget the scents of beer and take-out buffalo wings that often filled my kitchen back home—here the aroma is a mix of sweat, poor hygiene, and urine. And oh yeah, I'm living behind metal bars, in a six-by-eight-foot cell.

"This your first time in the joint?"

Rambo's first words to me since our break-the-ice conversation before dinner. I see him lying down on his side in the darkness.

"Yeah."

"You scared, right?"

I unconsciously started shaking once the lights went out, as I have the previous two nights. In the darkness, the reality of where I am sinks in more. Rambo is pretty perceptive.

"I haven't gotten used to this place yet. I wasn't planning on being here this long. Wasn't planning on being here at all, actually."

"You ain't need to be scared. I've seen ya the last couple a days. You ain't no smartass and ya don't run your mouth. You'll be okay."

"Thanks. I appreciate you saying that."

He's snoring away before long. He may be small time, but I'm pretty certain this isn't his first stint.

⁂

Five thirty a.m. Wake up time. Not that I need the clanging of night sticks on bars and

yelling from the COs to awaken me. I've never required more than five or six hours sleep. Here, I get about half of that, in spurts, and I'm up well before the "Get up now or else" threats.

Before breakfast, we get a chance to make a phone call. We're granted this privilege several times a day. My mental Rolodex only has entries for Pluto Dan and my parents. I don't have a woman in my life. The last one receptive to my charms ended things after a few weeks. Getting to know me better became synonymous with boring her out of her wits. I use the time to do a little reading. I chose a book on the life of Tiger Woods from the small selection of available literature.

My parents came to visit after I called to inform them their only child is in prison. They tried putting up a brave front, but once my mom began crying, it was too much for me to handle.

I begged them not to come back. They ignored my request and now sit across from me, phones pressed to their ears, waiting for me to pick up the phone on my side of the glass.

"Oh Peter, this is so awful. Why won't they let us be in the same room with you? A mother should be able to hug her own son."

"Hello, Mom. I agree with you, but I don't make the rules."

My mom's graying blond hair, usually perfectly groomed, seems as if she barely combed a brush through it. My dad appears haggard, as well. Dark circles are visible under his eyes. I inherited his physique—tall and thin. He never really lost his boyish looks, and if not for his salt and pepper hair, he'd be mistaken for a much younger man.

"How are you holding up, son?"

"I'm fine, Dad."

We all know I'm lying, but what else can I say? If I tell the truth and admit my skin crawls every minute I'm in here, my mom will burst into tears. Witnessing my parents' disheveled state makes me uneasy. I smooth a hand through my black, wavy hair I planned to get cut this week. It's greasy now.

"You really didn't need to come back here. I already filled you in on my case."

Parents are supposed to love their kids unconditionally, regardless of circumstance. My folks have always stuck by my side, been my biggest fans. I wonder if people like Rambo have such parental support, and if lacking it is what leads to a life of crime.

"Tomorrow is my arraignment. My lawyer has everything under control."

Another lie.

"Are you getting anything to eat? You look emaciated."

My mom, not mincing words. She stares at me like I'm a zoo animal. Even my dad, the strong one, appears shaken by the sight of me in prison garb. He thinks he's masking his feelings, but his right leg bouncing up and down gives him away. It's his tell when he's nervous. Luckily, he doesn't play poker.

"I'm fine. Really. It's no country club, but I won't be here long."

"What makes you so sure of that?" my dad asks, hoping I have news regarding my release. I don't.

My poor folks. Were they disappointed I gave up trial law? Yes. Did they envision me married by now, having provided them with grandchildren to spoil? Sure. Did they foresee, in their worst nightmares, their son incarcerated, relegated to communication over recorded phone lines? Likely not.

My mom's voice crackles. She struggles not to cry, but a teardrop makes its way down her cheek. Pretending not to notice, I do my best to reassure them.

"This is all a huge misunderstanding. Circumstantial evidence never holds up. I wasn't present at the murder scene, meaning no physical evidence ties me to the crime. No hair fibers. No fibers from my clothing. None of my DNA. Surely the ongoing investigation will bring all this to light. Police detectives will find physical evidence left behind by the real killer. Criminals always make mistakes."

My dad echoes my sentiments, pegging my analysis as right on. We talk a little more until an approaching guard lets me know we need to wrap things up. As we say our goodbyes, I interject a final message.

"Mom. Dad. I'll be sitting at your dining room table, the three of us enjoying one of Mom's legendary meals, in no time."

I wish I could give my tearful mom a hug. I force a smile as I meet their eyes before they rise and walk away. They remain my biggest supporters. Okay, my only supporters. They truly believe in my innocence. Not like the folks of real murderers, who don't believe their own proclamations of outrage over the injustice taking place.

Time. Wishing there were more hours in the day is a common sentiment. Here, the days are painfully long. It's worse than watching the clock when you were in grade school, waiting for the bell to ring. I have made zero headway trying to decipher how I wound up in this hellhole. I curse Hank countless times a day. I can only pray the city's finest are working diligently to uncover the truth, what really went down. Tomorrow can't come soon enough. I've been clinging to the hope the words *bail is waived... released on his own cognizance...* will be resonating through the courtroom. This expectation keeps me going.

CHAPTER 6
JASON

I PULL OFF US-80 AT A rest stop, just outside of Dallas, and fish out a phone from my gym bag.

A few days before the Quincy tragedy, I purchased fifteen disposable cell phones from Best Buy. Anonymous, untraceable, burner phones. I gave one each to Hank, Tess, and my mom, keeping the remaining dozen for myself. A condition of the deal I struck with Hank was to be available, via his new phone, so I could contact him after the sting, to get a report on his interaction with Garrison. Really, I want to make sure he keeps his mouth shut and stays out of the country. I made this stipulation clear right after handing him a thick envelope filled with $67,500, the ninety percent I owed him, in hundred-dollar bills.

I could have given Poodle Boy even more money, but didn't want to incite his suspicions any more than they already were. About a year ago, my mom came into an inheritance of three-quarters of a mil. Some distant, wealthy relative whom I barely knew. Matthew and I each saw our measly bank account balances grow by $200,000. The money was intended for college, but not a cent has gone toward advancing my education. I have kept my newfound relative wealth quiet. I didn't go crazy, spending wildly. On occasion, I would buy my buddies a round of drinks, even splurge on a bottle of champagne to impress Tess. But I tempered my impulses. I've been saving it for a rainy day. Since the Matthew incident, it has been pouring.

The only other condition, an obvious one, was to get a case of amnesia regarding the entire situation. Failure to abide by these terms will result in unpleasantness. I don't expect Hank to disappoint.

Hank picks up on the fourth ring, muttering hello as if unsure who is on the line.

"Hank, old pal. Guess who? You enjoying the good life?"

"Hello, Bernie. Yes, life is good. Better than I ever imagined."

"Excellent. Am glad to hear it. Tell me about St. John."

I'm sitting on the hood of my car, the bright sun providing warmth amidst a blowing wind. I speak loudly, to be heard above the steady *whir* of traffic.

"It's the smallest and most beautiful of the U.S. Virgin Islands. I've only been here two days, but it feels like home. Natives are friendly, ocean is aqua blue, beach is clean, sand is white. Just got back from snorkeling at Trunk Bay. You wouldn't believe the colorful fish and coral out here."

I try picturing him in snorkeling gear. Pudgy with scraggly hair, he doesn't exactly cut an attractive figure. He seems oblivious to Quincy news. If he knows what I did to Chang, I'd expect him to show some anger.

"Where are you staying?"

"An overpriced hotel for now. Need to start looking for a place."

"Have you purchased a boat yet? You've been paid handsomely, but you'll need to find work soon."

A family of weary travelers stroll by, heading for the convenience store. Kids needing a bathroom, adults stretching sore muscles, grunting audibly.

"Sailing is real big here. I'm gonna take some lessons, buy a big sailboat—maybe a catamaran—and start up a chartering business."

"So, you've sailed before?"

"Yeah, back in college. A buddy of mine had a sunfish, the smallest sailboat out there, a twenty footer. It tipped over a lot, but we had a blast with it. By the time we graduated, I was pretty proficient at keeping us dry."

"For your sake, I hope you're not bullshitting me. But really, I don't care whether you're living like a fucking king or a peasant. Just remember: if you even think about setting foot anywhere near Quincy, you'll regret it. As of now, I'm your best friend, your ally. You do something stupid and you'll get to see my dark side."

"I get it. I won't cross you. You can count on that."

His voice wavers as he speaks, unable to hide his nervousness. This is good. I want him nervous.

"Good. Now, get out and enjoy your new life. I'll be in touch."

Luring Garrison to the scene of the crime necessitated the involvement of someone he trusted. Tess handled the initial interaction, a meeting at Jethro Memorial Park, a place Hank frequented to let his *dogs* run loose. I don't consider poodles real dogs. A grown, single man walking poodle screams nut job. I have followed Garrison to the same park on several occasions, where he meets Poodle Boy and a few other guys for some basketball. Despite appearing a decade older than the others, Poodle Boy is a follower, passive by nature. Not surprisingly, he can't shoot worth a crap. Surprisingly, Garrison plays a decent game.

Tess approached him with our proposition. She didn't divulge the full plan, only the part requiring his involvement. It took some persuasion, a woman's touch. It took guaranteeing Garrison wouldn't be physically harmed. Tess's beauty didn't hurt our cause. She fed him a vague story about me being an eccentric millionaire who enjoyed playing practical jokes. She promised a large sum of cash. He was skeptical about what he was getting himself into, though he certainly didn't realize he would become an accessory to a murder. He demanded details of the so-called prank. Tess wouldn't oblige, simply stating she'd find another of Garrison's friends to play along. She even walked away, giving him time to think it over, before returning from her parked car, half an hour later. In the end, money beat out friendship.

Not wanting to turn over his entire incentive, $75,000, up front, Tess gave him ten percent, $7,500, as a show of good faith, with the remainder to be delivered after he took care of business. We figured he knew Tess wasn't acting alone in whatever scheme she was selling. We also figured he was aware that, having been able to track him down once, we'd be able to do so again should he decide to take the money and run. Yeah, flight was a risk, but I counted on greed keeping him in the game.

⸺◦◖✿◗◦⸺

I finished the last stretch of driving and am standing beside my illegally curbside parked car outside the Dallas/Fort Worth airport terminal. With the car's title in hand and the Seller portion filled out and signed, I scan weary departing passengers heading towards the parking lot or in search of a taxi. I'm holding a cardboard sign reading: MOVING TO HAWAII. NEED TO SELL '88 FORD MUSTANG NOW. PRICE $100. No, I haven't changed my itinerary, but surmised that a sign advertising LEAVING THE COUNTRY would ring *drug dealer* or *escaped felon*.

A twenty-dollar bill, along with a promise of a sale within ten minutes, keeps the traffic control cop off my back. No test drives is part of the deal, which scares off the first interested party, a big dude in a cowboy hat. A kid who looks like he just got his license, approaches me next.

"Does thing this run?"

"As good as new." A lie.

"Does it have a stereo system?"

"You bet. It rocks." No lie.

"Can I start her up and hear it, along with the engine."

"Sure thing brother. Hop in." I hand over the keys and

slide into the passenger seat. He fires it up, liking that it starts without incident.

Looking at the odometer, he says, "Mileage is kinda high."

"Price is kinda low," I reply.

"Good point." He's got the radio on now, bopping his head to The Who's "Pinball Wizard". "This car isn't stolen or anything, is it?"

"Nope. Got the title right here. All you have to do is take this to DMV to complete the transfer of ownership. I'm just a guy getting away from it all. Tired of the rat race. Time to enjoy life. Just came into a big inheritance." Mostly true.

He revs the engine a few more times, unable to mask his smile. "You've got a deal, sir."

I didn't go through the trouble of trying to change my identity, so the cash I'm handing over to the woman at the American Airlines counter in exchange for a one-way ticket to the Cayman Islands won't hide my existence. If the investigation progresses to where I'm being sought out, all I'm accomplishing by paying cash is buying the small amount of time a fruitless credit card activity search consumes.

Although my brother and I grew up together, we have different last names. My dad left home when I was six months old. I have no recollection of him. Before I turned one, my mom hooked up with another loser, and a year or so later, Matthew was born. Loser number two stuck around a little longer than the first, but when I try conjuring up an image in my mind of what he looked like, a tall, fuzzy outline is all I can muster. My mom married loser number one, so her last name matches mine. She considered legally changing Matthew's name on a few occasions but held out hope for a reunion with loser number two, who stayed in touch for a while by phone and even sent financial

support, until he remarried when Matthew was five. In any

event, this name thing plays to my advantage now, making my connection to Matthew a little less obvious.

With two hours to kill before my flight, I grab one of my burner phones and make another long-distance call.

⸺◦◖◈◗◦⸺

"Hi. Is everything okay?" Greeting from Tess.

I'm standing near my gate, by a large window, watching a plane land.

"Just fine, Tess. My plane takes off in less than two hours. Then, four hours in the air."

"I still don't understand why you couldn't just fly out of Miami with me. Why you had to drive halfway across the country and take a longer flight."

For now, at least, her anger has subsided. I'm hopeful she's ready to go with the flow, to make the best of a bad situation. Her tone is friendly, caring even. Maybe she has pushed the unpleasantness out of her mind. Whatever the case, I'm thrilled and not about to question her.

"Serpentine, my dear."

"Serpentine? What is that and what does it have to do with your cross country detour?"

"Serpentine means resembling a serpent, as in its movement, which is not a direct path from point A to point B. Rather a winding and turning one. Peter Falk shouted 'Serpentine!' to Alan Arkin in the 70s movie *The In-Laws*, as they were running for their car while being shot at."

"Okay, whatever. Since when do you watch 70s movies?"

I'm momentarily mesmerized by the efficiency with which a ground crew unloads luggage from a just-arrived plane.

"Let's discuss my movie preferences another time. Tell me about our paradise."

She sighs. She prefers being the one controlling conversation, determining when to switch topics. Today, she's a good sport and moves on without further ado.

"It's amazing here. I must admit, you couldn't have picked a better destination. Flying in was so cool. Nothing but ocean for miles and miles and then, out of nowhere, this little slab of land appears, which we make a nosedive for. The beach here goes on forever. Get your ass here fast. We have a lot of exploring to do."

Her enthusiasm is contagious, causing my excitement level to rise.

"I can't wait. I'll be chugging rum punch with you in no time. Rum is so big there they serve it free in flight on Cayman Airways. I'll be wasted by the time I land."

"I'm reading through the brochures to find a fancy seafood place you can take me to for dinner tonight. Shall I come meet you at the airport?"

"No, you stay put. I'll take a cab. Toss the phone you're on now in the trash after we hang up. I'll see you soon, babe."

"Okay, babe. Bye. I'll be waiting for you."

Entrenched in my payback plan and all, there hasn't been a lot of time for intimacy, but as time is about to become a plentiful commodity, I expect that to change.

Hunger pains remind me it has been a while since I've last eaten, so I navigate the airport crowd, locate a burger joint, and grab a quick bite. Soon after inhaling two hamburgers, fries, and an iced tea, I hear a voice over the intercom announcing that flight 2047 to Grand Cayman will commence boarding momentarily. Almost an hour later, my plane leaves the runway in the dust and a hot stewardess makes the rounds passing out rum.

CHAPTER 7
PETER

I'M BACK AT THE VISITATION booth, awaiting the arrival of my replacement representation.

Over my objections, my parents hired a real lawyer to defend me. All right, *you don't really have to do this* isn't technically an objection. Pluto Dan is out of the picture. In the picture: an immaculately dressed graybeard, with perfect posture, approaching his designated seat.

"William Douglas, attorney at law."

"Nice to meet you. I'm Peter Garrison, as I'm sure you know."

I glance at his briefcase, certain my folder is among its contents.

"I do. Your parents impressed upon me the urgency of your matter, so I got here on the double."

"I appreciate that. How are things looking for me?"

He sidesteps my question, attending to his own agenda first. "The case file your previous attorney put together blows. Granted, he was only on the job a couple of days, but your plight didn't cause him any sleep disruption."

He pauses, shaking his head in disgust, before continuing his admonishment. "The representation he provided is an outrage. It's idiots like him who keep lawyer jokes alive and well."

I nod my agreement, anxious for him to get on with it.

"The minimal time I've been on your case, I have spent judiciously."

Another pause. Is he fishing for praise?

"What I've learned gives me reason for optimism. I've read the police reports and spoken with the prosecution. Other than your fingerprints on the murder weapon, and witnesses placing you at the scene of the crime, nothing ties you to the felony. Now I realize this is akin to saying *other than **that**, Mrs. Lincoln, how was the show?*"

My lawyer smiles, amused with himself. "I must be missing something. What makes you so optimistic?"

"As a fellow member of the bar, you surely are familiar with the concept of reasonable doubt."

My repeated nodding signals him to continue.

"That, Peter, is your way out. But let's not get ahead of ourselves. My focus at the moment is convincing the judge to set bail at an amount your loving parents can afford."

A figure that took a sizable hit after paying this guy's hefty retainer fee. He goes on to enumerate people he has represented and his track record, both impressive lists. He then outlines what I can expect at my hearing tomorrow. Our chat ends with a proclamation.

"Peter, I possess a knack for reading people. I believe in your innocence. I believe in your case."

"Thank you, William. I appreciate it. And thanks for jumping onboard on such short notice."

He packs his briefcase, signaling the winding down of our conference. "That's what I do, Peter. I'm good at what I do. You get some rest, and I'll see you tomorrow."

He stands up and walks away briskly, disappearing from my sight in seconds. I rise deliberately, dreading the return to my cell.

My takeaway is that Sir William is pompous, though quite competent.

A good lawyer will fight his damnedest for a client, even if he thinks said client is guilty. From the client perspective, knowing your lawyer believes in you can do wonders for your state of mind, your well-being. It suddenly strikes me as funny how criminals are referred to as clients. Not just those, like myself, awaiting judgment, but convicted felons as well, who require representation for appeals and whatnot.

⸺◦◦⧳◦◦⸺

I survived another night and am in my cell with Rambo, counting down the hours until my courtroom escort arrives. We just returned from lunch. Yet another gourmet meal. I've perfected the bypass-the-taste-buds routine by swallowing whole chunks without chewing. I can almost hear my digestive system cursing me out by meal's end.

Calling Rambo my friend is a stretch, but since our forced rooming arrangement two days ago, we have taken to hanging out some.

We've graduated from grunts and small talk to getting to know a few things about each other. I've learned, for example, Rambo doesn't talk much because when you talk, it comes at the expense of having to listen. With the majority of people he runs across being assholes, he has come to prefer silence. I told him, and only him, the story of my unjust incarceration. He has a gentle side, one most would never imagine exists. I feel safe around here with Rambo as my de facto bodyguard. *Following him around like a puppy* probably more accurately describes our dynamic than *hanging out*.

"You gotta relax, man. You makin me dizzy with all your pacing."

"Sorry. I guess I'm a little anxious."

"A little?"

Rambo lies on his back, his hands interlaced behind his head, staring at the cement ceiling.

"It's just that being in here has made me realize I'm not living life to the fullest. I tend to play it safe instead of taking risks. I have feelings of inadequacy that I do nothing about. I view myself as a lesser man than most—although I'm not sure that applies to the masses I'm currently surrounded by. I've always felt like something of an outsider. I'm not exactly a charmer with the ladies. In short, I live a quiet life of desperation."

I'm rambling. It's driven by nervousness. I stop pacing and glance at Rambo, as if suddenly aware I have a captive audience. His gaze remains affixed to the ceiling. Moments of silence pass.

"You done?"

"Yeah. Sorry about the whining."

"Hey, we all got problems. You ain't alone."

This is all he says, yet his words comfort me.

I still hate it here, hate everything about this place, hate that I've had to spend even a minute here, much less four days. Hate that I'm treated like a kindergartner, being told what to do and when to do it. Make that treated *worse* than a kindergartner. They get to finger-paint, and run around and play. While Rambo has made the past couple days somewhat tolerable, this remains, by far, the most horrific experience of my life.

Half an hour before my escort is due to arrive for my three p.m. court appearance, Sam, a CO with whom I've become acquainted, slips a package through the bars in my general direction. Minutes later, I'm dressed in a black suit, white shirt, and muted yellow tie. My mom did the shopping. My dad delivered it to the appropriate prison personnel, which, in turn, triggered Sam's appearance at my cell.

"Docket number 131457. People versus Peter Garrison," the court officer announces as I'm led into the courtroom.

Seated next to Sir William at the defense table, I feel my nerves kicking in. My left leg involuntarily bounces up and down like a jackhammer, and my heart races. Glancing at my parents a couple rows back doesn't calm me down. My dad wipes sweat off his forehead, despite the chilliness in the room. My mom bows her head, as if anticipating the worst. Across the aisle sits the prosecution team, two guys dressed immaculately in three-piece suits. Who wears vests anymore? And why isn't my attorney sporting one?

The judge, a youngish man with a tidy beard, chats with his court reporter. I never tried a case before him, and am attempting to get a vibe from him as to what my chances are.

The judge raps his gavel several times to call things to order. My appearance has triggered some chatter and finger pointing—as in *there's the son of a bitch that killed Michael.* Considering this is merely an arraignment, likely not to last more than twenty minutes or so, there is sizable gallery presence. The sea of Asian faces tells me Chang was part of a large, close-knit family. Their facial expressions reveal a mix of grief and anger, the latter funneled in my direction.

With relative quiet achieved, the judge begins in a deep commanding voice.

"Will the defendant please rise." I cooperate. "Please identify yourself, by name, to this court."

"My name is Peter Garrison, Your Honor."

"Mr. Garrison, you have been charged with the crime of the first degree murder of one Mr. Michael Chang, taking place on July 28th, 2015 at approximately eight thirty p.m. A crime punishable by twenty years to life imprisonment. Do you understand the charge?"

"Yes, your honor, I do."

"How do you plead to this charge?"

"I plead not guilty, Your Honor."

The collective attention of the courtroom audience focuses on me. It's human nature, during a proclamation of innocence, to scrutinize. Am I lying? Is my voice trembling? Do I exhibit physical cues indicating deception?

"A plea of not guilty is so recorded. Mr. Garrison, you have the right to hire an attorney to represent you or have the court appoint one for you. Is the gentleman seated beside you, Mr. William Douglas, your attorney of record?"

"Yes, your honor, he is."

You can't overdo the *your honor* thing. I've been around enough judges to know they all have egos. A show of disrespect will land you on their bad side in a hurry.

"Very well then." Addressing Sir William, "Mr. Douglas, will you please rise and state your name for the record."

"Of course, your honor. My name is William Douglas, hired attorney representing Mr. Peter Garrison." I'm expecting an admonishment, or at least a long look, from the judge for stretching a two word response—William Douglas—into a mini-monologue. Instead, the judge plows on, not missing a beat.

"I would like to rule on bail now. Before ruling, I will hear statements from first the prosecution, followed by the defense. Mr. Jamison, as the lead prosecutor of record, do you wish to enter a statement regarding bail?"

Tony Jamison, the Assistant District Attorney (ADA) for the Vermont district encompassing Quincy, rises and addresses the judge.

"Thank you, your honor." Looks like both sides are prone to grandstanding. He answers a question with *thank you, your honor?* Tony straightens his tie and clears his throat before continuing. "Given the heinous nature of the crime, and the fact that the defendant, a single man with no children and no home or land ownership, presents a flight risk, I propose that bail be denied."

"Thank you, Mr. Jamison. Mr. Douglas, your turn."

I meet Sir William's eyes, nodding to convey my confidence in him. William matches Jamison's theatrics by rising slowly, glancing at the scribbling on his legal pad, and takes an exaggerated sip of water.

"Your honor, Mr. Garrison has absolutely no criminal history. He is a United States citizen, a Quincy resident for more than twenty years, employed in Quincy, has strong ties to the community, and has family with similarly strong community ties. His supportive parents are present in this courtroom."

I gaze into the gallery and observe my parents gripping each other's hands, listening intently. Sir William pauses to face the prosecution table, then proceeds.

"With due respect to my adversary, Mr. Jamison, Peter Garrison is not a flight risk. He doesn't even possess a passport. I humbly request that Peter be released on his own cognizance, with the promise he will remain available to yourself, court officials, law enforcement, as well as the prosecution."

I relax a little, content with the argument put forth by my counsel.

The judge ponders the arguments and quickly arrives at a decision, likely one formulated well in advance of this proceeding. "Bail is set at one hundred thousand dollars." Before he gets the last word out, an eruption of disbelief and outrage echoes throughout the room.

I breathe an audible sigh of relief. Well, it would have been audible if the gallery were simmered down by now. I clench my right hand into a fist and shake it up and down emphatically, a few times. I turn around and make eye contact with my dad, who shoots me a *we've got it covered* nod. Luckily, my folks and I anticipated this predicament the moment the shit hit the fan Friday morning. A few hours later, they arranged for a fast-tracked home equity loan at our local bank. To be safe, they also made a withdrawal on their 401K plan, incurring the twenty percent forfeiture of funds to the government—ten percent up front, another ten percent at tax time. Several pounds of the gavel, accompanied by strong words from the judge, are needed to restore order.

"Moving on. Mr. Jamison, I expect you to turn over all discovery materials to the defense. Today is Tuesday. Let's say you'll have them available for pickup by Mr. Douglas by Thursday."

"Certainly, Judge. My office will contact Mr. Douglas' office."

"Swell. Now, just one last item remains, which is the scheduling of the preliminary hearing." Flipping through a calendar, he looks up and proposes two weeks from today.

After getting both sides to agree, the judge adjourns us. Just as my escort approaches to lead me out of the courtroom, Sir William whispers, "You'll be out before dinner," as he discreetly flashes a cashier's check, made out for $100,000.

———————◦◦◦◦———————

I'm sitting on my parents' living room couch, the three of us sipping gin and tonics, in celebration. There's just one problem: I'm not a free man. I'm an *in limbo* man. A man awaiting judgment. I can't leave the county. Not the country, the county. Don't get me wrong, I'm thrilled to be out. As we raced off in my dad's beat up Toyota Tacoma pick-up truck, leaving my gated community residence in the dust, I rolled down my passenger side window and yelled, "Yahoo!" loud enough for Rambo and the others to hear.

"Mom. Dad." I wait for their full attention. "Thank you both! I can't put into words how grateful I am to be out of jail."

I stretch out my limbs, hogging couch space, soaking in the comforts of being back *on the outside.*

"Of course, son," they reply in unison.

My mom has a stuffing-filled Thanksgiving-sized turkey in the oven, side dishes simmering on three of the four stove top burners, and a fridge packed with desserts and late-night snack goodies. She swears I've lost fifteen pounds over the course of my confinement, and appears intent on me gaining it all back tonight.

After managing to survive my homecoming meal without a hint of serious conversation, I notice my mom turn grave while we're cleaning up in the kitchen.

"Your father and I are worried about you. We have spoken with a nice detective named Fred Murray, who is assigned to your case. The police don't seem to have any leads. Your lawyer is supposed to be among the best in Quincy, but likewise hasn't come up with anything concrete."

My mom wraps leftovers, depositing them into the refrigerator, while I do the dishes. The feel of the warm water, and the relief of doing something mundane and normal, comforts me. I've never thought of rinsing dishes and stacking them in a dishwasher as unwinding and therapeutic, but right now that's the case.

"Your father has followed through on your request to hire a private investigator.

Detective Murray will meet with you if you can provide him with any new information. He hasn't come out and said as much, but I don't think he believes you're a cold-blooded killer. Which, of course, you aren't."

She neatly and obsessively wraps each dish in aluminum foil, ensuring airtightness.

"But he doesn't know you like your father and I do. I told him you're kind of naïve and don't always make the best decisions, but there's not an evil bone in your body."

"Mom, I'm a lawyer. I'm trained to make good decisions. And I'm not naïve!" I hate the way she still thinks of me as a kid.

"Oh Peter, how did you get yourself into this mess?" My reassuring words didn't register with her, or she simply chose to ignore them.

"Mom, you're babbling. Don't worry so much. I believe in our legal system. Granted, my faith has taken a hit these past few days, but I'm innocent. The truth is out there. It will be uncovered, and I will be vindicated."

My mom reloads some plates I apparently misplaced in the dishwasher.

"That's your naivety talking, honey. How do you know the truth will come out? If you get sent back to jail, it will be more than I can bear."

"Believe me, Mom, it wouldn't be a picnic for me either."

My dad enters the room, temporarily saving me from the onslaught. He pours himself a cup of coffee, then motions with his head for me to follow him into the den. I top off my mug and follow. Only once settled into his beloved, worn, and admittedly quite comfortable recliner, does he speak. I'm sitting across from him in a not-as-comfortable leather sunken chair. I realize most people love leather chairs, but I stick to them when I'm hot and slide around too much when I'm not, so it's not something you'll ever find at my place, even if I could afford it.

"Son, it's great to see you out of prison garb," he says, slapping my shoulder. "Orange has never been your color."

"I look good in mandarin orange. Felony orange, not so much," I respond, playing along.

"I thought your mom's stuffing was kind of salty tonight. Maybe we can get some takeout tomorrow from that place you've been dining at."

"Yeah, I didn't want to say anything, but the mashed potatoes were kinda dry, too." In reality, my mom's mashed potatoes are the best. Garlicky, just the way I like them.

With that, my mom comes bursting into the room. "What do you mean 'the potatoes were kind of dry'?"

Did I mention she is sensitive? Serious and sensitive. I wonder how my dad puts up with her. That they have remained together for thirty years amazes me. It must be the opposites attract thing, something I've never understood, but then again the sample size of my relationships with the opposite sex hardly qualifies me to weigh in on the subject.

"Dear, did you tell Peter about the private investigator?" My mom brings us back to reality.

"I was just about to, sweetie." He doesn't like being called *dear*, and lets her know this by using an endearment she equally dislikes. I, again, marvel at how they put up with each other. Maybe neither has the youthfulness or energy to pursue something fresh and new.

Maybe they have contentment, if not excitement; tolerance, if not compatibility. Maybe if I find myself a girlfriend, I'll stop obsessing over my parents' dysfunctional dynamic.

My dad interrupts my compulsive analytics. "Son, your PI idea is a good one. I hired someone this morning."

"Thanks, Dad. My thinking is, while the police attempt to piece together the jigsaw puzzle, much of their focus will be on me. I am, after all, still their prime suspect. To even things out, I need this PI guy on my side. His sole driving force will be to gather evidence to help my cause. That's what you paying him buys us."

I rise and walk over to my dad, and pat him on the back, a show of gratitude for putting up the money. I then walk over to my mom, seated on the couch, and give her a hug, thanking her as well.

"It's no problem, Peter." My mom still has her arms around me as my dad fills me in.

"As you suggested, I've asked him to start on the trail of Hank. He says he can get phone records on his landline and mobile phones. I told him Hank appears to have fled town, but he seems confident he'll be able to track him down—and quickly."

"This is great. If we can locate Hank, we'll be well on our way to solving the mystery ourselves." I wonder again how Hank got involved in this.

After polishing off a huge Mom-prepared brunch—eggs, pancakes, bacon, and cinnamon rolls—I know that my transformation from skeletal-like to skinny is well underway. Following a walk around the neighborhood, at the urging of my digestive system, I join the already gathered Team Garrison in the den.

Along with my dad, relaxed as ever in his recliner, Sir William and a rugged looking chap I've never met fill out the room, both seated on the couch. My dad introduces me to Jack Brady, private investigator. Jack runs his hand through his thick black hair. He is easily six feet and three inches tall, and solidly built. Casually dressed in jeans, a polo shirt, and sneakers, he strikes a sharp contrast to Sir William's suited look.

Jack lists surveillance, manhunts, background investigations, and basic detective work as his areas of expertise. I suppress a *what does that leave* comeback. My mom precariously enters the room carrying a large tray of coffee-filled mugs, a small pitcher of cream, and a sugar bowl. I help her get the tray onto the coffee table without spilling or breaking anything, and we take our seats.

My dad kicks things off. "William and Jack, I've asked you here together to facilitate the sharing of information. I realize neither of you have had much time to do your thing yet, but I want us all to be on the same page. My wife, Karen, and I, along with Peter, of course, are at your disposal in any way we can be of assistance. William, could you start, by filling us in on where you are at?"

"Certainly, Doug. The DA's office turned over their discovery materials this morning, which I've got with me here." He makes a show of waving a folder. "I've got police reports, the autopsy report, pictures of the murder weapon, crime scene photographs in all their gruesome glory, and LUDs—that's Local Usage Details, as in phone records—for Chang's phones. Let's start with the murder weapon, the letter opener."

Sir William's dissemination of information comes across like an opening statement. I suppose having practiced law for so long, the lines between conversational and theatrical blur.

"It's a Westcott eight inch serrated blade with a porcelain handle. The serrated blade gives it about the equivalent potency of a standard kitchen knife. This is why, in my humble opinion, to ensure death, twenty-some stabs were delivered."

Jack rubs his eyes, appearing disinterested.

"From the autopsy, the medical examiner concludes, with ninety-nine percent certainty, that based upon the depth, width, gap, and shape of the stab wounds, the blade of the weapon is over seven inches long and the *teeth* are consistent with those of the letter opener. Further, the blood coated on the letter opener is type B – —that's blood type B with Rh negative—a blood type which only 1.5 percent of the population has. This 1.5 percent minority includes Michael Chang. As we all know, the lab guys were able to lift several full fingerprints matching yours, Peter, from the letter opener. There were no other fingerprints—not even unidentifiable partials—found."

I'm angered by the mounting evidence against me. Maybe the unfortunate situation is a signal for me to turn my life around. A loud and clear message. I don't normally believe in *signs* or believe things *happen for a reason*. I don't believe in fate, or even in God. I fall somewhere between atheism and agnosticism. How does one explain murderers and rapists bequeathed with perfect health while upstanding citizens, and worse yet, innocent children, are stricken with disease and ailments, if a higher power is watching over us?

My thoughts are pushed aside as I return my attention to Sir William.

"Now, while a murder weapon dripping with the victim's blood and your fingerprints may seem ominous, from a juror's perspective it raises a red flag."

William rises as he continues, seemingly more at ease delivering speeches on his feet. As usual, he is perfectly groomed. His thinning white hair, combed and shiny, never moves, even as he saunters across the room. He must use product. That's the term my barber uses at the conclusion of my haircuts. Would you like any *product*? Not hair spray, or gel, or mousse.

"You see, the autopsy also revealed no defensive wounds on the victim. This, combined with other factors, imply the murder was premeditated as opposed to spontaneous. If you, Peter, were the killer, the fact that witnesses saw you enter the restaurant alone brandishing the *weapon* in plain view, only supports the theory of premeditation."

Assuming my remaining days aren't spent on death row, I have an opportunity to reinvent myself. I can be a winner as opposed to merely a survivor. This can be my defining moment. My take charge moment. My opening to start taking risks, to stop playing it safe, to develop into something more than I am today, more than I've ever been.

Sir William is still going strong. "Casting aside, for the moment, that premeditation carries a heftier sentence, consider this from the jury's standpoint. How stupid would you have to be to leave behind the murder weapon covered with your prints? There's no trace of such stupidity surrounding any other aspect of the plan's execution. Further, stupidity and your law school diploma make for quite a nice oxymoron."

Jack, twirling his thick mustache, jumps in, unable to contain his impatience any longer. "It's nice that you've been rehearsing your closing arguments, but do you have any hard evidence we can use? Maybe something implicating someone else, or proving Peter here isn't the killer."

Sir William grimaces. "Do you have someplace else you'd rather be?"

"Actually, I have a plane to catch."

"A plane?"

"A plane."

This bickering, while entertaining, isn't constructive. I want everyone's energy and focus on the real enemy, the bastard who set me up.

After sneering at Jack, William turns toward my dad. "Your PI friend lacks an understanding of how the system works. It's not all about evidence, rather the interpretation of such evidence and how it is presented. Had I been allowed to finish, I would have informed you all that I've got copies of the LUD's for Chang's phones as well as Peter's."

He swivels his head until he meets my eyes. "Your incoming and outgoing calls around the time of the murder reveal nothing incriminating, which is good news. The bad news is, there is nothing suspicious, nothing out of the ordinary, with Chang's call history either. Now, back to the letter opener, the DA's office is attempting to track down its origin. I have an investigator at my firm's disposal who is working this angle as well."

He hesitates, perhaps to let the fact he has an investigator as his minion, sink in. Of course a fellow lawyer like myself knows that law firms employ investigators.

"Additionally, I plan to dig into Chang's life, determine who had motive. Chang must have really pissed somebody off, and there must be a thread to this end out there."

Viewing the pause as completion, for the moment anyway, my dad keeps things moving.

"Thanks William. Let's hear what Jack has come up with. Jack, would you enlighten us?"

"You bet. First, everyone, I apologize for my gruffness. William, I don't have the charisma you possess. You are eloquent, educated, and proper." Translation: *pompous, a know-it-all, and some more pompous.* "Me, I'm a straight-shooter. I'm substance over style. I don't care about hurt feelings or about being liked. Hank Simpson flew from Burlington, Vermont to St. Thomas, Virgin Islands three days ago. I don't know if he's still there, but figure my chances of finding him will increase by flying out there and asking around in person. He isn't a registered guest at any of the major hotels, but I didn't expect he would be. He could be in St. John or St. Croix, the other U.S. Virgin Islands, or he could be in Timbuktu. Hank's phone records don't reveal anything out of the ordinary. Criminal types today realize phones leave a trail, just as credit cards do. There's something to be said for the in-person rendezvous, like the way old school gangsters conducted business in the back seats of limousines."

Jack's no-nonsense manner and straightforward delivery is appealing. His voice is deep, his message resonating. My mom appears mesmerized by his words. Jack catches my mom's stare, and smiles at her, before diverting his attention toward the rest of the group as he finishes.

"The only other item I have to report is that a law enforcement friend of mine, familiar with the case, says Chang is a model citizen. His record is clean, not even a speeding ticket. If he has enemies, it is not clear who, when, or where. This is consistent with what you reported, William, with his phone records."

Out of her trance and back into *worried mom* mode, my mom asks how long these cases typically take to resolve. Neither Jack nor William supply a satisfactory answer. My dad regains control of the meeting as he senses Jack preparing to make his exit.

"While you professionals are doing your thing, what can Karen, Peter and I be doing? Other than sitting on our hands waiting for your check-in calls."

I have no intention of standing by idly and resent my exclusion from the professionals group.

Jack beats William to a response. "The waitress. We don't know anything about her, other than our assumption she was in cahoots with Hank. Locating Hank will tie up this loose end, but if you'd like to help, learn all you can about her. Peter, you've seen her, so ask around about her. Let's think about how we can get our hands on the employee contact list at Chang's restaurant. Do any of you know anyone who works there?"

My dad acts as our speaking representative. "Unfortunately, no. Not even Peter."

"I might recognize one or two of them, but that's about it," I contribute.

"The grieving wife may have access to this information. In the name of justice, she will hand it over to someone *on the case*, like us," says Jack, thinking on the fly.

"I can pull this off, using my influence and connections," William offers, breaking his silence drought, long by his standards.

I'm sensing he's making a promise he can't keep. Jack, with an *I know you're full of shit* look plastered on his face, mutters,

"We all would appreciate that." Addressing my parents, he adds, "Karen and Doug, thanks for your hospitality. I need to head to the airport now."

Jack's somewhat sudden, if not unexpected, departure announcement breaks up the party. We agree to meet again as a team, at my dad's insistence, in a few days' time. Jack will be conferencing in. Handshakes all around, then our visitors depart.

I felt like a bystander at the powwow, content standing by idly while others plotted to save me. I want to be the one—make that, I *need* to be the one—to not only save myself, but bring the offenders to justice.

I feel a jolt of self-confidence, a strong sense of purpose. I don't know how all this will play out, but I'm certain of one fact: If I go down, it will be fighting.

Two nights is about my limit for camping out at my parents' house. Expressing my gratitude for everything, I accept a pan of lasagna, promise to call often, and head to my place. My exit is anticlimactic, seeing as my parents have to give me a lift, with my car still parked at my complex.

En route, Sir William calls to say he'll be sending his investigator to Mrs. Chang's residence, in hopes of obtaining employee information. The investigator will carry an official-looking law enforcement badge of some sort. With the Peking Dragon still closed for business, this is deemed the best avenue available.

Since getting into the car, I've been resting my head against my backseat window, battling lethargy. William's call snaps me out of my funk. I'm sitting upright, steaming again over my predicament. I pound my fist against the door, prompting my mom to ask if I'm okay.

I suppose it is not uncommon to experience bouts of depression and anger following a prison stint. The thing is, though, I can't truthfully attribute how I'm feeling to the hellhole that was home the past few days. I mean, sure, the lion's share of my boiling blood is thanks to Hank, but I'm livid for allowing myself to be a victim. I realize Chang is the real victim, but I'm a victim as well. I'm the idiot who willingly walked into quicksand. Chang wasn't afforded the luxury of time to prepare, or even react. He wasn't provided the freedom to opt out of his predicament. I need to figure this out for both of us.

<hr/>

Back at my place, sipping a cup of coffee on my couch, I sift through a pile of mail that accumulated while I was away. Nothing important. Wait… a letter from work. I called my boss while in jail, letting him know my situation and that I'd be out soon. Still, my pulse quickens as I tear open the envelope. The opening words—*We regret to inform you*—confirm my fear. I've been let go. Since I'm still on probation, I have no recourse. They can fire me without cause. My hatred for Hank, and more so for the unknown ringleader who involved Hank, intensifies.

The ironies keep piling up. An ex-defense attorney requiring a defense attorney. Shortcomings in the legal system, which drove me out of litigation, lead me to jail. And now, I'm jobless because my employer, a law firm, presumes guilt.

My mind jumps back to my more pressing situation. I want to catch the next flight to St. Thomas and help Jack track down Hank. I have dreamt of the moment, confronting Hank face-to-face. I can't imagine any spoken words, any outcome, from such an encounter that would derail my *I want to rip his head off* urgings. A small part of me, a part which dissolves away under the light of rational thought, clings to the hope my pal Hank didn't really turn on me, that he was coerced, threatened, even beat up physically. Of course, any wounds he suffered would have been internal, if such beatings occurred while he was conning me. I grin, imagining him hanging in a gallows chamber, limbs restrained. My grin quickly fades as I try envisioning a scenario in which such torturous tactics require being carried out in the Virgin Islands.

Reality sets in, snapping me out of dream land. I can't leave the jurisdiction, let alone jet to the Virgin Islands. Or can I? Sure, it would be a rebellious, law breaking thing to do; something which, in all likelihood, would culminate with me back in jail; something the old Peter wouldn't dream of doing. But I'm not feeling, or thinking, like the old Peter. Where have the decisions the old Peter made gotten me? What has being the conservative, nice guy done for me? I mull over the situation. Guesstimate some probabilities. Like, what are the chances I would get caught, should I disregard the no-flight condition of my bail? And if I locate Hank, what are the chances it will lead to charges against me being dropped? And if I stay put, what are the odds Jack delivers Hank to me?

While I embrace integrating risk-taking to my persona, there's no need to recklessly splash in heavy doses of stupidity. Seeing myself in a new light—with me playing a key role in uncovering the truth, in extricating myself from my legal troubles, in bringing the bad guys to justice after perhaps subjecting them to some of my own justice— I can't take myself out of the game. Perhaps there's a perilous activity I can partake in here in Quincy. Maybe tail somebody or track down a lead.

Of course, I have nothing to go on. Four days in the slammer, thinking of little else besides the wreckage which is now my life, has netted nothing. I decide to call Jack. He may have something for me to do. If Sir William's guy strikes out with Chang's wife, I could break into the restaurant to get what we're after. I'm pretty certain Hank isn't the mastermind of the operation—he's not conniving or smart enough, for starters—so once Jack or Sir William get so much as a nibble on that front, I'll jump right in.

Having your life intruded upon, turned upside down, your rights violated, can do wonders for snapping one out of observer mode, out of sleepwalking-through-life mode. I feel more alive than I have in years.

CHAPTER 8
JASON

TESS ORDERS A GYRO AND a Greek salad. We found this Greek joint yesterday, among the sea of beachside eateries. I'm no expert on Greek cuisine, but for me it's all about the tzatziki sauce. The meat, prepared the same everywhere, roasted on a vertical spit, tastes about the same at every Greek restaurant I've been to. Ditto that uniformity for the pita bread and Greek salad. Tzatziki sauce, however, varies wildly. I like mine thick and garlicky. Just like they make it here.

"I'll have the same," I tell the tanned brunette waitress. "With extra tzatziki sauce. And bring us another round of drinks while you're at it."

"Certainly, sir. Coming right up."

Three days into island life and we're acclimating like pros. Of course, when getting into the swing of things involves lounging on the beach, soaking in the natural island beauty, eating and drinking to excess, and sleeping in, the transition isn't too difficult.

Tess breaks her stare from the tranquility of ocean waves splashing into the pristine white sand. "We should go scuba diving."

Scuba diving is big here. We've been told by several people we *have to* try it. Tess surprises me with her newfound sense for adventure. I'm picturing myself hooked up to an oxygen tank as our waitress returns with our second round of drinks, some rum concoction with a fancy name. I'm convinced there's an island edict to rush drink orders and hold up food orders. You can wait half an hour for a hamburger, but never more than a couple of minutes for alcohol. Getting customers drunk must be the first thing servers learn in training. Happy, inebriated patrons mean less complaints about the food and bigger tips. Not that the food is bad here. Between the beach-side ambiance and the liquor-induced state I'm in by the time the food arrives, I'm a teddy bear food critic and tip like a millionaire.

The lifestyle here is laid back. If you're in a rush, your blood pressure will get sky high waiting for someone to give a shit. Yeah, the servers want good tips, but if you stiff them for lollygagging, they still live in paradise and won't lose sleep over your irritation. They'll also remember you next time and do who knows what to your entree.

Halfway through our second rounds of drinks, Tess segues from scuba diving to this evening's entertainment. We drank and danced last night away at a disco club. As a rule, I don't dance, however the strobe lights, funky music, and alcohol, along with Tess's prodding, got me grooving. We closed the place down. Today, feeling earthier, she wants to spend the night on the beach. Who am I to argue?

Any uncertainty concerning the status of our relationship was erased the night I arrived. After landing and grabbing a taxi to the hotel I had booked before Tess's arrival, I was greeted with a shower of affection. Dressed in a cleavage-bearing, mid-thigh length negligee, she wrapped her arms around me and planted kiss after kiss upon me. Before I had the chance to tour our suite, we were naked on the carpet, intertwined.

Despite her misgivings surrounding the way things played out, I can only conclude she has pushed aside feelings of remorse regarding Chang and her anger towards me. History has proven power to be an aphrodisiac. Our little Bonnie and Clyde routine must be contributing to my sexual fortitude.

We've managed to avoid talk of the future, including possible upcoming confrontations with law enforcement. We've steered clear of any kind of serious conversation. This is nothing new for me, a live-for-today type of guy. Tess adopting this attitude represents a divergence from the *new Tess*, a regression to the pre-college Tess.

While Matthew and Tess's sister, Tina, branched out in high school, making new friends, joining clubs, and playing sports, Tess and I were outsiders, keeping to ourselves, getting wasted, and analyzing life together. Tess was always popular, due to the goddess-like aura she exudes, but like myself, was never at ease in the domain of high school cliquism. She understood my dark side, and didn't try to change me.

Midway through junior year, our relationship leapt to a new level. We skipped the dating thing, jumping from friends to lovers. It happened one cold, wintry night. With most of the student body watching our basketball team getting trounced by our arch-rival, Tess and I kept each other warm in a nearby abandoned barn.

Once our senior year rolled around, things changed. Tess, always the more serious student, began talking about college, about bettering herself, becoming a societal contributor. The following fall she left for Schenectady, New York, a smallish city upstate where she attended Union College, earning an accounting degree. She had been a victim of layoffs in the firm she worked at back in Quincy, and I feel bad about postponing her promising future.

As for Tess's current contented state, the real world and all that comes with it—dreams, aspirations, pressure, competition, setbacks, disenchantment—overwhelmed her. There's something to be said for setting the bar low, for equating happiness with success, where life's highs include a six-ball run on a pool table, downing Jack Daniels shots faster than your buddies, and sleeping in.

Our food arrives and my attention returns to the present and the good-sized bowl of tzatziki in front of me. I dip my gyro in the bowl, holding it there until drenched, before each bite. Tess, having drained her second drink, flags down our waitress and orders us another round.

"Since we're in *live it up* mode…" she says, as our waitress strolls away from our table, headed for the bar.

Before everything happened, Matthew would have loved it here. He's a nature lover. He could gaze at the night sky for hours. Here, nature's beauty is striking.

Tess stares at my face. "So, are you just being lazy, or is this beard here to stay?"

I laugh, running my fingers over the growth on my face. I haven't shaved since leaving Quincy. Playing with my coming-in-quickly beard has become an obsession.

"Do you like it? I'd like to keep it, but only with your approval."

"I'm not usually a beard fan, but it works on your handsome face."

She understands the motivation behind growing it. I need to change my look.

Our bellies full and satisfied, we stumble out of the place, head back to the beach, lay out towels, and fall asleep on our sand-bed. A few hours later, at sunset, a cool breeze nudges us awake. The light from the full moon guides us back through the darkness to our hotel.

"Ahhh, that's cold."

We're sobered up, back at our suite, sitting on the edge of the bed. Tess applies lotion to my sunburned neck, shoulders, and back. I skipped sunscreen today, thinking I was beyond the point of needing it. I was wrong.

"Don't be such a sissy."

"Hey, I didn't know you'd be torturing me."

"Since when is having lotion rubbed lovingly on your body by a woman in a bikini torture?"

"Okay, you've got me there."

While Tess showers, I select a phone from my collection and

dial up Hank. Ten rings later, I give up. I cuss him out, resigning to try again later.

Doubt enters my mind. Did I pay him enough? Is enough ever enough? How long will that silly-ass grin on his face, after sending him off with his payday, last? What happens when his boat-chartering-enterprise plan goes to hell? When he discovers none of the countless island beauties dig him? When he spends night after night alone? I can't get into his mind, can't predict his thoughts, can't dictate his actions. Will he turn on me? Blackmail me? Report me to the authorities?

Knowing his information on me is sparse calms my nerves. I only met him once, to give him his money, shortly after knocking off Chang. I was still in disguise at the time. I can hear the pigs laughing now when Hank tells them he doesn't know my real name. A potential problem occurs to me: what did he do with those god damn poodles? If he left them behind, will he be making calls to Quincy checking up on them? I fight the sensation something is terribly wrong.

"Will you stop with the tossing and turning? What's the matter with you, anyway?"

It's three in the morning and my restlessness bugs Tess. I tried Hank three more times, all with the same result. I called the bungalow rental complex where he *was* staying. The manager said he checked out two days ago. No forwarding information.

"Earth to Jason. Hellooooo." Tess mixes annoyance with humor.

"I'm here, babe. Just distracted. Go back to sleep. I'm gonna take a stroll outside and clear my head. I'll be back soon."

"What's going on, Jason? Is something wrong? Because if there is, I need to know about it. Remember, I'm in this with you."

Shrugging, I say, "Nothing's wrong. I need some fresh air is all." I kiss her forehead, and roll out of bed.

There's a nip in the air. A crispness. It's chilly, but the cool air feels clean, fresh, and invigorating. Despite my calm exterior, knots invade my stomach. I've been haunted these past few days by the real possibility of getting caught. These thoughts have crept their way into my dreams, dreams that end badly and violently. Sometimes I get shot, sometimes stabbed. It's not clear if I survive. I wind up in a half-alive, half-dead state. It would come as no surprise to hear an authoritative knock at my door, armed men primed to bust in.

I've been waiting for something like this, preparing. I can make it out the bedroom window, dash through the hotel property, up and over the six-foot fence separating the hotel from the neighboring liquor store, and into the adjacent alleyway. From there, I'd run like hell, as fast and as far as I can. I can't, of course, ditch Tess. I need to share my getaway plan with her. She's athletic, and shouldn't slow me down too much. A practice run may be in order.

I considered taking up a brief residency in the Virgin Islands to keep an eye on Hank. Maybe make a friend there to continue the surveillance once I left. In the end, I conclude learning Chang's fate will put the fear of God in him, thus securing his loyalty. I put my mind at ease somewhat with some rational thinking. Worst case scenario, if Poodle Boy's conscience gets the best of him and the fucker rats me out, the pigs are looking for someone—me—whose name and whereabouts they haven't a clue. Still, if his story gets out...

Shifting gears, I pull out yet another virgin phone and make a long distance call.

"Hello," an exhausted voice answers.

"Hello yourself, Mom."

"Oh Jason, it's so good to hear your voice. Music to my ears. Are you all right? I'm worried sick about you. You were so mysterious when I saw you last."

It pains me to hear her distraught tone.

"I'm fine, Mom. No need to worry. You didn't tell anyone where I am, did you?"

"Of course not. When my son swears me to silence, silence it is. Besides, I don't know where you are. All you told me was 'some Caribbean island.'"

This is her way of needling me for information. I change the subject.

"How is Matthew?"

She sighs, realizing I'm not going to divulge my whereabouts.

"I just visited him. He's doing better. He's still depressed, but showing signs of bouncing back. They have him off suicide watch. He was talkative, and he asked about you. He wants to come home. I talked to the staff about his release. They say he's made progress but want to keep him for observation for another couple weeks. Matthew's happiness is my only concern, and if he wants to come home, that's good enough for me. I'll give it another few days, and if he still seems fine, I'm getting him the hell out of there."

"That's good news, Mom. He's been in that place long enough. When Matthew's back home and I'm a little more settled, I want you both to join me." I hesitate, breathe in, and let out a deep breath. "My stay here might be more than temporary."

The line goes silent for a moment as my mom digests this.

"I can't just pick up and leave everything behind. I know I have some money, but my whole life is here. I only want to know you are safe. And Matthew won't be in shape for a big trip anytime soon. He needs stability, not to be running himself ragged with you."

Hesitation creeps into her voice, as if she has something to say, but isn't sure how to say it.

"Look, Jason. I… I watch the news. I know about that Chinese restaurant owner getting killed."

Silence again, then she blurts out the rest. "You're mixed up in this, aren't you? Is this why you're running away?"

I don't respond. I should have known she'd figure it out. I didn't want to burden her with this now. Guiding Matthew back to health demands all her energy.

"Don't think I don't know what's going on. I'm not an idiot," she adds in a scolding tone.

So much for keeping her fears to herself. So much for avoiding bluntness.

"We can discuss all this later. I need to get going. I'll call again soon."

"Jason! Talk to me. Please. How do I reach you if I need to?"

"You don't. I'll call you soon. Bye, Mom."

I disconnect the call and drop the phone to the ground, stomping on it, smashing it to bits. I kick the remnants into nearby shrubbery, exerting more force than necessary. Worrying my mom wasn't on the agenda.

It's six a.m. now. I'm back at the hotel. The past hour or so I spent assessing the Hank situation and have come up with a plan. Hungry, I rummage through the mini-fridge and settle upon Tess's leftover sesame chicken from dinner last night. The appearance of Tess as I'm closing the fridge door startles me. It's disturbing I didn't hear her approaching footsteps. I'm supposed to be on high alert.

"Where have you been? What's going on with you?" Tess stands behind me in her pajamas.

"I need to make a quick trip to St. John."

"St. John? Why? When?"

"I fly out in a couple of hours. Don't worry about the why part. You stay here and enjoy the good life. I'll be back in a day or two."

I plop a thick wad of hundred dollar bills on the living room table and walk back to the kitchen, where Tess stands in disbelief. She sidesteps my attempt to kiss her goodbye. Her glare tells me I'm not leaving anytime soon.

"You either fill me in right now, or I'm on the next plane stateside." She folds her arms across her chest.

"Okay. I need to do some damage control."

Her hands move to her hips, like a mother chastising her child. Her neck stretches out toward me, her glare intensified. If Tess were a cartoon character, there would be steam coming out of her ears. She wants to hear more, and pronto.

I oblige. "Hank checked out of his hotel and isn't answering his phone. I want to find out what he's up to. Make sure he's sticking to the plan. That's all."

We're silent for a beat, as Tess takes a deep breath, formulating her response.

"I can't keep pretending." Her head bowed, she mutters more to herself than to me. She meets my gaze again. Her eyes are squinted, her brows furrowed, and she's scowling.

"I've been pretending everything is all right. That what you did—what we did—didn't really happen, or that it had to happen, like it was fate or karma. I've been behaving like we're on vacation, when in reality we're hiding out, dodging responsibility, eluding the law."

"Babe —"

She lets me know she's not finished by talking over me. "I knew in my heart what we were doing was wrong. And that's when I thought you were gonna just *scare* Chang. I let you persuade me into believing Chang needed to know what his action triggered."

I allow her to vent. I suppress a combative reply, deciding against reminding her of the opportunity to get out before all this went down.

"How many more dead bodies will there be following your trip to see Hank?"

Her voice is calm now, devoid of emotion. I turn my palms up, with shoulders lifted, in concession.

I regret involving Tess. From the beginning, back in the early planning stages, I tried to find a way to exact revenge without dragging Tess into it. Ultimately, it boiled down to me not trusting anyone else.

"No more killing. I promise."

Killing isn't something I expected to enjoy. I saw it as a necessary means for retribution. What caught me off-guard is how the act itself made me feel, which was powerful... killing made me feel... powerful. It's a thrill, on par with my first sexual encounter and the first homerun I hit in pee wee baseball. I liked the torturing part. Seeing the fear in Chang's eyes, the sense of futility as I carved him up. It's a rush, a feeling of power. I liked it so much that doing it again would be something I'd relish if it was someone who angered me. No, I don't aspire to be a serial killer, eliminating random innocent targets. If pushed, however, if given a reason, a need to right a wrong, I would embrace the opportunity. It's like I've acquired a hunger.

With no retort forthcoming, I continue speaking, fast, minimizing the opportunity for interruption.

"Now, I'm gonna go and hang out a little with a member of our team. When I'm back, my mind will be clear, and you'll have my full attention. We can talk for hours."

She doesn't respond verbally, merely shrugs her shoulders, her face unreadable. I tell her I love her and slither out, hoping she'll still support me when I return.

CHAPTER 9
JACK

I'M LEANING OVER THE RAILING on the balcony of my third-floor Best Western hotel suite, breathing in the fresh ocean air. It's a little cool, as the sun rises along the eastern horizon.

I spent yesterday peddling Hank's picture all over the island. I phoned forty-two St. Thomas hotels, hoping to learn Hank's name made it into a reservation system. No such luck. I drove to some of the nicer hotels, including the Ritz Carlton, Frenchman's Reef and Morning, Windward Passage, Bunker Hill, and Bolongo Bay Beach Resort, shoving Hank's mug in front of desk clerks, bellhops, and maids. No recognition. I invaded countless restaurants, disturbing wait staff, bussers, hostesses, and bartenders. More futility. I tried taxi companies, getting the same blank stares from drivers. I roamed beachfront properties, inquiring at boat rental outfits, snack bars, snorkeling and scuba shops. Either Hank is invisible, a recluse, or isn't living on the island. I returned to my hotel at midnight. Consumed by exhaustion, I quickly fell asleep.

Twenty minutes later, I'm boarding a ferry. It's a fifteen minute ride to St. John, the most logical destination for someone laying low near St. Thomas. An airline check of outgoing flights from either St. Thomas or St. Croix came back negative for a Mr. Hank Simpson. Between the ocean breeze and the stench of salt water filling my lungs with each deep breath, I momentarily forget I'm on a business trip. Luxury cruise ships, docked in both St. Thomas and St. John, add to the vacation-like atmosphere.

Now on St. John soil, and back in business mode, I give Peter a call. He picks up on the first ring and I update him. His lack of immediate response conveys disappointment. I set expectations before my jaunt, explaining that manhunts like these don't usually yield immediate results, and patience is paramount. I don't have much to report. This is a courtesy call.

"Could he have left the island? Did you check outgoing flights? Hell, he could be living in a secluded hut."

I detect a hint of panic in Peter's voice. I go with my reassuring tone.

"Hey, he's human. Humans leave a trace. I'll find him."

I end the conversation, borderline-rudely cutting off another stream of questions.

Dressed in slacks, a polo shirt, and loafers, I blend in reasonably well as a tourist, despite the long pants in eighty-degree, sunny weather. I'd prefer to be in shorts, but then concealing my Colt 45 revolver would be more difficult. I don't have my full arsenal of surveillance equipment with me, but am carrying a top-of-the-line Konus long-range Spotting Scope in a knapsack, casually flung over a shoulder, as well as a pack-of-gum-sized Sony digital voice recorder in my trouser pocket. More gadgetry, including long range audio devices and night vision scopes, are back at the hotel. In my wallet, I have an authentic looking police badge. It comes in handy for eliciting cooperation.

My picture of Hank in tow, I resume my search. I cover a lot of ground in the morning, yet have nothing to show for it other than sore legs and a lion-sized appetite. Walking through the downtown Cruz Bay Area, scattered with places to take a load off and quench your thirst and hunger, I spot a hip seafood joint, the Fish Trap, its sign sporting a cartoon-like fish at the apex.

Jovial chatter resonates through the place as I'm led to one of the few vacant tables. Glancing around, I observe the common theme of alcohol. Pitchers of beer, margaritas, rum punch, and wine. Waitresses huddled by the bar, empty trays awaiting drink orders. Laughter, loudness, slurred words. It really is the good life down here.

"Can I get you started with something to drink?"

An attractive blonde, medium height, twenty five or so, greets me, poised to scribble down my request. As a rule, I don't drink on the job. Of course, work doesn't often take me to a tropical island. Fatigue and frustration break down my resolve.

"I'll have a bourbon on the rocks, please."

I'm perusing the menu as Tiffany—so says her name tag—returns with my drink, bread and butter. She pulls a pad and pen from her skirt pocket as I ask what she recommends.

"My favorite is the ginger-seared salmon. It's a house specialty."

"That's good enough for me. Salmon it is."

She's bopping to the pop music, piped in through big speakers in all corners of the large dining area.

"Tiffany, I have a question for you, if you don't mind."

"Sure, shoot."

I reach into my pocket and flash the picture. "Have you seen this man before? He's an old friend I'm trying to reconnect with."

She takes a long look before answering. "Well, he has a beard now, but I'm pretty sure I've seen him a few times in the cafeteria."

"The cafeteria?"

"Oh, sorry. Yeah, the cafeteria at the hospital in St. Thomas. That's where I work. Well, it's actually a medical center. The Schneider Medical Center. This is just a moonlighting gig a couple days a week. It's a happier environment here, though doesn't pay as well. Is it still called moonlighting if I work in the afternoon? Anyway, I'm rambling now."

My speech is delayed as I process this potential breakthrough development. "Have you spoken to him?"

"Well, not to sound full of myself, but I think he hit on me the other day, as he was paying for his cheeseburger and fries. Said he lives here in St. John and owns a nice sailboat."

"If this is my friend, his name is Hank Simpson. Does that ring a bell?"

"No, sorry, I never got his name. He isn't really my type. Too skinny and I don't like beards. Plus, you know, I've got a boyfriend. I better get your order in now."

"Yes, of course. Thanks for your time. You're going to get a good tip."

"Cool." She smiles as she saunters away.

I hope Tiffany is as right about Hank as she was about the salmon. My plate cleaned, and having resisted the urge to have another bourbon, I exit the restaurant with a spring in my step.

⋅∘⫘∘⋅

Sitting dockside at the St. John Marina, home to a hundred or so boats, I consider the odds Tiffany's information will lead me to Hank. I'm having trouble accepting that Hank would be spending time in a hospital. Having been on the island for only a week or so, he likely wouldn't have made a close friend yet, let alone a sick one requiring hospital visitation. Going with her story, the only plausible conclusion would be Hank himself required repeated medical attention. This seems unlikely for a guy in his mid-thirties. Still, with nothing else to go on, I pursue the lead, a lead which has landed me on the largest marina on the island. With an island population of only four thousand, finding his alleged boat is certainly possible. A quick count of sailboats docked in slips reveals about forty.

I head inside the marina, my mind piecing together a cover story.

"Can I help you?" asks a pimply-faced teenager behind the counter.

"Yes, I hope so. My name is Jack. I'm supposed to meet my

friend Hank Simpson by the docks for a ride in his boat, but I can't find him and he's not answering his phone. I'm a little concerned and am wondering if you may have seen him."

The kid makes a weird thinking expression. Without responding, he wheels around and yells in the direction of an older gentleman, whose leather-like face and arms indicate a life spent in the island sun. The kid's boss, perhaps.

"Hey, Mac, remember the guy who rented a slip for the orange Hobie Cat he bought from Bill Weathers? Is he Hank Simpson?"

"Yup, that's him. He's out in it all the time. Can't sail worth a shit. Who's asking?"

By the time the kid spins back around, I'm talking into my phone. Sensing his gaze on me, I pause, covering the receiver with my hand, and look up.

"I just got ahold of him. I'm good now. Thanks."

I resume speaking into my phone, continuing the charade, as I briskly head for the exit.

Playing it safe, in the event Mac or Pimply Face have a suspicious side, I slip into a men's room, unzip my backpack, and alter my appearance. I trade in my trousers for shorts, my polo shirt for a tank top, put on a baseball cap—bill down, hiding my face—and apply a fake beard.

Back at the docks, I wander by the boats, searching for a smallish sailboat with a Hobie Cat inscription. Having never sailed and not being a boat person, I hope I'm looking for an orange hull, as opposed to an orange sail. Spotting an orange sail would be difficult since all the sails have been removed from their masts, customary when docked, as a security measure. Twenty minutes later, I've examined all the sailboats. Five Hobie Cats, but none are orange. Of the several sailboats visible on the water, none have orange sails. They are too far out to identify hull colors or manufacturers.

Time to play the waiting game. Patience is a trait PI's either have or develop. Surveillance is lonely, time-consuming work. All

I can do is wait for Hank to show up. This could mean coming in from the water or heading out into it. If he doesn't show up by nightfall, the latter becomes the likelier scenario.

Scanning the area for a lookout location, I spot a shady stretch of sand at the beach's entrance, under a large green tree. I'm a good hundred yards from the docks, but with my scope, getting a close-up view isn't a problem. Not only do I have a clear view of faces, I could detect a mole on someone's neck. Having secured my residence for the next several hours until nightfall, I grab a large coffee from a convenience store down the street. Real coffee drinkers aren't deterred by warm weather.

Coffee in hand, I settle in. I spread out the blanket I picked up at a beachside shop, next to the convenience store. I may as well call Garrison, so I fish out my cell phone. Once again, Peter answers before the second ring. His folks are with him, and after some muffled chatter, I'm put on speaker. Following a quick debriefing, Peter speaks up.

"That's great news, Jack. I want to be there to confront him. I could fly out right away." Before I can respond, Doug jumps in.

"No, Peter. Not a good idea. Let's hear Jack out."

"I'm with your dad on this, Peter. I understand how you feel, but I've got experience in situations like this. I'm not gonna lose him. I've got a few ideas, and I have the upper hand. For starters, I'm armed. He most likely won't be. I'll also have the element of surprise in my favor. I've learned when you catch someone off guard, you get more genuine information out of them. They don't have time to rehearse a story."

"What's your plan?" ask Peter and his parents in unison.

"I'm still formalizing the details, but the end game will be getting his story and bringing him back to the States to face justice."

"Okay, we'll trust your plan, but please let us know as soon as you find him," Peter says, displaying a take-charge attitude.

"Roger that," I answer with a hint of sarcasm. But I get it.

Peter's future is on the line. His freedom. His dignity. "Oh, I almost forgot, one last thing. Peter, does Hank have any health issues you're aware of?"

"No, not that I know of. We weren't best friends, and he's a private guy. He wouldn't necessarily share something like that. Why do you ask?"

"He may have been at the hospital down here. It probably means nothing, if he was there at all, but I'll follow up just the same."

I promise to stay in touch, knowing the three of them will camp out by the phone, awaiting news.

I steal a moment to appreciate my surroundings. The beach, ocean, boats, breeze, and serenity all make for easy living. Pulling out my iPhone, I jot down some follow-up items.

Bill Weathers: sold Hank boat, may know where Hank is staying.

Schneider Medical Center: find out why Hank was there.

Sailing instructors: if Hank lacks sailing skills, he might be taking lessons.

Now time to iron out my plan of attack when confronting Hank. There's the bully approach. Strong-arm him onto his boat, getting him alone offshore, where screams are muffled. Cops routinely beat confessions out of perps. A tried-and-true approach. An approach I'm physically capable of pulling off. I've used intimidation before, scaring the shit out of a few guys. Today, though, I'm feeling politically correct, preferring a reasoning tactic. As with most plans, circumstance often dictates action. As long as Hank cooperates, there'll be no reason to inflict pain.

Back to my list. I dial four-one-one, requesting the number for Bill Weathers. Unlisted. I could go back to Pimply Face, but that would draw attention to myself. Besides, Weathers knowing anything useful about Hank is a long shot. I'll try the hospital next, but if patient confidentiality here is anything like in the States, obtaining information will be tricky, my mastery of deceit notwithstanding. With time to kill, I give it a shot.

"Hello, Schneider Medical Center," says a youngish female voice.

"Yes, hello. I'm Jack Simpson. I just flew in from Vermont. My cousin, Hank Simpson, has been getting treatment at your facility. He doesn't want to worry anyone in the family, but we're all concerned and I've been selected as the family representative to check up on him. He says he's doing great, but Hank always puts up a brave front. If there's anything at all I can do to help…" Playing a hunch, I pause for air.

"Umm, Mr. Simpson, I'm afraid I can't give out patient information."

Switching gears. "Can you tell me what services your center performs?"

"It's pretty much like a hospital in the States. Whatever ails you, we'll fix you up. We're the largest medical facility on the island." Gushing with pride, she continues. "We recently added a new division, the Charlotte Kimelman Cancer Institute. It's state of the art and critically acclaimed."

I'm beginning to wonder if she's a stockholder.

"That's impressive. If I get sick while out here, I'll know where to go."

I end the call on that note. Last on the list: the sailing instruction probe. That'll work better in person, with a picture in hand.

A sea of sails glide into my peripheral vision. Grabbing my scope, I scan the boats. There must be ten of them headed ashore. Gazing from boat to boat, I abruptly jump up as an orange hull floats into view. I make out the words *Hobie Cat* at the stern. Raising and steadying the scope, I lock in on the skipper.

"Fucking A." I'm tightening my grip on the picture I've been holding onto like it's gold. A glance back at the boat, once more back to the picture. It's him all right. Bearded, just as Tiffany described.

I pack up my knapsack and advance towards the docks.

CHAPTER 10
PETER

I'M DOWNTOWN AT THE COUNTY office building, waiting for a computer to free up in the public records room. I'm waiting for my number to be called.

Dissatisfied with the progress being made on my case—both the police and Sir William have disappointed—I'm taking matters into my own hands.

Proving a negative is a difficult thing to do. You can make a strong argument, but definitively stating something *didn't* happen—in this case, that I *didn't* kill Chang—is nearly impossible. It's akin to proving a squirrel wasn't in your backyard last night. You could say there were no squirrel tracks discovered, no acorns left behind, no squirrel noises heard throughout the night. But none of this *proves* there wasn't a squirrel presence. Maybe one scurried across a small portion of your yard, seeking a nut it spotted. Maybe a larger animal chased it, covering the squirrel's prints.

A guy in overalls, architectural drawings tucked under his arm, bumps into my chair on his way to a permitting window. Based on the glimpse I get of the papers, he must be applying for a building permit. Acknowledging his clumsiness doesn't occur to him as he barrels past me.

Tracking down the waitress and hunting down Hank are fine, but neither of them stabbed Chang enough times to ensure he'd never see chopsticks again. Nailing the butcher requires finding a motive. *Means, motive, and opportunity,* sums up the three aspects of a crime that must be established before determining guilt in a criminal proceeding. The pool of people with the means and opportunity to take out Chang is quite large. The pool diminishes exponentially when adding motive to the mix. My angle of attack must be finding someone with an ax to grind. This wasn't a random killing. Not an accidental thing. It was vicious and personal. I need to uncover the motivation.

Figuring I'd have some idle time, I brought along my laptop. Exploring as many avenues of information as I deem relevant, I start by Googling Chang. I did this upon my release from prison, but want to be thorough. Some hits on his restaurant, but little else. Nothing controversial. No signs he was an activist, no political ties, no public views on abortion, or the right to bear arms.

I had Jack run a background check. Only moving violations reported by Motor Vehicle Division came up. It's a little unsettling how your past indiscretions are obtainable by others without your consent or knowledge. I could have run the check myself—an online search for *background check* nets a host of companies, each offering a better deal than the next—but presumed Jack could obtain a more comprehensive report.

An elderly woman exits the public records room, allowing my entry. A dozen computer terminals, with direct access to databases housing public information, line the back wall of the room. A service personnel lady, sitting behind a desk in the front of the room, fields questions. I'm not sure what I'm looking for, but figure I'll know when I see it. Like cops executing an open-ended search warrant. Going in, they aren't specifically looking for bloodied tan loafers, but if their search uncovers such said shoes, the footwear will no doubt find their way into a sealed evidence bag.

Some of my curiosities can't be quenched via public information. Things like: was Chang being blackmailed? Did he beat anyone up? Blow the whistle on someone? Piss someone off? Maybe he gave *the finger* to the wrong person. I've tasked Sir William with getting access to his bank statements, in search of large withdrawals.

I spend some time sifting through land ownership. Chang and his wife owned the land on his primary residence and the small lot Peking Dragon stands on. He had no construction plans, was never divorced, had no pending lawsuits or complaints filed by or levied against. I make a note to check on complaints called into the cops, which wind up in a police-managed database. The complaints I'm rifling through have been lodged through the county.

The Quincy Municipal Court, located on the second floor of the Police Court Building, houses civic and criminal records. I approach two server windows, neither, surprisingly, with a line. I choose the girl over the old man. She's a little chubby, but cute. She has large brown eyes with long lashes, and a friendly demeanor. As she explains the procedure for accessing the information I'm after, which involves going into a back room with computer terminals, she smiles. Could she be flirting with me? She breaks off her spiel and stares at me, puzzlement in her expression.

"You look familiar. Have we met?"

"No. I would have remembered you for sure. Maybe you've seen me on TV or in the papers."

Before I can explain further, she excitedly asks, "Are you famous or something?"

"No, not famous, but, yes, *or something*. I'm accused—falsely, I assure you—of killing Michael Chang, the guy who owned the Chinese restaurant Peking Dragon."

Her jaw drops in amazement and disbelief. "Wow, that's you? You don't look like a killer."

"Thanks. That means a lot to me."

A line has formed behind me, but I'm only vaguely aware its presence. I'm monopolizing their resource, with no intentions of releasing it. I'm smitten, and in no rush for our playful exchange to end.

"Aren't you supposed to be in jail? I mean, I thought you were arrested." She seems oblivious to the line, as her smile and expressive eyes remain focused on me.

"I'm out on bail. If I had a passport, it would have been confiscated."

She smirks, appreciating the humor of my situation.

"Since you know about me now, could you tell me your name?"

She shuffles papers, pondering my request. "I'm Amy. And you? I'm guessing Killer is just a nickname."

This elicits a hearty laugh from me. "I'm Peter. Very nice to meet you, Amy."

Formalities out of the way, Amy jumps back to my situation. "So, hypothetically speaking, you iced this Chang dude, and had no plans to flee afterwards. In all the legal books I read, the bad guy hits the road pretty quickly. If I'm recalling correctly, you were picked up the next day at your apartment. Forget leaving the jurisdiction, you didn't even leave your neighborhood." She grins, proud of her assessment.

"You know, that's a good point. My folks are shelling out a lot of money to a lawyer who didn't pick up on this. How would you like to represent me? You're smarter, and cuter, than the old geezer I've got now." The cuter part slipped out, atypically for me.

Amy blushes, before responding. "Cuter than an old geezer? I'm not sure that qualifies as a compliment."

"Sorry. I can do better. I must be nervous."

"I'm just giving you a hard time. If you weren't a murder suspect, I might even find you a little charming." Amy flips her hair back, flirtatiously, momentarily mesmerizing me.

Behind me, someone clears their throat. Other folks in line mutter their impatience.

"I won't be a suspect for long. It's all a big misunderstanding. Does anyone ever get framed in those books you read?"

"Well, yeah, it has been known to happen. You know, the more I think about it, I can't recall a killer voluntarily showing up at a police building. I'd say you're either innocent or an odd bird." Pausing to appreciate her humor, she adds, "Actually, I think you may be both."

I place my hands on my hips, feigning indignation. Amy holds back laughter.

"Okay, I see no interpretation where being called an *odd bird* is complimentary."

She giggles at this, and I think I'm in love.

The chatter volume behind me increases. Any minute now, the crowd could turn unruly.

"Well, I better get on those records." Not wanting to press my luck, I start walking away, but stop after a few steps, turning back towards her. Exhibiting uncharacteristic boldness, I ask, "Hey, when I get exonerated, can I come back and take you out for a cup of coffee?"

Amy mulls over this proposition. My heart races.

"I'm not really a coffee drinker, but lunch might be ok." I smile as she adds, "But I reserve the right to change my mind if you get off on a hung jury or some technicality."

Before she can add anything further, I go to her, extending my hand. "You've got a deal."

Amy leans forward, venturing across the employee/customer boundary. We shake on it, our hands clasped together a bit longer than necessary. Ignoring dirty looks from members of the line, I exit again, this time without a glance back, trying to hide my swagger.

In the computer room, it doesn't take long to learn that Chang isn't referenced in either the civil or criminal records database.

On my way home from downtown, noticing the late hour, I pull over, into a McDonalds parking lot, and dial a number I have programmed in my phone. Debbie, Chang's wife, picks up.

"Hello?"

"Hello. Mrs. Chang, I'm Detective Louis Simmons with QPD. Might you have a few minutes for some questions?"

"Sure, Detective."

Compared to homicide, impersonating an officer is small potatoes. Besides, it will be overlooked once the truth comes out, especially if I assist in catching the perpetrator. I provide some case details not made public, as validation of my official capacity. I gain her trust with sincere sympathy, and she opens up.

"Michael had something of a temper. And little patience for incompetence." She speaks softly, anguish evident. She pauses, unsure how to proceed. I prod her.

"Did you see or hear him arguing with anyone?"

"Well, he'd yell at the neighborhood kids when stray balls landed in our yard, and they trampled through his garden, retrieving them. He went off a few weeks ago on our next door neighbor, Barry, when his barking dog wouldn't shut up."

So the guy is a hothead. Surely, his temper rubbed some folks the wrong way.

"I know this is difficult, Mrs. Chang, but all this will help us catch whoever killed your husband. Is there anyone else you can recall Mr. Chang having a conflict with?"

A pause.

"The police already asked me all this. Don't you guys compare notes?"

Exhaustion and exasperation seep out. I need to press on, but finish up quickly.

"Please, Mrs. Chang, bear with me for just a moment longer. I wasn't available for the initial questioning. I'd prefer to hear directly from you rather than reading a report."

She sighs, before relenting. "Nobody specific, no. Daily life would just get to him. He got under my skin, on occasion. So it wouldn't surprise me to learn there were people who didn't like him."

Another pause.

I can picture her drawing an imaginary cross over her chest as she says, "I'm only telling you this so you're best equipped to find who did this to Michael. And don't get me wrong, Michael is... was... a wonderful man."

She's an emotional wreck, on the verge of tears. We're both silent for a beat as she composes herself. Mrs. Chang mentions that no one has kept her in the loop concerning progress on the case. I promise to call with any new developments, and we say our goodbyes.

⟡

Following my call with the widowed Mrs. Chang, I swing by Subway for a chicken teriyaki foot-long. I'm a regular here, on a first name basis with some of the *sandwich artists*. Mary slips me a free bag of chips, proclaiming me as her favorite customer. Knowing my dilemma, she discreetly asks how I'm holding up. She's attractive and personable and if it weren't for the giant diamond on her ring finger, I would have asked her out long ago. Settled at a corner window table, I unwrap my sub.

Three bites in, my phone rings. Sir William summons me to his office. I hang up, wrap my sandwich, and make the ten minute drive.

A large oak desk bisects his large office. His chair resembles a throne, with its high back and jeweled arms. I pull up a plush chair, next to my dad. We're both dressed comfortably in jeans and T-shirts, while William wears his uniform, a suit and tie. I sometimes wonder if he sleeps with a tie on.

"Thank you for joining me on short notice. I just had coffee with my friend on the force. As I've mentioned, he works in the Burglary Unit, but he's plugged in to the goings-on of the entire Quincy Police Department. Being a small department, sans a vast homicide presence, this isn't surprising. Anyway, Bob shared some news I believe will make you both quite happy."

William sips coffee, for dramatic effect. The pause, too long for our liking, prompts my dad and me to speak up in unison. My dad's deep voice drowns out mine.

"For Christ's sake, William, get on with it."

William brings his leather recliner to an upright position, placing his elbows on his desk.

"Right. The prosecution of your case is going nowhere. Both homicide and the DA's office keep running into dead ends, which, parenthetically, is consistent with the grumblings I'm hearing from my contact in the DA's office. They can't find a motive."

My dad makes a fist, shaking it in celebratory fashion.

"That's because I don't have one," I say a little too loudly. "I didn't *know* Chang. Never met the guy. Had no ill will towards him."

My dad places a soothing hand on my shoulder, which I brush away.

Sir William leans forward, across his desk, and delivers his next bundle of information in a hushed tone. "I think they're finally getting that. They know you've been snooping around downtown, and they know about Jack. They figure either you're expending a lot of time and money on misdirection, or you may be innocent."

My dad grins. I do as well, but a little more frustration seeps out. "They could have saved a lot of tax payer money by simply believing me from the onset."

Sir William has had enough of my victim act, and feels a need to defend the legal system.

"Yeah, well these gentlemen can be pigheaded about due diligence. They have a funny thing about thoroughness before eliminating their prime suspect." Sarcasm laces his words, before he eases up and turns serious again. "The good news is they've got detectives now looking for other suspects."

"Great. Tell them they're a little behind, but I'll be happy to share what I've got."

"You? *We* don't have anything concrete, Peter."

My dad shoots both myself and William a disappointing look. He's not amused by our petty exchange.

"When will they be dismissing the charges against Peter?" asks my dad, tired of waiting for William to broach the subject.

Sir William smiles as he extends his palm towards my dad. A *whoa* gesture.

"Let's hold our horses on that. I voiced my news would make you happy, not delirious. Someone in top brass isn't ready to cut you loose just yet."

"You *voiced*?" I can't help myself.

Ignoring my sarcasm, my dad picks up the conversation. "So, they plan to proceed with the preliminary hearing?"

William leans back in his recliner, clasping his hands behind his neck. Sure, now that he has our undivided attention, he responds.

"As far as I know, yes, they do. If Jack can deliver Hank, as you gentlemen seem to think is imminent, and his story is compelling enough, and they can verify even parts of it, we're in business. Further, when, and I stress *when*, as opposed to *if*, I come up with something to support our *some other dude did it* theory, it's a brand-spanking-new ball game."

"William, it's not a theory. It's a fact. The theoretical part is that you'll be uncovering the evidence supporting such fact." I'm incapable of keeping the snide remark to myself.

Sir William directs his retort at my dad. "What's gotten into this boy of yours, Doug. He used to be a nice, respectful kid."

Before my dad can respond, I jump in. "What's *gotten into me*, William, is my life is hanging in the balance, and I'm not getting warm fuzzies over the fact I remain the only suspect, and am awaiting trial for a murder I didn't commit!"

Sir William reclines in his chair, smirking.

My dad plays mediator. "Hey, we're all on the same team here. William, Peter is not a boy, rather a grown, intelligent man. And son, despite the lack of results thus far, I trust William will come through for us, with a breakthrough imminent. Maybe we should call it a day. William, did you have anything else?"

William stares at the ceiling, probably considering, then rejecting, a sarcastic comeback. "Nothing pressing. I've interviewed most of the help at Peking Dragon and have a couple leads on our mystery waitress, including a detailed sketch of her."

"What kind of leads?" I've already provided a description. A sketch won't lead to her whereabouts if her appearance has changed. Even if it hasn't, she's likely left town.

I'm on the receiving end of a glare from William, obviously not pleased with my message and tone. He directs his response toward my dad. "Places she frequents, people she associates with, that sort of thing. I have an assistant out canvassing with her picture. Admittedly, it's a long shot, but I don't like leaving stones unturned."

"So, nothing on the identity of our Jack the Ripper?" If he had something, he would have led with it, but I want to see him squirm.

"Well, I have some irons in the fire, but nothing to report on yet."

Growing tired of his metaphors, I let him off the hook. I remain silent, as does Sir William. My dad breaks the standoff by rising and initiating the goodbyes.

CHAPTER 11
JASON

MY TIMING HAS NEVER BEEN great. Lady Luck is rarely with me. The saying *if it weren't for shit luck, I'd have no luck at all,* should include my name as a footnote. The first time I bought a pack of smokes, at fifteen, at the corner convenience store, a cop wandered in as I was leaving. He confiscated the cigs and read me the riot act. When I used to skip school back in the day, I'd invariably run into a friend of my mom's, who would report back to her. I've never won at anything. Not cards, despite possessing an awesome poker face. Not being the third radio station caller. Not even a raffle.

The break I caught today though makes up for all of it. A resident at the dive Poodle Boy moved out of happened to notice him loading up his shit. Later, they headed out at the same time, in the same direction—my new best friend for groceries, Poodle Boy to his new, luxurious dwelling at Turtle Bay Apartments.

A walk around the premises yields two pieces of information. First, I found no indication of a security personnel presence. Secondly, I count about forty units in the complex. The front office is the logical place to inquire about Hank, but I don't want to get on management's radar. With the sun shining, and the temperature in the eighties, I'm not surprised to find the pool hopping. Only a grey-bearded man floating on his back, and three teenage boys tossing around a beach ball, are in the pool. The rest, sprawled out on lounge chairs, work on their tans.

Time to disrupt the tranquility.

"Hey everyone!" I shout, capturing the attention of all. Ignoring glares from an elderly couple, each with a hard-cover book in their lap, I continue. "My buddy Hank Simpson and I are throwing a big bash this weekend at his apartment to celebrate my visit from the States. There will be free food and drinks, and lots of alcohol. Hank is making up flyers now, which will have all the details. You're all invited."

The reaction to my phantom party announcement, overwhelmingly, is indifference. A dude with long, dark hair and a lip ring gives me a thumbs up.

"Cool, bro," chimes in a middle-aged man in a speedo. He's pretending to read a magazine, while not-so-discreetly checking out a couple of young women lying face down a few chairs away.

One of the sunbathers, a cute blonde in a black and white bikini, says, "Sounds like fun. I'm in twelve C, right next door, so it'll be a short walk."

Neglecting the others, I advance to the blonde. With a cat-that-ate-the-canary grin on my face, I respond, "That's great. Hank didn't mention he lived next door to a beautiful woman."

Blondie blushes and keeps the chatter going. "You must be a good influence on Hank. He seems like the quiet type."

The three-quarters empty wine glass in her hand aids her loose lips. I'm tempted to hang around, but maintain my focus and politely excuse myself.

Apartment twelve C is a corner unit, meaning the adjacent eleven C belongs to Hank. I circle to the rear of his place, encountering a lush wooden area beyond it. The bathroom window appears just large enough for me to squeeze through.

Breaking into the apartment proves easy. A fierce blow with my elbow shatters it—the window, that is, not my elbow. No alarms go off, nor does anyone notice my intrusion. I gather the jagged pieces of glass and dispose of them in a nearby trash receptacle. I'm satisfied the open window won't raise suspicion today. Tomorrow, the odor of a decaying body, not the window, will be the attention attractor.

Inside, I plop myself down on a comfortable suede couch in Poodle Boy's living room.

My first stop, upon arriving in St. Johns, was at a hiking and camping store where I picked up a carving knife that makes the letter opener look like a toothpick. I decided on a knife over a gun for a few reasons. First, and foremost, guns make loud noises. Further, I'm not familiar with the gun laws here. There could be a required waiting period before purchase. Traceable records might be kept. Buying a knife with cash is quick and leaves no footprints. The appeal of the more intimate nature inherent in stabbings clinched it.

While I'm prepared to kill again—it could happen within the hour, if Poodle Boy gets home soon—I'm not a shoot first, ask questions later type of guy. I'll give him a chance to explain himself. To tell me why he broke two of our established ground rules. He must always carry his cell phone with him and must notify me immediately if he moves. *Fucking with me is not in the rule book.*

I must admit, this guy does a good job spending his newfound money. I find a bottle of Grey Goose vodka in the freezer and steaks thawing in the fridge. Waiting for him to show up won't be as boring as I thought.

CHAPTER 12
JACK

HAVING STEERED HIS BOAT INTO his slip, Hank prepares to jump out, rope in hand, to perform the dock line tying ritual. Stern lines, bow lines, spring lines. If you don't know what you're doing, you could find your boat has drifted off somewhere the next time you want to take her out for a ride. Before Hank can steady himself and get onto the dock, I make a running start, leap onboard, and land a few feet from where he stands.

"What the hell! What're you doing, mister?"

His voice is high-pitched, as if he has just inhaled helium.

"I need to get off land for a bit. Can you take me for a quick spin?" I flash a wad of bills, mostly Washingtons and Lincolns, but they are sandwiched between a pair of Jacksons. "I'll pay you well. I missed the last charter of the day and am going stir crazy. If you charter, I'll book you for the week. My name is Bill Foghorn. You're the lucky guy I've run into first." Sensing Hank's bewilderment, I add, "I didn't mean to startle you."

"Startle? Try *scared the shit out of*. Ever hear of asking permission before boarding a stranger's boat? A lesser man would have cured your stir-craziness by tossing you into the water."

Suppressing a hearty laugh at the image of this smallish, out of shape guy trying to lift me, I throw my hands up in surrender. "You're right. My approach needs work. My sincerest apologies. Honestly, I just flew into St. Thomas, caught a ferry here, checked into my hotel, threw on some chillin' clothes, and hopped a taxi back here. The ferry ride was so intoxicating I have to get back on the water." I'm fighting off a smirk, one that developed when I said *chillin'*, a word that's never come out of my mouth. I'm not sure what chillin' clothes are, but doubt my garb qualifies.

"I'm not the best sailor. And I'm not running a charter business. It'll be dark soon, anyway."

"Half an hour would do wonders for me. I'll pay you a hundred dollars. You haven't tied up yet."

Hank considers the offer for a moment. "Sorry pal. I'm gonna call it a night. There are lots of charters you can catch in the morning."

I take a couple steps forward, eliminating the space between us. I lift my shirt, exposing my gun. "Please reconsider. I'm not gonna hurt you, just want to talk."

Hank's entire body shakes. He scans the area around us, likely gauging whether screaming or running are viable options. With the barrel of my gun now pressed against his belly, he acquiesces.

"Okay, you win."

Moments later, having navigated us into deeper water, Hank breaks the silence. "So, who are you? And what do you want with me?"

"Does the name Peter Garrison ring a bell?"

Hank does his best to disguise his uneasiness at the mention of Peter's name. "Are you a cop or something?" His voice crackles.

Playing out the two scenarios in my mind—cop versus PI—I go with the truth, confident I'll get results either way.

"I'm a private investigator, hired by Peter. Listen Hank, the cops are looking for you too. They've eliminated Peter as a suspect. I know you aren't a killer. Just tell me what you know, come back to Vermont with me, and clear Peter's good name."

Sensing him weighing his options—denial versus a soul unburdening—I add, "I know you want to do the right thing. Give up who got you into this and you'll get off with a slap on the wrist. If you choose the devil, however, I have no problem using this gun. Maybe I'll just wound you, shoot you in the leg, causing amputation. Then again, the truth will come out, with or without your cooperation, so I may just blow you away because I can't stand lying weasels."

More silence. Still mulling? Defiance? I play a hunch. "I know about your cancer. I visited the medical center in St. Thomas. They filled me in. Amazing what you can learn by donating a large sum of cash."

Hank's facial expression shows exhaustion, defeatism. Living with a huge weight on your shoulders can wear you down. Many criminals carry with them a burden of inevitable capture. In Hank's case, I suspect he's guilt-ridden, as well.

Sure he will spill his guts, I'm content waiting, listening to the squawking seagulls, overhead. It's not long before my mind-reading skills are validated. Hank lets out a deep breath and steadies himself by grabbing onto a side railing.

"All right. I'm not cut out for this bad guy stuff. I've been looking for a reason to turn myself in, and apparently you're the nudge I've needed. I feel terrible about what I did to Peter. He's a good guy and I took advantage of his good nature." He pauses, shaking his head from side to side. "I can't believe my health issues were divulged to you." His indignance doesn't last long, as his focus returns.

"You're right, I do have cancer. The same kind that did my mom in ten years ago. I was diagnosed six months ago and the prognosis isn't good. With my mom passed and my dad remarried, living in Arizona, I have nobody to help me through this. I became bitter, angry at the hand life dealt me. My *why me* questions have gone unanswered."

He talks fast, consumed by nerves. I play the role of a priest during confessional, allowing him to purge himself while I listen.

"Having been relatively poor my entire life, I couldn't pass up a chance to spend whatever time I have left on this planet in style. It was an omen or something. Life's way of throwing me a bone. A consolation prize. *You're gonna die soon, but have some exotic island fun before you go.* And all I had to do was betray Peter. I knew he'd get off and be fine. I knew he'd be steaming mad, but figured he'd forgive me once I'm dead."

"But your conscience starting getting in the way, right?"

Waves from a nearby speedboat rock us, causing us both to grab onto the railing which runs around the boat's perimeter. Once stabilized, Hank replies.

"Yeah. I started thinking my spot in Heaven would be given away to someone else. That I needed to cleanse my soul."

Cleanse away, I'm thinking. I provide a final nudge. "It's not too late to turn this thing around, Hank. Why don't you tell me what happened. Take it from the start. I won't contact the authorities until we're back in Quincy. You have my word on that. And, by the way, I'm sorry about the cancer. You're too young for this to be happening. Life isn't fair."

I tuck my gun back into my pants.

"I appreciate that. As far as what went down, I'm not sure how much help I'll be."

He has my full attention, as well my digital audio recorder's, which has been on for a while now.

"A few days before the Chang murder, a young woman approached me in a park. She outlined a plan in which I had to get Peter to deliver a letter opener to her. She told me she was a waitress at Peking Dragon. I'm sure Peter has shared the ruse with you, as far as me claiming the opener was a gift I wanted him to give to her. I know her as Cindy, though I doubt that's her real name. I didn't know Chang would wind up dead. Really, I didn't. I knew something shady was in the works, but I guess the money dampened my skepticism. And skewed my judgment."

"How much money?" Curiosity triggers my interruption.

"Seventy-five thousand. Ten percent handed to me in an envelope right there at the park. Anyway, shortly after I sent Peter into the restaurant, I met Cindy's partner to receive the rest of the money. This guy, Bernie—again, probably not his real name—delivered as promised. He let me know, in no uncertain terms, should I sing, I'll be a dead man."

Hank brings his right hand to his temple, his pointed index finger and raised thumb forming a resemblance to a gun. I nod, letting him know I get it and prompting him to continue.

"Bernie gave me a disposable cell phone, which he required me to carry around so he could check up on me. I didn't like this development, but the time for bargaining had passed. I didn't know yet about Chang, but figured foul play had taken place at Peking Dragon."

"So has Bernie been calling you?" I realize you can't trace throw away phones, but hope to garner information regarding Bernie's state of mind, even a tip-off about his whereabouts or plans.

"He called a two or three times, but I lost my phone yesterday when I capsized this baby. I searched for it, futilely. Must be karma."

Turning off the recorder, I lay out the plan. "Here's how this is going to play out. We're gonna head back to the docks, drive to your place, gather your belongings, and catch a ferry to St. Thomas. They leave on the hour until 11 pm, so we have plenty of time. We'll bunk at my hotel tonight and catch an early morning flight to the States."

Hank wearily nods his consent and murmurs, "I just want to put all this behind me."

CHAPTER 13
JASON

Fatigue has set in by the time I hear a car pull into the parking lot, its headlights beaming into the living room, where I'm watching the tube. Pushing aside a bottom corner of the drapes, I observe the action. The driver side door opens, and it's not Poodle Boy. This guy, taller and better-looking, moves with a self-confident swagger. *Shit*. I'm in for more waiting. As I'm releasing the curtain, I glimpse a skinny figure emerging from the passenger side of the car. A few seconds later, I get a clear view of the face—Poodle Boy.

I didn't expect this monkey wrench. Thinking quickly, I head for the bathroom to buy some time. Who the hell is this other guy? What do I do when Poodle Boy needs to pee? What if the other guy needs to take a leak? I hear a key in the lock, and then voices. Assessing the situation, I yank the door closed, my ear pressed against it. Fortunately, Mr. Confidence speaks authoritatively, as in loudly. The picture quickly becomes clear. This guy is a PI who has tracked down my accomplice with the intention of dragging him back to Quincy. I can't let this happen.

Fighting off panic, I take several measured deep breaths. I pat the material of my pants at the sock line feeling my weapon securely intact. *Be cool*. I repeat this in my mind as a mantra. Thinking clearly, again, I devise a plan. There won't be time for conversation, only swift force. Positioned behind the door, I ready myself for the ensuing excitement.

A few moments after the PI implores Poodle Boy to get his shit packed up, I hear footsteps drawing near. His bedroom is past the bathroom, down the hall on the left. As I ponder my next move, the approaching footsteps slow. Then stop. This is it. The doorknob I'm staring at turns. In an instant, Poodle Boy will cross the threshold. It's game time.

Inside now, his back faces me, just inches away. Time seems to stop momentarily. He freezes for a beat, as the large mirror above the sink reveals my presence. This hesitation is all I need. In an adept coordination of movements, I wrap my left arm tightly around his torso, restricting the movement of his arms. With my knife poised in my right hand, in a wide-arcing motion, I then slice across his throat with the blade. Blood gushes out in buckets, drenching him, my arms, and the tiled floor. A muffled *yelp* escapes his lips as he appears to choke, gasping for breath. His head isn't severed from his body, but the blade cut deep. Hopefully deep enough to have severed the carotid arteries, as well as the jugular vein, which would bring on death within minutes, due to blood loss to the brain. That's what my internet research yielded, anyway.

I feel the familiar adrenaline rush flow through my veins. Once again, I'm surprised how easily and naturally killing comes to me. I'm tingling like I'm electrified.

I dart for the window, the mirror appearing in my sight-line en route. The vision catches me off-guard. Not the bloodied and bludgeoned Poodle Boy. Rather, my reflection. Sweaty, beady-eyed, gruff beard, a blood-soaked knife in my hand. Dismissing the feeling that I look psychopathic, I get a move on and slither out the window. Awkwardly, I drop the few feet to the ground. I instantly right myself with a roll, launch to my feet, and dash. Looking over my shoulder, I see the PI charging like a bull through the bathroom, to the window. Peering out, his head swivels back and forth between myself and the limp body on the floor. Fortunately, he does the right thing, backtracking to attend to Poodle Boy.

Once in the clear, I ditch the bloody gloves covering my hands, gloves I've been wearing since breaking into the apartment. The smart move would be a mad sprint to my car. Instead, pure adrenaline takes over as I dash off into the darkness without concern for direction. I realize it's now too late to head back for my car. The place will soon be infested with ambulances and cop cars. I'm akin to a fugitive on the lam. In my favor, I don't believe the PI got a good look at my face, despite my lapse of judgment by momentarily turning around to meet his eyes.

I disappear into the woods behind the apartment, not slowing down until I'm off the complex grounds.

CHAPTER 14
JACK

AVING CHOSEN *SAVING A LOW life* over *apprehending a lower life*, I follow protocol for these types of situations. I'm kneeling beside Hank, the index and middle fingers of my right hand applied firmly against his neck. He has a pulse, albeit faint. He's unconscious, not responding to my voice. My left hand presses my phone against my ear. I'm barking instructions to a 911 operator, securing a medical and law enforcement presence.

He's still losing blood. Rushing to the bathroom, I grab a white towel off the rack across from the sink and apply pressure to the wound on Hank's neck. I feel bad for the guy. Yeah, he dug his own grave, with his willing involvement in the criminal underworld. But the poor slob has cancer. A guy trying to enjoy his scarce remaining time. A guy lured into a sinister plot, which has led to this brutal attack, and probable death.

I'm replaying the rapid-fire sequence of events surrounding the bathroom beat down. How did I let the perp get away? By the time I got to the bathroom window, the perp was on the run. He turned back to look at me. I took my gun out of my pocket, released the safety, and took aim. I didn't have a clear shot. The perp vanished into the woods. I curse myself for not stopping him.

The sound of blaring sirens can be heard now. The cavalry nears. I check on Hank. No sign of life. The towel on his neck is more red than white. I feel for a pulse again, this time unsure of a beat. Moments later, paramedics fill the bathroom. They get him on a stretcher and hurry to the open-doored rear of the ambulance. The vehicle is running, the driver waiting for the *go* signal. The expression on the face of the head blue-masked guy, Hank's first respondent, isn't encouraging.

The excitement having dissipated, I again admonish myself for allowing the perp to escape. What do I do now? Track him down? With what to go on? I don't know the guy, never met him before today, don't have a name, and only saw his face for half a second. The alternative? Run back to Quincy with Hank's taped confession. Hank doesn't identify the killer, but it should be enough to get Peter off. Delivering Hank will be quite the coup. On audio or in person, dead or alive, it will be compelling testimony.

Less than half an hour after paramedics carted off Hank's body, I get a call from the police department. Hank is dead. So much for my first aid skills. They want me downtown at the station for questioning. Pronto. I was told, amidst the earlier chaos, to keep myself available for questioning. With a homicide now on their hands, the urgency for questioning has sky-rocketed. I opt to drive myself in, bypassing the official escort.

The irony hits me. I let the perp get away so I could save Hank. Only I couldn't save him. Does this mean I made the wrong decision? Would I have tracked down the perp? I'd like to think so, considering I'm armed. A gun beats a knife. Of course, he may have been packing as well. I didn't scrutinize the decision at the time. I wasn't afforded the luxury of time. The scenario that played out in my head had me chasing, shooting at but missing, and failing to catch the perp. The conjured scenario rolling in my mind now, knowing Hank couldn't be saved, has me chasing the perp with abandon. Giving it my all. Catching the bastard. Shooting him in the leg and bringing him down.

My imagination leads to a gut-check moment. Was my choice the honorable one, the humane one, or did fear drive the decision?

Was I hesitant to pull the trigger? I've never shot anyone, only fired warning shots on a couple occasions. To scare.

I use the remaining time of the drive to catch up on correspondence. *Ring ring ring.* Moments later, the Garrison clan is conferenced in.

CHAPTER 15
PETER

I 'M DIALED INTO THE CALL from my car, my time too valuable now to make side trips to my parents' house. I'm en route back to Police Records. Okay, maybe my time isn't so valuable. I don't have a need to pore over any records. The purpose for this trip is to visit my girlfriend. Okay, *girlfriend* is a little premature. I don't want Amy to forget me, so am visiting on the pretense of providing an update on my case.

"Peter, Doug, Karen, I found Hank. He exonerates you, Peter. I recorded his recounting of events, including his involvement, as well as that of others. He outlined how you were manipulated and framed. Hank died a few minutes ago."

I nearly drive off the road.

"What?" my parents and I utter in disbelief.

"I strongly suspect the guy responsible also bumped off Chang. Unfortunately, he got away. What's important is me getting back with my tape recording and turning it over to the proper hands. This could free you, Peter."

Pushing shock aside, I allow Jack's message to register. "Awesome, Jack. He would have made a better witness alive, but this is big." I speak for the family. "Where do we go from here? How soon until my kangaroo court trial gets dropped?"

"Good questions. A lot depends upon the judge's belief of Hank's credibility."

"Can you play us the tape now? How long is it?" I want to hear the weasel's sorrow.

"It goes on for about twenty minutes. Let me get back on U.S. soil and I'll play you the whole thing in high definition audio."

"Could you play us a snippet, the key parts?" my mom pipes in. It's a reasonable inquiry. A few seconds later, Hank's voice fills the phone lines. It's the part where he details the plan. Jack plays another part, where Hank expresses remorse for turning on me.

"This is damning stuff, Jack. He gave you all this willingly?" my dad asks.

"He's been struggling with what went down. He's been looking for a reason to turn himself in. I just jump-started things a little."

"Did he die because of you?" my mom asks, trying to clear her conscious.

"No. The perp was waiting for Hank in his bathroom. I'll fill you in later on the full story. It has a few tentacles."

I pull into a parking garage, two blocks away from Amy's workplace. "Jack, don't play games with us. If you have something of interest, please share." I don't mince words. Directness gets results.

"I'm driving to Police Headquarters now for my grilling. I don't exactly have a lot of time to chat. Hank had cancer. I don't know what kind, but I'm guessing it was advanced and that the prognosis wasn't good. His trip to St. John was a going away party. A party made possible by the seventy-five thousand he was paid to deceive you. I hope this offers a little solace, and resolution, Peter."

The news of Hank's cancer shocks me. Why didn't he confide in me? On some level, not burdening me with his illness strikes me as admirable. It seems like yesterday we were high-fiving each other after made baskets, and now he's gone.

The silence reminds me I'm expected to respond to Jack. "My desire to kill Hank has subsided. Forgiveness is even a possibility, with him being dead and all."

"It doesn't excuse what he did," my dad adds. "What he put you through."

"I'm just thrilled to have anything resembling an explanation, after going so long on conjecture."

"Barring a delay, I'll be on the first flight out of here in the morning. We get this tape to the authorities, and you should be a free man soon."

While technically free now, until the DA's office relents, their claws remain lodged in me, and I am not *free*.

"Thank you so much, Jack. I knew you would come through." My mom lets out a sigh of relief.

"Now, just to throw it out there, instead of rushing back, I could try to find Hank's killer. It's a real long-shot. Honestly, the tape recording should provide the reasonable doubt to get Peter off, and my staying would get expensive."

We agree Jack should catch the next flight home. He could stay and mail the tape, but that means extra sets of hands on the evidence. We need to minimize the links in the chain of custody. Jack has the tape sealed in a large plastic Baggie. He promises to check in after his interrogation. We thank him again for his good work and say our goodbyes.

While obtaining Hank's confession validates my story, it also confirms my theory about Hank merely being a pawn, and that someone else—Bernie—plotted to ruin my life. A renewed hatred washes over me. I won't feel contentment until this animal gets taken down, preferably by me.

At Police Records, I work myself to the service counter, where Amy awaits. Dressed in a white blouse and black skirt, she looks great. Her dark hair is up, held in place by a large clip. She greets me with a full smile.

"Hi." A harmless enough opening.

"Hi yourself. Back already? I haven't seen your case folder in the dismissal pile yet."

"Not yet, but it's in the works." Okay, I'm stretching the truth a bit. "I stopped by to debrief you. Things look promising. I'm being proven innocent. I'll return when it's official. Just wanted to let you know it will be soon. You should start thinking about cuisine preferences." My newfound confidence boils over.

After pausing for air, I proceed to fill her in on the latest developments. The lack of motive. The investigating of other suspects. Hank's confession and subsequent death. She takes it all in with a grin. Her smile radiates playfulness. I feel like an adolescent.

"Does this mean you won't be requiring my legal assistance?" she asks.

"Yes, it sure does. I figure I wouldn't be able to afford you, anyway. What it also means is any day now you'll be finding my paperwork in that dismissed pile. It's becoming clear I'm one of the good guys."

"Oh, is that so?"

"Indeed it is." This exchange, this back and forth, this flirtation, sends jolts of electricity through me.

Going with the *leave them wanting more* philosophy (translation: scared of screwing up by saying the wrong thing), I check my watch, explain my appointment-filled rest of the day, and dash off. I'm hoping the notion I had time to drop in for a hello during my ridiculously busy day hasn't gone unnoticed. Of course, it isn't the truth, what with my day being ridiculously idle.

I've been approaching this case from the viewpoint of why Hank involved me. What I did to piss him off. I've been concentrating on Chang being the real victim. Trying to ascertain who wanted to harm him. Shifting the focus to myself as a target provides new perspective.

The guy who iced Chang doesn't like me, either. Doesn't like me to the extent he set me up to take the fall for murder. He wants me imprisoned. He *put* me in prison. The question *who hates me?* should be easier to answer than *who hates Chang?* Easier for me, at least.

I've been downplaying the notion I was framed. I've been seeing myself as a cog in the wheel that is the assassination. A member of an ensemble cast. Somebody had to take the fall and I was convenient. A sucker. It was nothing personal.

I don't see myself inspiring hatred. I'm a peaceful guy. I'd like to think I inspire harmony. Or, worst case scenario, indifference. But what if I consumed someone's thoughts? And what if these thoughts weren't pleasant? And what if this *someone* disliked Chang more than myself? Having never met Chang, I have trouble believing we are hated for the same reason, that Chang and I are somehow connected. I task myself with solving the riddle: who despises me? I believe Hank's recorded words, that he was just a pawn in the operation. I also believe his implication—he was chosen as a pawn due to his friendship with me. I'm not a random puzzle piece, rather a guy some psychopathic nut hand-picked, due to his having a beef with me.

Armed with a pad and pen, I start a *who could be the psycho* list. I spin around in my chair several times, stand, pace the room, sit back down. Chew on my pen for a while. Nothing comes to mind.

My time spent fixating on Hank made sense from the standpoint that in order to be hated, you have to be known. Altering my approach a bit, I scribble down the names of everyone I consider more than an acquaintance, excluding Hank and family. This doesn't take long. Which is good since it's a fruitless exercise. None of the ten people on my list could possibly be the psycho. More relevantly, since you can never tell what lies beneath one's exterior, I can't come up with a reason why any of them would have it in for me. Sam Murray, an old law professor, for example, used to push me to realize my potential. Hardly a murderous trait. It's a stretch including him on the list, but we did form a bond after his generous grading policy led to me enrolling in a bunch of his classes. Despite misjudging Hank, I eliminate friends from the psycho list. Back to a blank slate.

A fast memory-scan disqualifies law school classmates. Only the top-dog students had enemies. I cross off neighbors too. I'm not loud, don't have pets, and am courteous. I eliminate basketball opponents as well. I'm not a trash talker and don't *dis* those I score on. Disrespecting some of the street-ballers I play with is akin to a death wish. I leave the *in your face*, and like comments, for those brasher than myself.

I list coworkers and bosses at places I've worked. Satisfied the list is exhaustive, I consider each one. Minutes later, I have crossed out all the names except for Jerry Henderson, a partner at Henderson & Gates. For some reason, Jerry never liked me much. He has a temper and I was on the receiving end of a few verbal onslaughts. He also didn't appreciate me leaving his firm. While I have a hard time believing I remained on his radar after quitting, I make a note to follow up on him.

As I'm trying to envision a scenario where a probate client I've represented would seek revenge, it hits me that I've omitted the clients I represented at Henderson and Gates from the list. Most of the cases I worked were settled out of court, and of those, I don't recall any bitterness towards me from our clients. Those that made it to court were relatively minor cases, again with none standing out in regard to potential client retribution. I start with the most recent cases—the three I handled in the past six months or so. Since I didn't get any of them off, there could have been hard feelings.

In the most recent case, I defended Tom Collins (his name stayed with me since he shares his name with a gin drink), a fortyish man, on assault charges for punching a fellow patron in the face at a local bar. The victim had the gall to bump into Tom without saying *excuse me*. The victim required medical attention and sought payment to cover his expenses. Forced to turn over his hard earned money to a 'scumbag' didn't please Tom. Although he had a temper, setting me up for murder for failing to twist the facts of the case in his favor is a long-shot. Still, I don't dismiss him as a candidate.

My first case was an elderly woman accused of shoplifting from a grocery store. Caught red-handed with a roast stuffed into her oversized purse as she was leaving, I never really had a chance. The statement made by the employee who stopped her was compelling. Along with having to return the stolen meat, a meager fine represented her only punishment. Not much of a motive. Not list worthy.

The middle case. I defended a seventeen-year-old kid the cops busted for underage drinking. The arresting officer played hardball and the kid got sentenced to a couple of nights in jail. He was probably out after a night. He was a scared, timid teen. He never expressed anger towards me. I would think if he had a problem with anyone, it would be the hard ass cop. The kid, whose name I can't recall, definitely warrants a follow up.

<hr />

I look up Tom's number on the Internet and catch him at his listed home address.

"Yeah?" He hasn't upgraded his phone etiquette since we talked last.

"Hello Tom. This is Peter Garrison. I'm —"

"I don't know a Peter Garrison. What do you want?"

"I represented you in a bar fight a while back and —" I'm zero for two at finishing sentences.

"Oh yeah. Okay. You're not calling to tell me I owe you money are you? I paid your bill."

I've heard enough to cross him off the list. I'm also anxious to end this call. "No, Tom, you don't owe me a cent. It's our firm's policy to check up on past clients. I just want to make sure you're doing okay and don't require more legal assistance."

I'm holding my breath, hoping like hell he doesn't. Getting caught in my scam won't go over well.

"Yeah. Yeah. I'm doing fine. I do my drinking at home now. Keeps me out of trouble."

Next, I call my former employer, Henderson & Gates. I'm pleased to reach Diane, the long-standing, loyal, and grossly underpaid receptionist. I assure her I didn't kill anybody and thank her for being in her prayers. Diane, the defacto mom to most of the staff, must be pushing seventy. I want to talk to Henderson so I can clear him, but first I need to exploit Diane's good will. She puts me on hold for a few minutes before supplying me with the information I'm after.

"His name is Matthew Rincon. I really shouldn't be doing this, Peter, but seeing as this was your case, and you're in trouble..." Her voice trails off as I promise not to reveal her as the information source.

She gives me his phone number and address, then reads the pertinent facts in the case, a consolation for not being able to send me a copy of the file. I thank her as she transfers me to Henderson.

"What the hell do you want, Garrison? I hope you aren't calling for legal aid. And I hope, for your sake, you didn't do what you're accused of."

"No, Jerry, I don't need a lawyer. I appreciate your concern though."

He's still an ornery bastard, but his apathy for me clinches crossing him off the list. I tell him I was going to ask something, but, upon hearing his voice, changed my mind. Lame, I know. To which he responds "Whatever" and hangs up.

Fifteen minutes later, I'm parked on the street in front of Matthew's house. One hundred fourteen Cherry Lane. I considered calling, but want to gauge his body language and reaction to my presence and questions. Mustering the courage to get out of my car—if he's the one trying to ruin my life, this could be dangerous—I approach the front door and ring the bell. Silence. Letting a minute pass, I ring it again. Another minute passes before I hear footsteps. Yet another full minute later, the door cracks open. He looks me over. It takes a few seconds before he places me.

"What do you want?"

Thinner now, Matthew is dressed in a T-shirt and sweat pants, hair unkempt, several days removed from his last shave.

"Hello Matthew. I wanted to check up on you and offer my apologies again for not getting you off."

"Since when do lawyers make house calls?"

"I'm not a trial lawyer anymore. Soon after your case, I parted ways with my law firm. I just want to see how you're doing."

He rolls his eyes, clearly annoyed by my presence. "I'm doing just fine. Kind of busy, so if there's nothing else…"

Matthew leans against the door, still not fully open. Not that I expect to be invited inside for coffee and pastries. Standoffish and sarcastic, with a matter-of-fact attitude, his reception doesn't surprise me, given my inability to get him off. He doesn't strike me as cold-blooded or calculating, however, just a rude kid. I wish him well and am off, ending the uncomfortable visit.

I didn't get the chance to inquire about his brief prison stint, but given his distaste for conversation, I wasn't going to learn anything. I conclude because he's still in Quincy, as opposed to having fled the country, he probably didn't kill Chang, meaning I can cross him off my list. So, I'm back where I started. A blank slate.

On my ride home, I reflect on my first meeting with Matthew in my office. He was nervous about what happened, but good-natured and gracious. He was also neat and clean shaven. How can this be the same kid I defended?

Following a sleepless night and uneventful day without an epiphany, I'm back with my dad in Sir William's office. We were convened on short notice. It's the eve of my preliminary hearing. William pours us each a cup of coffee from his Keurig machine. Once we've gotten a few sips of the admittedly delicious coffee into our systems—I need to get myself one of these fancy machines—and the suspense has sufficiently mounted, Sir William divulges what's behind his smirking. In his usual dramatic fashion, he insisted on sharing his news in person. My patience would be running out by now if he was holding onto bad news, but for good news I'll let him have his fun. Satisfied he has our undivided attention, he proceeds.

"Well, gentlemen, it appears our cool customer killer wasn't so composed after all."

"What do you mean?" asks my dad through clenched teeth and a tight frown.

"What I mean is whoever ended Chang's life slipped up. The DA's office sent over new discovery material. While our mystery murderer didn't leave behind any fingerprints or blood, he did deposit three drops of sweat onto the victim's bloodied shirt."

"Sweat." My heart thunders. This is my exoneration. I chuckle at the overwhelming odds modern day bad guys are up against. Combating DNA is next to impossible. If you're trying to create an illusion you weren't present somewhere, short of really not being there, there's no foolproof formula.

"Yes, as in perspiration." William says.

My dad looks puzzled. I jump in to explain.

"Dad, DNA can be obtained from anything containing body cells. This includes skin, semen, saliva, tears, and yes, sweat."

My dad nods his understanding, as I motion for Sir William to continue.

"Lab technicians tested the residue from said sweat droplets and now have his DNA. The running theory is while leaning over Chang to stab him, sweat dripped off his forehead. The location of the droplets on Chang's shirt is consistent with the line where the perpetrator's head would have been given the angle of the stab wounds."

He holds up his hand as I start to speak, signaling he has more vital information. After a beat, he proceeds.

"The DNA from the sweat droplets doesn't match Chang's DNA. Peter, you probably recall when you were booked, submitting to a Q-tip cheek swab, the purpose of which was to obtain your DNA."

I feel a trickle of my own sweat running down my forehead. I'm sitting on the edge of my seat, knowing where this is headed.

"As we speak, your sample is being compared to the DNA secured by the lab techs."

This time it's my dad on the receiving end of the palm-in-face signal, suppressing his question.

"Almost done. Assuming you in fact are not the monstrous executioner, Peter, this comparison will not yield a match."

"Is this enough to prove Peter's innocence?" My dad doesn't wait for the pause, indicating we may speak.

I raise my index finger, letting William know I've got this. "Let me play devil's advocate for a moment. The prosecution will argue these drops of sweat could have come from anyone who had been in contact with Chang that day. Or even days previous, if his shirt wasn't recently washed. Additionally, unless the killer has a previous record, the DNA from the sweat may not match anyone in the criminal database, so that being the case, we wouldn't have anyone to pin the murder on. So, Dad, this doesn't prove I'm innocent. What it does buy us, however, is the prosecution's nemesis. Reasonable doubt. Reasonable doubt is my best friend. It's what will set me free."

Sir William nods emphatically. "There's nothing like new evidence to muddy the waters."

"This is amazing. It's a gift from God. It's karma." My dad punctuates his words by scooting his chair close enough to give me the sit-down equivalent of a bear hug. I'm not quite ready to celebrate.

"This is indeed a score for us good guys, but we need this DNA comparison be finished in time for tomorrow's hearing."

I turn my attention to William. "We also need the tape Jack dropped off to make it to a jury. The prosecution will challenge it."

Sir William clears his throat, indicating his anxiousness to speak. "Honestly, Hank's taped confession could get thrown out. The judge could rule it inadmissible. There's no evidence Jack didn't coerce the confession and then kill Hank himself. It may be admitted, but I wouldn't count on it. The good news is, between this DNA stuff and your lack of motive, the DA might drop the charges against you."

"Son, this nightmare will soon end. For you. For all of us. I just hope the media hypes up your innocence the way they did your presumed guilt."

"Dad, I don't care if they bury it in the fine print. All I want is my life back."

"Here! Here! To freedom." Sir William theatrically raises his coffee mug, we all clink, and drink the remainder of our now cold coffee.

We refill our mugs, spend a little more time chatting about tomorrow's hearing, and call it a night. My dad has my mom on the phone, sharing the good news, as we're heading out of the building. At our cars now, we hug again before parting ways. I'm exhausted by the time I get home and hope to get some sleep. Tomorrow is a big day.

Sir William wakes me at eight a.m. with the news the sweat droplets aren't mine. They also don't belong to anyone in the criminal database, meaning the identity of Chang's killer remains unknown.

An hour later, I'm in a booth at Leon's Diner, considered the greasiest in town, sitting across from my parents. My stomach is too queasy to handle the plate of scrambled eggs, bacon, and wheat toast in front of me. I mindlessly pick at the eggs as my mom attempts to divert my attention from the looming court date, with chatter about her latest quilting project. Neither I nor my dad really listen, but we allow her to ramble on as she's trying to calm her own nerves as much as she is mine. With our plates barely touched, our waitress asks if everything is okay. Something overcooked? Undercooked? Bad-tasting? We assure her the problem isn't the food. My dad pays the bill and we walk the few blocks to the courthouse. The crisp, fresh air delivers some anxiety relief.

We run into Tony Jamison, the ADA, the guy I hope feels charitable today, as we enter the building. He politely acknowledges us, giving nothing away with his facial expression. I wouldn't want to play poker with him. Once past the walk-through metal detector, we find Sir William at one of the long oak benches, scribbling away on a legal pad. Following an exchange of pleasantries, I get right to it.

"Did Jamison hear the tape? Has he filed a motion to get it thrown out?"

"Jamison is playing things close to the vest, but I know he's listened to it. Sans the ability to cross examine Hank, it's a longshot it will be admitted, so let's not fixate on that. I want you all to keep in mind the burden of proof, while still on the prosecution, is much lower at a preliminary hearing than it is at trial. Having said that, there is reason for optimism."

I don't want to distract William before court, but it bugs me that he doesn't treat me like an equal, like a fellow attorney. I'm not his typical client. I know all about preliminary hearings.

Sir William absent-mindedly spins the combination lock wheels on the briefcase in his lap.

"They have nothing more on you, Peter, than they had at the time of your arrest. This looms huge. At some point circumstantial evidence must be backed up, and there's a glaring failure on the part of the DA's office in this regard."

"In your experience, William, does this mean the ruling will go our way?" My mom wants assurance.

It also irks me the way my folks value William's opinion over mine. Yeah, he has an experience edge, but I didn't get my law diploma out of a cereal box.

"I wish I had a guarantee for you, but that's not how these things work. I can tell you my preparation for this hearing has been meticulous and exhaustive. I can also say I wholly and absolutely believe in Peter's innocence, and my strategy is to persuade the judge to feel similarly. Let's walk into the courtroom with heads held high, brimming with confidence."

Not exactly a Knute Rockne speech, but my mom's spirits have lifted, nonetheless. It feels strange being back in court. I've been in this very courtroom many times, defending clients.

A substantial contingent of the Asian community dominates the spectator section of the courtroom. The larger-than-last-time representation tells me more than just family and friends are in attendance. Once again, the venom directed towards me is unmistakable. I refrain from shouting *it wasn't me*. The clerk announces my case. With order in the room restored, the judge begins with some preliminaries before turning the floor over to Jamison, who gets to present his side first.

"Judge, upon vigilant consideration, having performed our due diligence, and in light of new evidence, it is the conclusion of the district attorney's office, the case against Mr. Peter Garrison is purely circumstantial. To this end, we are dismissing all charges against Mr. Garrison and humbly offer him our heartfelt apologies."

He glances in my direction as he speaks this last part. I let out a breath I wasn't aware I had been holding in. My entire body collapses to a limp-like state. A feeling of euphoria rushes over me.

A stunned silence fills the gallery. I turn around to see my parents embracing. As they catch my gaze, my mom blows me a kiss while my dad flashes a thumbs up sign. Sir William wraps an arm around me as we firmly shake hands. I thank him amidst the now chatter-filled room. The judge, who seems as caught off-guard by this development as the rest of us, raps his gavel a few times before speaking.

"Thank you, Mr. Jamison." He directs his attention toward our defense table as he proclaims, "Case dismissed."

My optimistic mom spent half the night preparing a celebratory Italian-themed feast. Italian beef, lasagna, chicken parmesan, baked ziti, antipasto salad, and garlic bread. Neither effort nor expense was spared. She said the time in the kitchen freed her mind from the uncertainty of my fate, but in reality she did all this for me. I suppose if things had turned out differently today, the food would have served as consolation. The atmosphere is electric. Horns blow (figuratively), and confetti fills the room (again, figuratively). My folks' place is hopping. Hopping in volume of people terms, though there isn't anyone here I particularly want to socialize with tonight. It's a bunch of my parents' friends, a couple of their neighbors, Sir William, and Jack, the most interesting of them all. His appearance is more a courtesy than a desire to be here.

Jack enthralls us with a recounting of events surrounding his capture of Hank. He details Hank's gruesome death, as well as the crafty escape by his killer. I wonder if I would have made the same moral decision Jack did, in trying to save Hank. Despite Hank's betrayal, I conclude, in all likelihood, I would have acted as Jack did. Although apprehending the butcher would have been nice, he seems at peace with his handling of the situation, content leaving matters to the authorities, satisfied the mission to vindicate me has been realized. He wishes me well, ready to move on to his next case. Before he leaves, I toast both he and Sir William for their fine work and diligence. I feel more indebted to Jack, seeing as he put his life on the line. Sure, he was well-compensated, and danger always lurks in his line of work, but still…

The food, laid out buffet style in the kitchen, with overflowing platters, pans, and dishes, covers the large table surface as well as most of the counter space. I'm receiving congratulatory handshakes, pats on the back, hugs, and kisses from the guests. My dad toasts me, speaking for everyone.

"We all knew this day would come. We all knew there wasn't a chance in hell you were mixed up in this sordid mess. I can't wait to see your good name cleared by the press."

Everyone drinks to this. I'm not much of a drinker, but am giving my best impression of a drunk, guzzling down beer after beer, with some whiskey shots mixed in. My dad, also a lightweight, keeps pace with me. I follow my dad's toast with a toast of my own, to my parents, thanking them for their support, financial assistance, and for throwing this party. This elicits applause and raised glasses, as well as some raised plates, in the direction of my mom. Her culinary skills are renowned.

A full plate of food in hand, Sir William whisks my dad and me away from the crowd, leading us through the sliding glass door, onto the patio, where we plop down at a wooden picnic table to eat. The unseasonably warm, mid-seventies temperature for early autumn enhances the jovial setting. As we devour the delectable entrees, William replays his post-hearing chat with Jamison.

"To be honest, I was a little surprised he caved in so easily. I asked what swayed him to drop the charges."

He takes a large bite of lasagna, necessitating a pause.

"And?" I don't care if he has to speak with his mouth full. He raises an index finger, swallows, emits an *Mmmm* sound, declares this the best lasagna he's tasted, and continues.

"Jamison says he knows Jack by reputation, and although he could have easily had the tape of Hank confession thrown out, in his heart he believed in its authenticity. This, on top of the sweat DNA mismatch, lack of motive, and lack of physical evidence, became the proverbial straw that broke the camel's back."

"I'm glad he finally came to his senses. I don't understand why it took this long, and why Peter had to be tormented the way he was."

"Well, our at-large killer went to great lengths to ensure you would suffer, Peter."

"He succeeded," I chime in.

"Jamison asked me to relay something to you. Since you didn't go to trial, double jeopardy doesn't apply. So, in the event you are guilty, you're not off the hook. He can charge you again."

"I know this, William. I'm a lawyer, remember? Besides, I have nothing to worry about. I'm innocent!"

"I know. I know. I told him the same thing. I'm just telling you what he said. It's time to put all this behind us now."

We enjoy the rest of our meal in relative quiet. Sir William makes his way back into the kitchen to deposit his empty plate in the sink and thank my mom for a delicious meal. Back on the patio, we wish one another well as he excuses himself.

I'm free now, but feel unsettled. Sure, I'm thrilled to be a regular citizen again, able to cross the county line with impunity. But I don't have closure. The guy who framed me, who has made my life miserable, remains on the loose. Given the progress tracking him down thus far, I have little assurance he'll be brought to justice anytime soon. My degree of confidence he'll get caught at all isn't exactly sky high. It occurs to me I may be in peril once again. My tormentor may not be thrilled with the news of my release.

My heart beat quickens and I catch myself clenching my jaw. My hatred for my unknown tormenter grows. I want him to suffer. I rise and take a loop around the perimeter of my parents' yard, calming myself down.

Forcing my mind to shift gears, I manage a grin. First thing in the morning, I'm gonna pick up a newspaper, find the story on me, and dash to Police Records to show Amy.

CHAPTER 16
JASON

KNOCKING OFF POODLE BOY was easier than I imagined. Even the monkey wrench of the PI showing up didn't deter me. It did force my hand, however, eliminating the opportunity for questioning. My options were narrowed down to two choices: flee before discovery, or take out Hank quickly. I'm satisfied I made the correct call. Considering the lack of planning and preparation, compared to killing Chang, this time around went pretty smoothly. Sure, my escape was a little hastier, but I pulled this one off on my own. An elaborate ruse wasn't required.

Despite all the blood and his lifeless body on the bathroom floor, I wasn't sure I had killed him. Ideally, I would have preferred complementing the throat slash with body stabs, but I was rushed. Last night, in the hotel business center, I confirmed his death when I found an article online detailing the horrid murder. The story included a picture of him *in happier times*. A witness, my PI buddy, didn't get a good look at my face. That he merely witnessed the getaway, and not the killing itself, has left authorities frustrated. The PI had been detained for interrogation, but it yielded little, except to clear himself as a suspect. He was released as the murder investigation ensues.

Carless and shirtless on a nameless St. John street, I hailed down a slow-moving car. I bribed the old lady behind the wheel to chauffeur me to the docks, where the ferries are stationed. My bloodied shirt was balled up and stuffed in my pants. I knew I needed to dispose of my clothes, as well as the knife still in my possession, someplace they wouldn't be discovered. At a waterside shop, I bought a change of clothes, depositing what I was wearing into the bag bearing the store's insignia. Before boarding the ferry to St. Thomas, I put a large rock into the bag. In ten minute intervals, I tossed the bag, and then the knife, into the deep water. Back on land, I caught a taxi to the airport and got on the next plane headed in the direction of Grand Cayman.

I'm going on little sleep as my catnap on the couch was cut short when Tess stalked into the living area half an hour ago. I didn't join her in bed last night so as not to wake her, and more relevantly, delay the inquisition.

Tess, normally immaculately groomed, hasn't brushed her long, black hair and her fingernail polish is cracking. Still, dressed in a T-shirt and shorts, she has an inner beauty that shines through.

"I don't get why you had to kill him."

I take umbrage with whoever said honesty is the best policy. I should have told her I couldn't find Poodle Boy. Apparently she took a liking to the wimp in the short time she spent with him.

"I didn't know you had a thing for him, babe." Wrong thing to say, I realize, but I'm tired and in no mood for a lecture.

"I don't have a *thing* for him. He was harmless, and now he's dead. You needlessly ended his life. I just don't get you. You're killing for sport now?" She's shaking her head, oozing disapproval.

"It wasn't just for sport. Besides, he didn't put up much of a fight, so it wasn't really sporting." I'm pushing her buttons. Back to my rationale. "Don't you get it? He betrayed us. This is a high stakes game we're involved in." This does little to comfort her.

"A game? Is that what this is to you? How many more players do you plan to destroy? Maybe it's time to remove my game piece before you decide I'm a threat. You do realize the more people you kill, the greater the likelihood we'll get caught, don't you?"

Her voice is piercing cold. She starts to say more, then throws her arms in the air in a show of disgust.

"Hey, Hank knew the rules when he accepted the money. There has to be consequences for breaking them." My nonchalant attitude pisses her off more.

"Did it ever occur to you he simply lost the phone you gave him? Or maybe he was robbed. He had no way of contacting you, ya know. And you didn't give him the chance to explain himself."

"Wow, I'm beginning to wonder if the two of you were fucking." I know I'm out of line, but I need her on my side, not his.

What I really need is her *by* my side. I feel her slipping away. Tess has always been my rock, my calming influence. I don't want to lose her. I can't picture my life without her in it. If only she could understand why I had to kill Hank. I harbor guilt for having selfishly dragged her into this mess.

"Fuck you! I didn't sign up for this. Chang was one thing. You sold me on him ruining Matthew's life. Now you're killing because it's *fun?*"

I wave my hand dismissively, a gesture which fails to slow her down.

"You're not the same guy I've known all my life. You've transformed from a citizen to a criminal. There's no crime more heinous than yours. You took the life of another. You took the life of *two* others."

This hurts. I hate that I've disappointed her, that she thinks of me as a criminal. I haven't really thought of myself in this context. The obvious strikes me, that if Matthew hadn't been violated, I wouldn't have killed. Unable to face Tess, I turn my back and walk away, as she finishes dramatically.

"I'm outta here."

With this, she heads for the door, slamming it behind her so hard I'm amazed it's still on its hinges. I don't make a move after her. I'll let her cool off. She'll be back, and we'll make up. All her stuff is here, so she'll have to come back.

I wish Tess understood my views. I couldn't allow Poodle Boy to start yapping about us. He and I shook hands like gentleman, and he went back on his word. Sure, in the eyes of the law, my actions were reprehensible. But there has been a warped sense of justice concerning this entire ordeal.

I find a beer in the fridge, return to the couch, and turn on the tube. Two laps through the channels later, I turn the TV off and am on the balcony getting fresh air. Thinking about my brother, I call home.

Matthew picks up.

"How are you, bro? I didn't know you were back home." I try to mask the surprise in my voice. I'm relieved and happy he has been released from the hospital.

"I'm good, bro. The needle pokers didn't want to let me out, but Mom raised holy hell."

He sounds subdued, but coherent. It feels good to talk to him again.

"I was worried those doctors were screwing you up. You sound good, though, so they must have been all right."

He ignores my commentary. "Mom says you're in the Caribbean somewhere. What's going on, Jason? Did you kill that Peking Dragon guy who ratted me out?"

"Is that what Mom said?"

"Mom hasn't told me anything. Just that you got yourself into some trouble and had to go away for a while. Said you'd be calling to fill us in."

"Look, Matthew, you're gonna have to trust me. The less you know right now, the better. If you don't know where I am, nobody can beat it out of you."

"Who exactly will be coming to beat me up? You killed Chang, didn't you?" I don't respond immediately, so he continues. "I appreciate the gesture, but you shouldn't have done it, Jason. Tell me what I can do to help you."

"What you can do is lay low until this blows over. If anyone comes by asking questions, you know nothing."

"Speaking of people stopping by, that dumb-ass lawyer of mine dropped by. Claimed he was checking up on me. Wanted to know how I was doing."

"Peter Garrison?" My chest gets tight and uncomfortable with the mention of his name.

"Yeah, that's him. It was like he was snooping around for something. He sure as hell wasn't interested in my well-being. He never *checked up* on me while I was in jail."

The noise level rises, as kids playing in an alley get excited. I head back indoors, leaving the balcony. We both start speaking at once. I let him go first.

"He parked across the street from our house, sitting in his car for half an hour before approaching and ringing the doorbell."

This isn't good. "What was he doing in his car? Peering into the house with binoculars?"

"I couldn't tell. Could have been jacking off for all I know."

I don't like Garrison. Haven't from the moment he didn't deliver on his promise to my mom and Matthew. My hatred level has just escalated.

"Did he mention Chang? Or me?"

"No, I got rid of him pretty quickly. Didn't let him in the house."

"Good." I'm relieved the encounter didn't spiral out of control.

"Oh, Jason, I almost forgot. The cops found DNA on Chang's shirt. The shirt he was wearing when he was murdered. Well, actually, they found sweat droplets, which contained the DNA. They're saying it came from Chang's killer."

Matthew, talking fast, breaks for air, giving me time to process this.

Interpreting my silence as panic, he adds, "But don't worry.

117

Unless you have an arrest on your record I don't know about, they won't have your DNA. Jason, I wish you'd let me help you."

"I'm good, Matthew. Really I need to get going now. I'll be in touch soon. Take care of yourself."

"You're the one who needs to be careful. Just say the word if you need me."

"You got it, bro. Later." I project a strong exterior, despite trembling on the inside.

I go through the ritual of smashing the phone. I still have plenty left. Besides the DNA stuff, I've got myself another problem. Peter fucking Garrison. I'm not sure how much he knows or what he's up to, but I intend to find out.

⸻

With all the excitement in St. John, I have been negligent in keeping tabs on Garrison. He had a court hearing scheduled the last I checked on him. Putting two and two together, I figure Garrison must have hired the PI. I hope the scumbag gets sent back to the slammer and becomes some big dude's bitch.

I'm back in the hotel business center, on a computer, the Google site up in my browser window. Typing "peter garrison quincy vermont" in the search box, I get several hits. The top one causes me to curse audibly. The title reads "Murder charges dropped against Peter Garrison." I brace for the worst as I click through to the full story. Fortunately, the reasons cited for the dismissal don't include the emergence of another suspect. The story mentions how the DA's office jumped to conclusions based upon incriminating, yet purely circumstantial, evidence. Reading on, the article explains the DNA stuff Matthew told me about. The fact that the DNA doesn't match Garrison's DNA went a long way towards his exoneration. So much for my image of him back in the slammer as some big dude's bitch.

The last paragraph, which details Garrison's recent signature in log books at county office and police records buildings (presumably an attempt to track down the real killer), disturbs me. Perhaps I've underestimated him. In conjunction with his unannounced visit to my home, I'm beginning to think he may be onto me. The urgency in finding out what he's up to has escalated. I can't count on him giving up the investigation, despite his newfound freedom.

I feel the walls closing in on me. If a punk like Garrison can home in on me, the cops can't be far behind. It's only a matter of time before the swarming begins. It's time to move. Time to ditch paradise. I can't be leaving footprints with my travels. I either need to go somewhere the United States doesn't have an extradition treaty with—my research says I'd be untouchable in Russia, China, and North Korea—or live in seclusion here, on some other island, or back in the States. Once my plane ticket to here gets uncovered, I'll be a trapped rat, given the smallness of the island. I'll be better off hiding in a small town stateside, far from Vermont. I could enter the country on the east coast and drive out west. If I'm careful, traveling by car won't leave a trail.

Tess, gone for much of the day, finally returns. I'm standing near the doorway as she brushes by me, without so much as an *excuse me*, and makes a beeline for the bedroom. I give her space, not anxious to launch into another war of words.

She emerges a few minutes later, advancing to within five or ten feet of where I'm standing in the living room. She has been crying. Her eyes are red, and a moist, crumpled tissue peeks out of her fisted hand. I sense apprehension.

"Babe, are you okay? What's up?"

"I need to tell you something." There's hesitation in her voice.

I let her words linger, waiting for more. She complies.

"I can't do this anymore, Jason. I can't support you any longer. I have to leave. I don't mean this to sound harsh, but I can't be with you. Not under the circumstances. I'm tired of running and hiding. I don't want to live in fear, knowing at any moment someone could come and take you away. And I don't want to be considered an accomplice."

This stings. It's worse than physical pain. My legs wobble. I love Tess! I can't get any words out. Her anger this morning has morphed into sadness. She goes on.

"I love you, Jason. I always have, and I always will. But it's not enough. It's too late for us to share a real existence. The thought of living without you scares me, but I'm frightened more by what our life together would be like."

She's talking fast, like she's been rehearsing and doesn't want to leave anything out. As agonizing as this is, I understand where she's coming from. Part of me has been thinking about cutting her loose for a while now. Not because I don't want her around, rather because endangering her gnaws at my conscience. Tess maintains eye contact, confident in her words.

"I completely understand, Tess. There's no need to explain. You have no reason to feel bad about any of this, so please don't."

Tenderly cupping her hand, I guide her to the couch. "I don't want to know where you're going. The less I know of your plans, the better it will be for you. I'm sorry I dragged you into all this. You have nothing to worry about as far as me mentioning your involvement."

I get a lump in my throat, making it difficult to speak. "They'll have to kill me before I give you up. I think you know that. Whatever happens, just know I love you. I know I fucked things up. Ruined any chance for us to lead a normal life. I just want you to be happy. You deserve that."

I surprise myself with my selflessness. She stuck with me when nobody else would have. I can't fault her for reaching a breaking point. The truth is, with my mission to take out Garrison, my last moments of freedom could very well be in Quincy.

"Thanks, babe, for reacting so well, and letting me go."

I respond by embracing her, only releasing her when the envelope I placed on top of the TV catches my attention.

"I have something for you." I rise and retrieve the envelope, labeled "Tess".

"What's this?" Tess asks.

"A little spending money."

We go back and forth, with Tess saying she can't accept it, and me insisting, until finally she relents and slips the unopened envelope in her pocket. The envelope contains $25,000, half of the sum I've been hiding in my duffle bag.

The $50,000 represents a third of my total net worth. The rest is tucked away at my bank back in Quincy. Not knowing where I'll be at any given time in the future, unsure of accessibility to ATM machines, along with withdrawal amounts limited to $500 per day—a threshold imposed by my bank, for my protection, certainly not for my convenience—I withdrew this chunk of change from my account before skipping town.

Tess risked everything for me. She made no demands on me. Such demonstration of unconditional loyalty deserves rewarding. Besides, she's the closest thing to a soul mate I've ever had or will have. If something were to happen to me, I wouldn't want her to suffer the same fate. Furthermore, I forked over more money to Poodle Boy than I'm giving Tess, and I didn't even like the weasel.

Tess has already booked a red-eye flight to the States, leaving tonight, and wants to go to the airport alone. Far from Vermont is all she says about her destination.

Honk! Honk! Her taxi awaits. We kiss, likely for the last time.

"Be careful," she says, in a volume barely above a whisper. "And good luck. You'll be in my thoughts and prayers."

Tears run down my face. I don't bother wiping them away. Tess, crying as well, softly says goodbye.

"Bye, babe," I say.

And then she vanishes. I watch as the taxi tears out, tires screeching.

I swing by the nearest liquor store, pick up a bottle of Jack Daniels, and head back to my room.

It's morning now. Maybe afternoon. I just stumbled out of bed, crashing onto the floor. My head hurts like hell. The room spins. I stand up for an instant, making the spinning sensation worse, so I plop back down onto the bed.

I glance over at the night table, an arm's reach from where I'm lying. Only a half full bottle of Jack sits on the table. More telling, I should say it's half empty. I've been trying to keep a clear head as of late, taking it easy with the booze, so drinking large amounts of straight whiskey probably wasn't a great idea.

Along with the pounding inside my head, I feel like puking. I need some ibuprofen, but seeing as this requires a trip to the hotel gift shop, it's not an option at the moment. Any further movement will cause me to upchuck. I try closing my eyes, waiting it out. It's not working. I race to the toilet and throw up.

Eventually making it to my feet, I stumble my way to the gift shop, where I find the ibuprofen.

An hour or two later, I'm up from a nice nap, courtesy of the pills. I drag myself into the car, needing to get food into my system. Finding a nearby diner, I order toast and coffee. Despite feeling hungry, I don't want to risk a repeat of this morning's episode. With my grogginess fading, I focus on strategy.

With two murders on my resume, authorities from the States, the Virgin Islands, or here in Grand Cayman could very well be on the lookout for me. Airports should be avoided, if possible, when you're on the lam. Unless you're traveling under an assumed identity, when you're being hunted, boarding a commercial airplane is akin to surrender.

Since surrendering isn't on my itinerary, I've chosen a different mode of transportation. A luxury cruise liner. A Carnival cruise ship. The idea came to me in my drunken state last night. I won't board with the rest of the passengers when the *all aboard* whistle sounds. Those folks will have purchased tickets in their possession, along with identification, which will be examined closely before passage onto the beautiful vessel is granted. I'll be traveling as a stowaway.

Sure, this violates federal law, but I have no intention of getting caught. I have seen the cruise ships dock here, hundreds of Americans disembarking for island adventure. A few strategies come to mind.

I could home in on a male passenger, traveling alone, bearing a physical resemblance to me. Since the ships remain at port for a couple of days, I'd spend day one selecting my victim and disguising myself to resemble him. Day two I'd make my move, overpowering him, stealing his clothes and wallet. Becoming him.

Bribing an official monitoring ship re-entry is another option. Another alternative would be boarding from the water. This would be tricky, but not impossible. Plan D, which comes to me now, is to create a diversion at an opportune time. Drawing ship personnel away from their posts, momentarily, could provide a window for me to slip through.

Compared to murder, sneaking onto a boat will be easy.

I spent the day arranging for my boat trip. Not the usual buying new clothes and packing type of preparation. A little research—a call to Carnival's customer service department, followed by more time logged into the hotel computer—netted key security policy information.

For starters, Carnival must provide the Department of Homeland Security with specific guest information. This confirmed my need to bypass the traditional registration process. Federal monitoring of the cruise industry has reached an all-time high. Apparently, crew members weren't behaving themselves while at port, including reports of sexual assault, so tracking their whereabouts, as well as passengers', became necessary.

The A-PASS, a computerized system, enables Carnival to record the identities of all crew and passengers through electronic photographs. Both crew and passengers must swipe their boarding pass at the ship's gangplank whenever boarding or leaving the vessel.

I'm in possession of a fake Carnival boarding pass. It won't hold up against close scrutiny, but appears legit at quick glance. Earlier today at the docks, I stopped a passenger, making an excuse to see her boarding pass. They should call it a boarding *card*, seeing as all other swipeables are cards. While handling it, I discreetly took a picture with a cheap flip phone I purchased. The card contains the company logo, along with trip specifics, like dates and boarding times, as well as lodging particulars—deck and stateroom. There's no picture, not a visible one anyway. Just an embedded digital image. My card has no such digital image, nor is it swipe-enabled. Which is fine, since I have no plans to use it. If necessary, I'm willing to display and flash it. If it gets confiscated for closer examination, my troubles will run deeper than forgery.

While at the docks, I got an appreciation for the sheer size of the yachts. Seeing the height above sea level where access onto the ship would be, I ruled out entering via the water. I also ruled out beating up a passenger and stealing his identity, determining I'd need to kill him or else he'd call the cops once he came to, which would result in a call to the ship's authorities, which in turn would lead to a bow-to-stern search. I'd be discovered.

I walked well up the detachable gangplank to get a feel for the boarding setup. Two officers man the card swipe area, a roped-off space just beyond the gangplank's end, onboard the vessel. Bribing them both is risky and complicated, and it would take only one of them to turn on me at any point during the trip back to U.S. soil.

I settle upon a plan involving diversion and enticing a local. The island resident local would ideally be a loner type. Loser type. Someone whose morals don't rival those of religious right groups. Someone in need of easy cash. Someone not inclined to ask a lot of questions.

It's dusk now and I'm back on the gangplank, a duffle bag containing clothes and a few other personal items, in hand. A line of about thirty passengers has formed, awaiting ship reentry. I'm positioned near the front of the line, off to the side, out of view of an overhead security camera. I give a subtle signal—removing my hat and holding it in the air for a second—and ready myself for action.

From the back of the line emerges a man, stumbling, shoving, and cursing, as he makes his way toward the front of the queue. A large, muscular fellow takes exception to the rudeness and pushes the drunk to the ground. Popping right back up, the obnoxious guy throws and lands a punch to the face of the body builder, catching him off-guard. With this, the employees guarding the entrance take the few steps to get to the midst of the skirmish— one which thankfully has captured the attention of everyone in line—intending to restore order. My guy, barely recognizable clean shaven and out of his flip-flops and dingy T-shirt, plays his role to perfection. He resists attempts to settle him down.

I don't stick around to see how it plays out. In a quick, fluid maneuver, I dart under the ropes designed to keep boarding passengers at bay, and get my body up and over a metal railing adjacent to the official entrance area. *I'm in.*

In my peripheral vision, I glimpse a figure, a snitch, pointing at me, his presumed yelling drowned out in the chaos, trying to flag down an official to stop the nut sneaking aboard. Seconds later, I've distanced myself from the commotion. The scene lasts just a minute or so, and doesn't register as a blip on anyone's radar outside the small radius at the gangplank's end. Locating a stairwell, I race up the first few flights, before settling into a normal-paced walk, until I reach deck nine (of about fifteen), the Promenade deck.

I have no clue what the hell Promenade means or what activities ensue here. I ease into a wide hallway and blend into the crowd. Snaking my way into a bar, I spy an apparent poker game transpiring in the back of the room. Men huddle around a large wooden table, chips and cards flying. I utter some "hey bud's" and elbow my way to the front of the room, where a drink line has formed.

A few details still need working out. Of all the staterooms in this luxury liner, none are reserved for me. Nor do I have a table assignment in the dining room. I'm not too concerned about my next meal. Cruises are known for serving exorbitant amounts of food at all hours. If I dress and act the part, I'll fit right in around here. Which is why a button-down shirt, a pair of trousers, and a tie made the duffle bag cut. Locating a place to crash, to hide out in, to store my belongings, will be my first assignment. I can't very well be dragging my bag everywhere. Talk about drawing suspicion. The Lido deck will have to wait.

CHAPTER 17
PETER

"**S**O HOW DOES IT FEEL, no longer being a murder suspect? Do you miss the limelight?" Amy ribs me.

We're seated at a corner table at Cafe Milano, an upscale, hidden away, Italian restaurant on the outskirts of town. *Nice choice, Amy.* I called in advance to reserve their best table and slipped the maître d' a five-spot as a show of appreciation. The large window adjacent to us affords a nice view of the setting sun. Amy is stunning in a black strapless dress, her long auburn hair flowing over her shoulders in contrast to the ponytail and pinned up hairdos she sports at work.

"It feels good. There's some lingering bitterness attached to being wrongly accused and imprisoned, but right now, being here with you, all that is pushed out of my mind. As for the limelight, I'll be quite happy living the rest of my life in relative anonymity. This experience did lead me to you, so it hasn't been all bad."

"Wow, pretty heavy for a first date."

The waiter appears to take our drink order—a bottle of cabernet sauvignon—giving me time to come up with a witty comeback. With nothing forthcoming, I settle for asking her to tell me about herself.

"Besides your penchant for sarcasm, that is," I sneak in, before she responds.

"You're a funny guy, Peter. Okay, in addition to giving you a hard time, I enjoy cooking, movies, yoga, drinking wine, and long walks on the beach. Sorry, I couldn't resist the last part. It was beginning to sound like a dating site profile. I do enjoy late night walks in my neighborhood, though. Especially when the moon is full and stars are visible. It's a nice way to decompress after a long day."

"I hope there aren't any nuts living near you. They tend to come out at night, you know." I instantly regret saying this and hope I didn't offend or scare her.

"It's a safe area, but I carry a Taser just in case. My boss got it for me when he learned I lived alone."

"Yikes. Remind me not to get on your bad side. Actually, that's a smart idea. I'm glad your boss set you up. He sounds like a good guy."

"Yeah, he is. Kind of a father figure. He worries about me and wanted me to carry a real gun. We compromised on the Taser."

Amy asks about my job. She read in the papers I'm a lawyer. I break the news about getting fired, assuring her I'll have no problem finding work with my law degree and experience.

"So, I'm dating an unemployed guy, recently released from prison. My parents will be so proud." We both burst out laughing.

Conversation flows throughout dinner as my nervousness dissipates. I've never hit it off with anyone this fast. The cliché *I feel like I've known you forever* comes to mind. We launch into story after story, aided by liquid courage provided by the now-empty wine bottle. She thinks it's cool I like sports. She used to play tennis with her dad until arthritis intruded his body. I'm smitten with her and don't want the meal to end.

Both the meal and the evening do conclude. We're back at her impressive house. Her street isn't lined with mansions, but it's upscale. Her house is large, with a good-size front lawn. Amy explained earlier she rents the place, and a guy paid by the owner comes to mow the grass. Her parents found the place and were happy she liked it. They feel more at ease knowing she's living in a safe area, since they live a little ways away in Burlington. Keeping my urges at bay, I am a gentleman, settling for a simple goodnight kiss at her doorstep. A second date seems promising as she gives me her phone number before heading inside.

Amy catches her breath, as we sit on a picnic table outside the tennis courts at a local park. It's sunny and cool, perfect tennis weather. We're sipping from our water bottles as we converse.

"So how did you become a tennis star? And why aren't you playing on the pro tour?" she asks.

Amy plays a pretty good game, but I'm out to impress her, and apparently succeeded. I give her my best *gee, shucks* look and shrug, telling her I'm not that good.

"Your *I'm okay, not great* modesty act lured me out here, but now forget it. I'm not in your league. Not even close."

"Well, we're even then, because I'm not in your league off the court," I respond truthfully.

She's successful, cute, and witty. I'm none of the above. Not even fully employed, although I aim to rectify that. She persists about the origins of my tennis prowess, so I dredge up my childhood years, describing my dad as distracted and distant, though our relationship has matured since. I paint my mom as a disciplinarian, but not so much a participant in my life. I credit my grandfather with exposing me to sports. Quite the jock in his day, he excelled at baseball and basketball, as well as tennis. He spent countless hours teaching me to play, as well as the respect and etiquette aspects of sports. "Athletes don't have to be prima donnas, you know. In my day, sportsmanship was more than just lip service."

"He was passionate and purposeful. His mantra was to master the fundamentals. With tennis, he had me hitting against a backboard for over a year before he let me play on a real court.

He had unlimited patience and pushed me to get the most out of my abilities. He also instilled in me a mental toughness, which complements the physical element of sport. Above all, he infused me with the notion that to excel at something—sports or otherwise—you must enjoy it. If you don't like what you're doing, stop doing it and find something you do like. He taught me a lot about life. I was lucky to have him around."

To my amazement, Amy leans forward, listening intently to my long-winded tale.

"He sounds awesome, Peter. My dad was the guiding light in my childhood. Really, he still is. I'm not as dependent on him now, but he introduced me to so much of what life has to offer, enabling me to make smarter choices as an adult."

She gingerly brings up the subject of Chang, and I find myself confiding to her my need for closure, my yearning to pursue the guy responsible for his death and setting me up in the process. She admires my stance, offering to help me however she can.

My ringing phone interrupts our conversation. I have no desire to pick it up, but Amy motions toward the phone, sitting on top of my racquet, along with my wallet and keys, and whispers "May I?" I nod, as she answers.

"Hello, Peter Garrison's office, this is Amy speaking."

I let out a hearty laugh. After a beat, she hands me the phone. "A Mr. Doug Garrison on line two."

Apologizing for the disturbance—he's intrigued by the female voice, but knows I can't fill him in now—my dad explains Sir William has confidential information regarding the Chang case, and he's anxious to share. Says we'll want to drop whatever we're doing (a greater sacrifice for myself than my dad) and get to his office pronto. I explain that *pronto* will be about an hour for me as I'm not ready to shoo Amy away just yet. I ask for a preview, but, of course, there are no details forthcoming, in typical teaser Sir William fashion.

Amy, in tune with my obsession to track down my tormentor, convinces me to take her home, so I can get the scoop on my lawyer's secretive news. Before agreeing to this, I make her promise there will be a date number three. She raises her right hand and solemnly vows to see me again, on the condition the venue is not a tennis court.

At her front door, she leans into me, draping her arms around me. Following her lead, I kiss her. She doesn't pull away. We remain lip-locked for what feels like an hour, and must have been a minute or two.

I'm still in an aroused state as I pull into the law offices parking lot. Walking through the building corridors and seeing my dad and Sir William snaps me out of my euphoria. I help myself to a mug of William's freshly-brewed coffee. It tastes even better than usual. When you're a free man, after having your freedom stripped away, life's simple pleasures are accentuated.

We zip past the pleasantries, and, atypically, Sir William gets right to it. I should show up near quitting time more often. He has glanced at his wall clock, reading almost five p.m., a couple of times since my arrival. My dad shifts around in his seat while I'm quite relaxed. Along with the dismissal of charges against me, Amy entering my life has resulted in my improved well-being.

"What I'm about to tell you won't appear in the newspapers or on the local news. My buddy on the force thought you deserved to know, however. If there's a leak of this information, my relationship with this guy will be compromised, as will his credibility. So please respect the sensitive nature of what I'm relaying to you."

Okay, maybe he's not in such a hurry to get out of here.

"You got it," I reply for us both, my dad nodding his understanding.

This prompts Sir William to roll his eyes, mistaking my good mood for attitude.

"Due to a night shift operator misspelling Chang's name as

C-h-i-n-g, this wasn't caught earlier, but one of the detectives, while searching the call logs for months preceding Chang's murder, got lucky. Instead of searching for Chang by name, he searched by location, looking for matches with Peking Dragon. Sure enough, Michael *Ching* lodged a complaint against a kid loitering and drinking in the parking lot of his restaurant."

The significance of this registers immediately.

"The kid was Matthew Rincon." It's not a question. I know I'm right. My dad whistles, picking up on the connection.

"The cops swiftly respond to Chang's snitch call, and arrest Matthew for underage drinking. Matthew is put in touch with your old law firm, and, well, you know the rest. Now the cops do as well. They know Matthew has Chang, and to a lesser extent, you, Peter, to thank for his jail stint."

The news stuns me. How did I miss this? I should have checked up on Matthew after his sentencing.

"When I was assigned to the case, the story in the case folder began with the cops' arrest of Matthew. I don't recall a mention of who called the cops. If there was, it didn't make an impression on me. It had no bearing on the case. Had the location of the arrest even been in the file, it would have listed the crossroads where Peking Dragon is located, which, likewise, wouldn't have set off any alarms."

I'm speaking out loud, but am re-hashing more for my sanity.

"It makes sense all this stems from your days in a courtroom," my dad says, playing Monday-morning quarterback. "Everyone hates lawyers, making them a target for all kinds of nut cases." He pauses, turning to face William. "Not that *I* dislike *you*, William."

Sir William waves off my dad's attempt to clarify. He gets it.

"You know, a few days ago I went to see Matthew. I didn't know about his connection to Chang, but I considered the possibility he harbored enough resentment to retaliate."

My mind drifts back to a boardroom discussion of the case

with my colleagues. They convinced me the kid would get a slap on the wrist. They said no judge wants to throw minors in jail, especially for petty offenses. Maybe I could have prepped more. I figured if the kid showed remorse, he'd get off. I figured wrong. My attention returns to my dad and William, who patiently wait for me to continue.

"I didn't really believe he killed Chang, but I wanted to see him to feel him out. Wow."

I'm shaking my head, bewilderment etched on my face. "Matthew didn't kill Chang. He has an iron-clad alibi," Sir William states dramatically.

Confused, we wait for him to elaborate, which he does. "At the time of Chang's murder, Matthew was in his bed at a mental hospital in Dover, forty miles from the scene of the crime."

He goes on to explain how his incarceration, while brief, wasn't without incident. He was sexually assaulted, which messed with his mind. *Wow.* This revelation saddens me. His offense didn't warrant jail time, let alone abuse.

"If Matthew didn't kill Chang, who did?" my perplexed dad demands.

"We don't know yet."

Sir William's liberal use of the word *we* doesn't escape me. Following a brief pause, he speculates.

"Maybe a friend or family member. The digging is underway. This link could be a huge coincidence, but we all know cops and the DA's office aren't big believers of coincidence."

—⋄◦⧼⧽◦⋄—

When you pay for a service, what can you rightfully expect in return? What constitutes justifiable actions if services aren't rendered to your satisfaction? You can ask for, even demand, your money back. You can spread the word how you were wronged. You can blow off steam by letting the person who screwed you know it, in the form of a nasty letter, email, phone call, or in-person berating. You can take legal action, suing the service provider for negligence and incompetence. You can ask a court for compensation due to financial loss and medical issues caused by the ineptitude.

But there's a line you can't cross. You can't harass, stalk, or physically harm. You also can't frame someone for a crime they didn't commit, especially when the framing leads to punishment. Particularly when sanctions include forfeiture of freedom and monetary loss. It's not like the DA's office, upon declaring me innocent, reimbursed me for incurred legal and investigative expenses. What often accompanies tangible losses are intangibles, such as emotional duress and a damaged reputation.

It would be easy to fall into a *why me* line of thinking. To wallow in self-pity. To curl up into a ball, shielding myself from the harshness of the real world. But that would be conceding defeat. It would be acknowledging my tormentor got to me. That he ruined my life. Stripped away my will to live.

I've spent a fair amount of time trying to assess my culpability in this ordeal. I gave it my all, but my all wasn't enough. I factor in that while Henderson & Gates is a respectable, and expensive, law firm, I wouldn't place it among the city's elite. Similarly, I'm a good lawyer, but not prestigious.

All things considered, Matthew Rincon broke the law and got caught doing it. I played no part in those happenings. While my legal defense wasn't spectacular, I didn't break any laws. I didn't deserve punishment.

Rather than harboring resentment and crawling into my shell, I'm choosing to channel my energy towards tracking down the inflictor of my pain. It's time for some undercover work.

Surmising my best shot at getting answers will come from a grandmotherly type, I stake out Matthew's neighbors, in search of a sweet elderly woman. I don't have to wait long before coming across just that, tinkering in her garden, three houses down from Matthew.

I wait until she turns to head back inside—a long forty-five minutes, long enough to formulate a hunch she's a widow—before jumping out of my car and walking briskly toward her. An earlier sweep of the neighborhood yielded a list of names painted on mailboxes, which I associated with their corresponding street number, on a sheet of paper attached to my clipboard. I yell out to her as she closes in on her door, quickening my pace to a borderline jog.

"Hello. Mrs. Johnson? I'm sorry to bother you on such a fine day, but I'm Samuel Sanders, an insurance agent for the Rincon family. I'd like to ask you a couple brief questions if you can spare the time."

I produce a business card I made up this morning at Kinko's. She examines the card, deems it legit with a barely perceptible nod of her head, and ushers me inside. Perfect. I want this chat to take place indoors, out of sight and earshot of nosy neighbors.

"Oh dear. I have an abundance of free time. More than I know what to do with. And please call me Gloria. Hearing *Mrs.* is a painful reminder of the recent passing of my poor Henry." Bingo. My gut was right on.

"I'm very sorry about your Henry, Gloria."

Once inside, she offers me tea and cookies. It's more of an insistence than a question. I politely accept. She leads me to a sitting room, before disappearing into the kitchen. Several minutes later, I hear the distinct whistle of a tea kettle. A few more minutes pass before she emerges carrying a silver antique platter, holding two teacups and a plate of homemade cookies. I sip my tea, have a cookie, and lie by uttering the word "delicious". As Gloria dunks her cookie, I get to it.

"I am representing Matthew Rincon, down the street. Do you know the Rincon family?"

"Oh, dear, yes. I watched those two kids grow up. Jenny did a fine job raising them boys." Translation: single mom. Matthew has a brother. "They are nice boys, especially Matthew. He shovels out driveways in the winter, and watches the Melius' cat when they go on vacation." She points at the house next to hers. "He is always pleasant. His brother, Jason, is quieter, not outgoing like Matthew. I didn't know him as well."

The mom and brother become immediate suspects. Without much prodding, I learn Jenny has had back luck with men, and the boys have different fathers.

I keep Gloria chatting—she's thrilled to have a captive audience—and a second cup of tea later, she reveals she hasn't seen either boy around for the past few weeks. She sees Jenny driving and walking around the block regularly. I know where Matthew has been. Locating Jason has just become priority one. Gloria has a wealth of information, and she shares for the price of keeping her company. By the time I excuse myself, I've learned even more potentially useful information. She has seen the boys hanging out with various guys over the years, but doesn't recall much about them. Since she can remember, though, the boys were tight with a couple of girls. Sisters, she thinks. The girls haven't been around lately, but when they were younger, the four of them were inseparable.

On my ride home, as I'm making a checklist (yeah, I'm obsessed with lists) I realize I'm in over my head. A list of questions is more accurate. Who are the sisters the brothers hung with? Where is Jason? Who has Matthew called and received calls from recently? Who has the mom called and received calls from? Do Matthew or Jason know any thugs? Are they thugs? I reach out to the best, and only, PI I know.

Having secured more money from my parents (plan B; plan A didn't pan out once my bank loan application got rejected), I can afford Jack's fees, and am on the horn with him now. I assured my folks I'll repay them with interest. They were skeptical, but didn't hesitate to write me a check, simply stating "this is a gift. Your last such gift." Of course, if I found myself in trouble again, such gifts would flow until they were destitute.

"Peter Garrison. How are you? I didn't expect to hear from you so soon. Shouldn't you still be celebrating?" He's in a great mood.

"I'd like to hire you again, Jack."

He laughs. "Really? Why?"

"To find Chang's killer."

"You do understand you're scot-free now, right?"

"Yes, I do."

"Then why not let the cops take it from here?"

"Because we'll get results quicker. By *we*, of course, I mean you. But I'd like to assist you. I'll work cheap—for free—and don't mind grunt work. Or dangerous work, for that matter."

I'd love to glimpse the expression on his face. He must think I'm crazy.

"Are you trying to be a hero?"

"Not at all. I'm fine with you getting all the glory. You can even share information with the cops. I'm in it for peace of mind, wanting only justice."

"A regular Atticus Finch."

Ignoring his sarcastic remark, I tell him what I've got so far. My stakeouts, scheming, and results both surprise and impress him. We agree in principle to a deal, one we'll finalize over breakfast tomorrow. Unlike Sir William, Jack dislikes spending time in his office. Having never seen it, I wouldn't be surprised if his *office* doubled as the den in his home.

Hanging up, I'm filled with excitement. I know little about the daily grind of PI work, but compared to probate work, it seems like a blast.

We're seated across from each other in a corner booth at Denny's. It's six a.m., and we've beaten the breakfast rush. Our waitress just delivered our meals. Between bites of his fried egg sandwich, Jack lays it out for me.

"For starters, I want to point out the real possibility of

interfering with an active police investigation is something we need to be cognizant of. Especially since they have dialed in on this Matthew kid as the source of motive for murdering Chang. Previously, when I chased down Hank, the cops were proceeding in a different direction, focusing their investigation around the premise you were the killer. Now, the circumstances have changed. We can't be stepping on their toes, screwing up their investigation." He pauses, allowing for my rebuttal.

"I appreciate the delicateness of the situation, but you're a professional. One who gets results. Besides, police often engage the public. You've heard the pleas. 'If you have any information regarding the whereabouts of this person…' or 'If you have information regarding this crime…' We're all on the same side of the law."

My turn to pause, anxious for Jack's reaction.

"Cops like information. It's why they use informants. What they're not as keen on is interference with their cases. They're sensitive and don't like being shown up. I'm not saying we need to stay away. Just that we have to be careful."

"So, does this mean you're in?" I key in on his last words.

"Yes, Peter, I'm in." He extends his hand across the table and we shake on it.

"I like the fire in your belly and find your attitude noble, especially coming from someone who has been beaten up by the judicial system."

Our waitress returns to check on us. Telling her everything tastes great, I wait for her to leave.

"Thanks, Jack. Now for the part you're not going to like. I want to work with you on this. I think I've got an aptitude, and certainly an interest, in PI work. I'm good with Google searches. And Facebook. I don't use Facebook like most people. I *lurk*, using it as an investigative tool. I never 'like' or post anything, just prowl in the shadows. And I think I'd enjoy the field work, if my brief experience with stakeouts and lying to people to get information is an indicator. I enjoy bending rules for the greater good, and am proficient at it."

I hand over a retainer check while he considers this. Jack appears torn. "Let's take this one step at a time. Give me a day or two to dig on my own. If there's any grunt work you can perform which will save me time, I'll let you know. I've never put a client in harm's way before and I don't wish to start now."

He succeeds in tempering my enthusiasm. Picking up on my disappointment, he goes on. "I'll keep you posted with every move I make, every move I plan to make. I can see you won't be sitting by idly, so by knowing my moves, you won't get in my way."

I'm a little confused, but figure I can work on him more once he has had a chance to dive into this. Declining a request to top off his coffee, Jack rises, says he has another appointment, and heads out, his trademark quick exit. I'll be out of here in a minute, as soon as I settle the bill. From the moment we shook hands, Jack has been on my expense account.

Two incoming calls keep me awake during my drive home. Sir William buzzes in first, with, of course, vital news. Since I'm no longer a paying client, or a client at all, he spills the beans over the phone. Keurig machine coffee notwithstanding, the phone is my preferred communication method. The *beans* is that Matthew Rincon's brother, Jason Felding, fled the country a couple days after Chang bit the dust ("proverbial dust" to quote William). He's hiding out in the Cayman Islands. The Quincy Police Department is teaming up with the authorities in Grand Cayman, with the unified mission to flush Jason out. They have no hard evidence against him, but his behavior warrants a visit from the men in blue, armed with a DNA lab kit, basically surgical gloves, a Q-tip, and a plastic Baggie.

I rush Sir William off the phone once the *flow of information* portion of our call concludes. His tone suggests I haven't suitably recognized his herculean feat of drawing case facts from his detective friend. It's not so much that I deplore acknowledging his accomplishments, rather his demand for praise on a regular basis that puts me off.

I call Jack, passing along the news. He promises to get back to me once he's had a chance to verify the story. I tell him to count me in if he intends to get some Caribbean sun.

My next distraction comes in the form of a call from Amy. I share the brother development with her. She adds to my fortuitous day with an invitation. A night of dinner and dancing. At her apartment. She wants to use me as a guinea pig for a chicken marsala recipe she's been anxious to try out. I accept, refraining from interjecting a comment about her feeling free to use me any way she likes. She tells me the dress code is business casual. I compliment her wittiness, ask what I can bring (bottle of wine), hold back another remark (this time "I love you"), and we say our *until later* goodbyes. My feelings shift from love to lust as I envision how the evening might play out. This could wind up being the best night of my life.

Jack calls back twenty minutes later. Jason was last spotted at a liquor store in Grand Cayman three days ago. He has prepaid his rent through the end of the month at the place he's been staying. He hasn't exactly been laying low as he's been seen at the beach, at restaurants, in the hotel lobby and bar. Jack doesn't plan to fly there. Says if Jason is still in the Caymans, he'll be apprehended.

"You don't think he's still there." I'm reading his inflections. "Didn't you say he hasn't flown anywhere since arriving?" I'm already mentally packed for a beach vacation.

"Here's what I'm thinking. A) He's now flying under an assumed name. Although, I'd be surprised if he has the means and forethought to obtain a falsified passport. B) If he's feeling any heat, he'll run. He'll run, hide, survive. I'm not usually an advocate of the wait-and-see approach, but in this case, I prefer to let the cops have a go at it in the Caribbean. In the meantime, you and I need to do some research."

"You and I?" I'm grinning widely. "So, you're finally seeing my potential?"

"Something like that."

More likely he's understaffed and has more questions than answers. I wait for him to speak again, hoping for a task. He squashes my curiosity for the time being.

"We'll talk tomorrow."

―――――⋙⋘―――――

My mind races with thoughts of the night ahead as I approach Amy's doorstep, bottle of Chardonnay in hand. I considered bringing a more lavish gift, jewelry perhaps, but don't want to scare her off. Okay, the expense may have been a factor as well.

In my typical over-analyzing way, I deem tonight as a defining moment in my life. The next couple of hours will bear out whether Amy will be anything more than a future distant memory. It's act now or lose your chance forever time. Embrace the moment. Perform at full capacity. It's like stepping into the batter's box with two outs and the bases loaded. You're either the hero or the goat. When I played sports with my grandfather, we had this thing where the loser would have to *wear the goat horns* for the rest of the day. When he won, he'd rib me with comments like "it must be hard walking around with those big goat horns on your head."

I take a deep breath before ringing the bell. Amy is decked out in a flowing skirt and silk top. A low-cut, cleavage-revealing top. My hormones do jumping jacks.

"Wow, you look amazing. The bar for business casual sure has been raised."

My comment evokes a devilish smile. I'm led to the living room as she inspects the wine bottle. My interpretation of the dress code was Dockers and a polo shirt.

"Thanks. I'm impressed with your wine selection. That you know white wine goes best with chicken. I thought you just got lucky last time, ordering red wine with our pasta dishes. Now I have to attribute it to sophistication."

She excuses herself to check on dinner and pour us some wine. I take in the dining room table, set up with the good china, candles providing mood lighting. Either she spent hours cleaning or she's naturally neat, as the place is immaculate. The décor in the living and dining rooms exhibit classic taste. I'm called into the kitchen, and obediently go to her.

Amy dips a spoon into the chicken marsala pan, feeding me sauce.

"Delicious." Without acknowledgement, she heads for a pot of boiling clam chowder soup. New England style. My taste buds get treated to the best clam chowder I've had in a long time. Ignoring another superlative, she leans toward the back burner. Mashed potatoes.

"Garlicky." Amy glares at me, theatrically. I expand. "That's a good thing. Really. I love garlic. My two favorite spices are garlic powder and garlic salt. I enjoy it in clove form, as well. Also —"

"Okay, okay. I believe you."

Taking a white apron off a hook adjacent to the refrigerator, she waves it in surrender above her head, with outstretched arms. She brings her wine glass to my lips, tilting it just enough to afford me a small sip. The next sample is her tongue. The best sample yet. Kissing progresses to groping, which following a brief pause to turn off the burners, advances to a tour of her bedroom.

"I figure this will break the tension," she whispers seductively. I simply smile in response, not wanting to risk words which could lead to a change of heart.

In none of the scenarios I played out in my head did we wind up in bed this quickly. She exposes (no pun intended) her soft, gentle, playful side. Despite deliberance in fully exploring each other, the physical part ends... umm... prematurely. I'm soaking up the cuddling. Amy's undivided attention. It's an unparalleled feeling. A nirvana. Sure, part of what I'm feeling can be attributed to *it's nice being with a woman.* But, this could be a budding love thing. I like her.

A *ringing* in the direction of my crumpled pants on the floor interrupts my bliss.

"Don't you dare answer that."

We're both laughing, realizing the timing could have been worse. One appetite satisfied, we return to the kitchen to acquiesce our growling bellies. The stove serves as a buffet table as we fix our plates, warm them in the microwave, and scarf down the gourmet meal. Amy's culinary skills only add to her aura. As we're polishing off dessert—banana splits!—my phone goes off again.

"Really? Your ringer is still on? You know, people turn off their phones at movie theaters. Does being with me rank below being at the movies?" She casts an indignant look my way.

"Certainly not." I turn off my phone, but not before scanning my missed calls. My parents and Jack. I'm dying to hear Jack's message but will wait a bit.

At my insistence, we do the dishes. I wash, she loads. She remarks how I've really taken to this team work thing my grandfather instilled in me. Settled now on her couch, the two of us cozily sharing a blanket, I'm flipping through the two hundred plus DISH network channels, searching for a romantic comedy.

"So what did your PI friend have to say?" She understands about the investigation going on and granted me phone time.

"He gave me homework. I'll be helping him with some digging. Nothing dangerous. I'll get the details in the morning when I officially begin."

"Is he discounting his rates seeing as you'll be performing

half of his job for him?" A fair question, although *half* is a sizable exaggeration.

"My contributions will fall under the apprenticeship umbrella. Kind of like an unpaid internship. The theory being I'll learn the trade from a master."

"I hope reality lives up to the theory billing."

I respond by kissing her on the neck. This phases out conversation, and leads to me giving Amy a piggyback ride to more comfortable quarters. As we approach her bed, I give my best *neigh* and buck her off, sending her airborne before landing, and bouncing, on the bed. Round two lasts longer, while matching the excitement level achieved earlier. Late now, there's an unspoken certainty I'll be spending the night.

The next few hours I watch Amy sleep. Between the foreign bed, my assignment from Jack, and Amy and I ratcheting things up a level, sleep eludes me. It's just as well since I'd probably be snoring, drooling, or doing something embarrassing in my sleep. I wait until six o'clock, with the sun starting to rise, before making a run to a local bagel shop. I pick up a half dozen bagels—don't know her favorite yet, so make my best six guesses—and two cups of coffee, tossing creamers and sugar packets into the bag.

Following breakfast in bed—scoring me chivalry points—I excuse myself to take care of some things, promising to call later. I'm anxious to meet with Jack and get started. It's what I'm going to be doing for the next thirty years. Yeah, I've already decided. I won't be returning to the legal profession.

I thought defense work would be more rewarding, helping clients in need, upholding the law. In reality, my level of influence and control was minimal. I was at the mercy of the whims of many: my firm's partners, prosecutors, judges, and expert witnesses painting pictures orchestrated by the counselors paying them. A flawed jury system, where deliberating jurors tire, lose their resolve, compromise their positions, or simply lack requisite understanding, contributes to the mayhem. Attorneys must follow rules and procedures.

Investigators cut corners. They work independently. Their movements aren't as scrutinized, able to serve clients with less interference. Stepping off the stage where judicial misconduct and unethical behavior runs rampant appeals to me. Investigators don't really have opponents the way trial lawyers do.

I'm gonna be a PI. I'm kicking off my new career today. I'm ready to track down, tail, and chase. I intend on catching myself a bad guy.

CHAPTER 18
JASON

I N A FEW MINUTES, THIS luxury cruise ship will dock in Miami, Florida. Ride over. And quite the ride it has been. Two days at sea, nothing but big, blue ocean. It's only 450 miles from Grand Cayman, in the Western Caribbean, to Miami, but we had to navigate around Cuba, a narrow, long island, and impediment to the beeline route. While being at sea is invigorating, I'm antsy to get onto dry land. Cabin fever has kicked in. I shared a room with some nerd, also traveling alone, feeding him a story about my girlfriend booting me out of our state room after a blowout. I assured him it would just be for a night, but since he took a liking to me, and the fighting with my girlfriend continued, one night turned to two. As for feeding my belly, I grazed at buffets on various decks. Ice cream sundaes on the Sky Deck were my favorite.

I've learned, from a discreetly posed question, disembarking will be a sans-security procedure. This suits me fine, since an hour ago I pilfered the largest, sharpest knife I could find in one of the onboard kitchens. Thinking ahead, it occurred to me ground transportation would be an issue. I can't rent a car. That leaving-a-trail thing gets in the way. Carjacking is my best option. Thus the need for the weapon tucked away in my duffle bag. Violating a random person doesn't faze me whatsoever. I won't target nasty-looking guys built like boxers, so a random old lady entering her car with an armful of groceries more accurately describes my intention. It's funny how, compared to murder, minor crimes don't even register in my mind as wrong. Once you've committed a heinous crime, the consequences associated with lesser crimes seem miniscule.

I'm headed for Eugene, Oregon. No particular reason, other than its remoteness from Vermont and the beauty and peacefulness it advertises. I don't want to settle in a small, hick town, where strangers don't blend in. Before heading west, however, I'll make a detour in Quincy.

I'm headed east in my new Lincoln Continental. The odometer reads just over 14,000, practically right off the lot. The heist didn't go as smoothly as I had expected. The old broad didn't turn over the keys willingly. She actually hit me over the head with her purse, making me laugh. So, our little encounter left her a little bruised up. But not cut up, as I had no reason to use my knife.

I ring my mom, who answers excitedly. "Jason, thank God. Are you okay?"

"I'm fine, Mom. What's the matter? Why are you panicked?"

"I've heard through the grapevine the cops are after you."

"Fuck."

"They think you killed Chang. You did, didn't you? I suppose I've always known, but didn't want to believe it. Where are you now? Are you safe? Are you going to turn yourself in?"

Her rapid fire flow of words blur into my subconscious. All that registered was *the cops are after you.*

"Jason, are you still there? Jason?"

"I'm here, Mom. Who told you this?"

"Rachel Connors, at the supermarket. She heard it from Beverly Jones. Rachel and Beverly play tennis together, you know. Anyway, Beverly's husband, Bill, is a cop, so a pretty reliable source, I'd say. They think you're hiding out in the Cayman Islands. I hope you're not there. If you are, you need to get out right away."

"Is Matthew there?" My mom's panic stresses me out.

"No. He's been up to something secretive and won't tell me

147

what. I don't know where he is. He left the house early this morning. I think it has something to do with you. He's worried about you, Jason." The inflection in her voice remains high pitched.

"Listen to me, Mom. First, you need to calm down. I'm not in the Cayman Islands. I'm not in any danger. I need to speak with Matthew. When you see him next, please give him the phone you're using now. Can you do that for me?"

"Yes, I can do that. I wish you boys weren't so mysterious. I thought the three of us were a team. I can't help you if I don't know what you're planning. I'm your mother and would sooner die than have something bad happen to either one of you."

I can do without my mom's dramatics right now. "Nobody's gonna die. Matthew is just trying to protect you, as am I. I'll be in touch soon. Please don't worry about me."

We say our goodbyes, my mind immediately shifting to Matthew. He must be tangled up with the lawyer. Or maybe the PI from the Virgin Islands. That's got to be the secret stuff occupying him. If he thinks Garrison is trying to track me down, as it appears he is, who knows what Matthew will do. With the pigs chasing me, the need to take out Garrison lessens. I need to communicate this to Matthew before he does anything stupid.

Speaking of stupid, showing up in Quincy now would qualify as such. I'll continue heading in that general direction, keep trying to reach Matthew, and take things from there. Suspecting the pigs are after me, and knowing it for certain, are very different things.

I no longer have the luxury of time. I need to get to Oregon. To begin my new life. I'll need to lay low for a while. I'll take a job where I get paid under the table. I'll work on getting a new identity. But first, I've got to find Matthew.

CHAPTER 19
PETER

MY ASSIGNMENT IS TO UNCOVER the identity of the waitress. The elusive waitress, whose magical repertoire includes a pretty good disappearing act. Jack warns me that finding her may be more difficult than hunting down Jason. She's not as brash, meaning not as susceptible to making mistakes. Jack's plausible theory pegs the waitress having strong prior ties to Jason—a girlfriend or good friend type. I'll need to rummage through his past.

My resources consist of my laptop computer and the citizenship of Quincy. An hour or two into online searching, it becomes obvious that hitting the streets will be the path leading to answers. Keyboard tapping has yielded little. Typing names into Google often returns pages of results. I don't get a single hit for Jason. His brother Matthew isn't quite as invisible, as I learn where he went to high school and some activities he participated in. Nothing on the mom.

I need to find out where Jason worked, what bars he frequented, who he hung with, who he dated, things like that. I'm not the cops and can't access phone logs, but I bet I can get useful information off computers in the family home. This, of course, requires a break-in, something I'm not ready to do just yet. I decide to follow up on the one lead I have. The neighborhood old lady who saw Jason and his brother hanging out with those two girls.

Did Jason date one or both of them? Is he still in touch with either of them? Could one of them be his accomplice? I need answers to these questions. If granny down the street saw these girls, some of the other neighbors must have also. It's a starting point anyway. As a bonus, spending time in the neighborhood will allow me to keep tabs on Matthew and the mother, as well.

I jot down a note, on my iPad, to ask Jack about getting myself some identification. I have no problem risking an impersonation charge, if it leads me closer to nailing the perps. I can pull off being a detective, a PI, or whatever the situation calls for. For now, I'll need to stick with the insurance agent cover, seeing as that's the only fake ID I possess.

With no easy targets milling about, I boldly select a large home two doors down from Jason's place. I say boldly because being discovered by Matthew would not be a good thing. Just lurking in the vicinity risks such discovery. The nearer I am to his house increases the odds of being spotted. I get lucky as a middle-aged lady greets me. I go through my spiel, and while this woman has seen Jason and Matthew with the two girls the old lady mentioned, she doesn't know names or specifics. She can't resist, however, sharing gossip about Jason and the red-headed older woman at the end of the block. Apparently, the two of them had a torrid affair a few years back.

I stroll down the street to her house. There's no name on the mailbox. As I'm contemplating advancing to her front door, the garage door opens and a car barrels down the driveway. I casually start jogging towards my car, opposite from where the street dead ends, in the direction she'll be heading. As the silver Mercedes races by me, I make out a fortyish, red-headed woman behind the wheel. I pick up the pace, deciding on a whim to follow her.

By the time I get to my car, she's turning left, out of the neighborhood. I start my engine and join the race. Risking a speeding ticket, I tail her to a dry cleaning store. She knows only one speed, as she briskly makes her way inside. Having a minute to catch my breath, I formulate a plan, beginning with letting her continue on her Indy 500 rampage solo. I don't expect to uncover anything running more errands with her.

Her business concluded, she peels out of the parking lot, leaving a cloud of dust in her wake. I wander into the dry cleaners, greeting the man standing between the motorized closet carousel and the service desk. My first attempt at getting the redhead's name fails.

"It's very important I know her name." I place a twenty dollar bill on the desk.

"Of course, the source of this information will be kept confidential," I add, pushing to clinch the deal.

It's amazing what you can pry out of people once you toss greenbacks their way. The twenty bought me her name, Gloria Stevens. It costs me another twenty to learn she has been living with some Italian guy for the past two years. Her relationship with Jason must have ended well before that, making her involvement in the Chang murder a long shot. The Italian, also a customer, a fussier one at that—*my shirts must not have a single wrinkle* was the imitation—is the possessive type. This makes the long shot even longer. Nothing can be gained by following her. I know where she lives and can talk to her anytime.

Jack calls to check in. I tell him about striking out online and the field work I'm exploring.

"Be careful, Peter. It's a dangerous world out there. There's an element of unpredictability inherent in this line of work. You never know how folks will react to questioning. Some don't like their privacy invaded. Tread carefully, okay?"

"Don't worry about me. I'll be fine."

"Keep your antenna up. If you sense trouble, get out. Always have an exit strategy."

"Really, Jack, I'm okay. I can take care of myself. Your motherly worrying is touching, though." Despite my sarcasm, I appreciate his concern.

While racing to the dry cleaners, we whizzed by a Subway, which I'm heading for now. Plotting my next course of action, I call Amy to thank her for a wonderful evening and let her know I'm still on cloud nine. Playing coy isn't my style. She impishly reminds me it was more than just an evening, before returning my sentiments. We make plans to catch a movie tonight, me giving her the selection responsibility. I suggest a later show to maximize my investigative time.

I'm mulling over a flowers versus candy gift for Amy when I realize the car behind me, a black Toyota pickup, has been trailing me for a few miles now. It's probably paranoia, but just the same I make a sharp left turn onto a residential street. Paranoia turns to fear as the pickup remains on my tail. And *honking* at me now. Someone I know?

Wishing I was armed, or at least had a baseball bat in the back seat, I cautiously pull over beside a large brick house with a nice, grassy front yard. The pickup parks behind me, and a guy wearing a baseball cap and jeans emerges from the car, heading my way. Curiosity getting the better of me, I exit my vehicle.

Not until the guy closes to about thirty yards away does recognition set in. It's Matthew.

⸺◦◦▰◦◦⸺

The irony of Jack's words of caution, imparted mere minutes ago, resonates in my head. How long has Matthew been following me? Watching me. I know this confrontation won't be pleasant, yet I'm immobilized, not making a move for my car, unable to avoid the imminent showdown. I don't back down, rather return the cold stare coming from beneath his lowered cap. For some reason, I'm not afraid. He's a bully, yeah, but he doesn't really scare me. He steadily advances toward me, each long stride evaporating distance between us. Just a few feet away now, he comes to a halt, still no words spoken. I maintain a cool, calm exterior. Physically, we are approximate equals. Matthew outweighs me by ten to twenty pounds, but I'm a couple of inches taller. His hardened glare tells me he's way past talking.

It's like a game of chicken. Who will speak first? Seeing as he's the one who arranged this impromptu meeting, I wait him out. I absorb a condescending glare before he gets around to stating his business.

"You've been quite the busy beaver, haven't you?" I wait for elaboration. "Sticking your nose where it doesn't belong." I'm beginning to get the picture. "Maybe you were never taught this as a kid, so let me educate you. Mind your own fucking business. Stop harassing my neighbors. Stay the fuck out of my neighborhood. I don't want to see you anywhere *near* my house. You got it?"

He inches forward and jabs his finger into my chest to punctuate his words. I take a step backwards as I respond.

"I got it."

My response gets him more keyed up. He takes a furtive glance around, presumably looking for witnesses. He steps back into my personal space before resuming his lecture.

"And in case you think you're still working my case, let me clue you in. You're fired. I stopped paying you the moment you got my ass sent to jail. You're a shit lawyer. You do shit work. I wouldn't hire you to wash my truck. Stay the fuck out of my life!"

"I got it."

A hard stare between us ensues. Sensing the scolding has concluded, I turn away to my car door, jittering from the adrenaline coursing through my system. I sensed wrong. As I'm reaching into my pocket for my keys, I catch movement in my peripheral vision. I instinctively, and foolishly, turn towards him. His fist connects with my jaw with a vicious *crack*. Stars fill my vision. For a second, I think I'm going to pass out. I stagger, lean into my car, and collapse to the ground. My jaw throbs as if alive. I want to puke. I do. The fucker sucker-punched me!

"Don't walk away from me when I'm talking to you. You think you're some kind of smartass?"

Now towering over me, he yells like a madman. The whole right side of my face throbs. He kicks me in the ribs several times for good measure, each impact eliciting an involuntary *yelp*. I'm writhing in pain, focusing only on the uniform blades of freshly cut grass a few feet away.

Taking a moment to channel my inner strength, I roll away from my attacker and stagger to my feet. Matthew, again upon me, laughs, taunting me. I take a couple slow, deep breaths, willing away the pain, focusing on keeping my balance. I close my eyes for a moment, trying to visualize the execution of moves I was taught almost ten years ago.

Assuming a martial arts sideways stance, creating a smaller target for my opponent to strike, I raise my left knee to just above waist level, then extend my leg in a quick, fluid snapping motion, catching Matthew squarely in the solar plexus with the full force of my foot. At the point of impact my foot is horizontal against his stomach, maximizing the surface area of the blow.

He doubles over for an instant, providing the opportunity to cock my right arm, my clenched fist strategically positioned behind my right ear. The moment his body returns to an upright position, I deliver a punch that connects with his face, making a resounding *crunch*, just like I learned in class.

Blood erupts from his nose as he grabs for it while falling backwards. I've clearly caught him by surprise, this display of strength from a scrawny guy. Exhibiting vengefulness, I can't resist kicking him while he's down, slamming my hiking-boot-covered foot into his ribs.

He's the one gasping for air now. A sadistic sense of excitement washes over me. The rush of adrenaline receding, I'm acutely aware of my pulsating jaw and cup my hand over it. I'm reminded of my sore ribs as I stalk away from Matthew. I turn around to face him, to convey some parting words.

"Hey Matthew, how 'bout we make a deal? I stay away from you, and you stay away from me."

Facedown on the asphalt, he moans audibly. I'm amazed we haven't attracted the attention of the owners whose home we've been using as a fighting ring. Not waiting for a response, I begin to turn back away, when I see him reach for his ankle and pull out a knife. He gets onto his feet and wobbles toward me. Images of Jason stabbing Chang and Hank jump into my mind. What is it with this family and knives? As if he senses my indecision—do I make a break for my car or try to wrestle the knife away from him?—his demeanor escalates to psychopathic.

"You fucker!" he growls, and wipes blood from his lips. He waggles the knife at me, taunting me.

My heartbeat quickens, aware the dynamic of this encounter has changed. I need to at least try to reason with this lunatic. He's no longer the nice, innocent kid I met in my office. Life has hardened him. The realization that things may end badly is unescapable.

"Don't be stupid, Matthew. As things stand now, this is just a scuffle. Nobody gets in trouble. I'm gonna get in my car and leave. I suggest you do the same."

He doesn't take my suggestion. Instead, he continues advancing toward me, with a little more steam. I dart for my car, rip open the door, and slide into the driver's seat. It's not so much that I'm afraid he'll stab me. I'm bursting with confidence, since dusting off the karate moves I haven't practiced in years. All sorts of scenarios dance through my mind.

What if, while tussling, *I accidentally stab him?* Assault with a deadly weapon is the type of thing that could land me a return trip to jail. And this time, the DNA evidence wouldn't be on my side. The split-second decision facing me is whether to spend the precious remaining milliseconds before he's on top of me, rolling up the driver side window and locking the door or starting the engine.

Cursing my manual roll-up windows, I stick the key in the ignition. I'm too late. Matthew thrusts his arm through the open window, knife in hand, poised to deliver a downward glancing blow into my chest.

I release the door latch and kick open the door, sending it into his midsection, causing his knife-wielding arm to swing wildly, missing its intended target—*me*. The jarring of the door into his body forces the knife airborne, out of his hand, onto the floor mat below the passenger seat. Matthew, sent backpedaling, stumbles onto his ass. Shaking out the cobwebs, he gets back on his feet.

I hoist myself back out of the car, assume my fighting stance, and before he can regroup, deliver a roundhouse kick to the side of his head, thwarting his impending bull rush attack. He goes down with a thud, his body sprawled out, once again on the lawn of our hospitable fellow Quincy resident. This time he's not moving, nor does he make a sound.

A woman comes running out of her house, *the house*, the one with a strange body on its lawn and two strange cars parked in front of it. She's yelling, "Hey!" I'm not inclined to stick around and chat.

Back in my car, one more decision awaits. The knife. There's no blood on it, nor my fingerprints. Frantically searching my back seat, I spot a piece of paper, a receipt from my last oil change. Using it to pick up the knife, careful not to leave any prints, I toss it in the general direction of Matthew's immobilized body. If questioned later, I'm just returning something that doesn't belong to me.

With the woman now halfway between her front door and my car, I throw the car in drive and stomp on the accelerator.

CHAPTER 20
JASON

I'M PARKED OUTSIDE A DINER in Albany, New York, gobbling down a triple decker turkey club sandwich. A heaping order of fries, my complement of choice to any sandwich, fill a Styrofoam box beside me. There's no way I'm crossing the state line into Vermont now. I've breathed a sigh a relief at each state line crossing since learning I'm a wanted man. It would be stupid to count on continued good fortune should I show my face in Vermont. I've had no luck reaching Matthew, and enduring my mom's escalating panic level exhausts me.

Readying myself for more high-pitched squealing, I call again, several hours having passed since my last call. The shrill level in her voice reaches an octave or two higher than in previous calls.

"Slow down, Mom. I can't understand what you're saying." It's not a volume issue as I'm holding the phone well away from my ear.

"I'm at the hospital. Matthew's in bad shape."

"What happened? Tell me everything you know." Panic enters *my* voice now.

"He looks awful, Jason. Someone beat him up pretty good." She's crying.

"Who beat him up? Do you know who did this? What's the matter with him?"

She sniffles before responding. "I only saw him for a minute before the doctors kicked me out. He has a black eye, swollen nose, and is in pain. He had trouble responding to simple questions."

I start to say something, but she cuts me off. "Hang on, Jason. Here comes the doctor."

"Don't hang up. I'm staying on the phone," I say to nobody, apparently, since I don't get a response. A few minutes later, my mom is back on the line. "Jason, are you still there?"

"I'm here, mom. What did the doc say?"

"Matthew's going to be fine. He'll make a full recovery. He has a concussion. The doctor says he's pretty coherent now. He has a broken nose and he suffered a little internal bleeding, likely from being kicked or struck with a blunt object in the stomach area. The bleeding has stopped and his spleen is fine, which the doctor says they were concerned about." She takes a breath for air and starts to cry again.

"Jesus Christ. Who the hell did this to him?"

"Jason, the doctor just gave me the signal. I can go see Matthew now."

"Leave the phone on. Please leave the phone on, okay, Mom? Okay? I want to talk to him," I interject, before she hangs up.

"All right, already. Hold your horses. I'm heading to his room now."

I hear a *crumpling* sound. Like she stuck the phone in her purse or something. Moments later I hear my mom's muffled voice. It's sympathetic as opposed to the shrill I've grown accustomed to. Now Matthew's voice, fainter, followed by some back-and-forth between them. I can't make out what they're saying. I let them converse for a minute or so before shouting to get my mom's attention. After a beat, her voice comes through loud and clear.

"Sorry, Jason. I almost forgot about you." Almost?

"Mom, let me talk to Matthew," I mumble. Her return catches me with a mouth full of fries.

"Okay, but don't get him riled up. He's been through a lot."

Some more jumbled words, followed by a few seconds of silence.

"Hey, bro." His voice sounds weak.

"Hey, bro. How're you doing?"

I roll up my window, as a strong gust of cold wind comes out of nowhere, sending a chill through me.

"I'm all right. Just a little banged up. I'll be outta here soon. They're just gonna run some tests." He's matter-of-fact, no enthusiasm.

"Matthew, who the fuck did this to you?" Enough with the small talk.

"That fucking lawyer. Peter Garrison. He's been hanging around our house some more. Talking to the neighbors. Asking about you. I confronted him today and he pulled some Kung Fu shit on me. I should have been able to take him. He's a wimpy punk. He just caught me off guard."

He's embarrassed he got beat up.

"That fucker. You take care of yourself and don't worry about Garrison. I'll handle him."

"No, Jason. Don't get mixed up with him. I know you can take him, but you need to stay away from Quincy. The cops are after you."

"Don't worry about me, bro. I can handle myself. You get yourself healed. I didn't say I'm coming to Quincy, anyway. I can inflict damage from afar."

I say this to put him at ease. Garrison has pissed me off for the last time. He will regret beating up my baby brother.

"Hang on to the phone you're on now. I'll be in touch with you. Mom has another phone where I can reach her."

"Why can't you just give me your number?"

"I have a bunch of disposables. I'm always switching them out. I'll contact you. It's safer for us both this way."

His silence says he's not convinced.

"Whatever you're up to, Jason, include me. I want to help. Tell me what to do and I'll do it."

"Think about if you're willing to leave Quincy. I'll be settled soon, far away from Vermont. Once the heat is off, I'll send for you if you're inter —"

"I'm interested. I'm ready to get the hell out of town." He responds emphatically, before I can finish the offer.

"Great, Matthew. That's fucking great. We'll be together again soon."

Before ending the call, he tells me how he has been tailing Garrison the past day or two, to see what he's up to. I learn the lawyer still lives in the same dumpy apartment complex on Broadway and that he spent last night holed up with some girl at 330 Pine Street. How that ugly, skinny bastard managed to get a woman is beyond me.

CHAPTER 21
PETER

I'M SIPPING A LARGE VANILLA milkshake, the most appealing no-chewing-required menu item. Our kind waitress, Cheryl, brought me an ice pack, which she secured to my jaw with a towel wrapped from my chin to top of my head. I look like Charlie Brown's sidekick, Linus, with a toothache. Across from me, Jack savors an avocado and bacon cheeseburger, today's Devil Burger special. He's the only one I was comfortable calling, the only person I knew wouldn't flip out upon seeing my swollen and bruised jaw. Following the obligatory scolding for engaging in fighting, Jack can't hide his fascination with my recounting of events.

"So, you pulled a Mr. Miyagi *Karate Kid* on him. I'm impressed. You must have had some martial arts training."

"It has been a while, but yeah, in my early teens my folks signed me up for lessons. I only advanced as far as an orange belt before realizing basketball and other team sports were more fun. I never tried it out for real until today. Luckily for me, it works pretty well."

"Did you hit him with the Crane move?"

Jack rises and assumes the stance, mimicking Ralph Macchio, who played Danielson in the movie, in the climactic scene. The one where he takes home the trophy. Jack has his arms raised in the air, bent at the wrists, one leg in the air, bent at the knee. I have to admit he has the position down, meaning he's probably seen the movie many times. I'm cracking up, which hurts my ribs, as he holds the pose, then executes the deceptive jump kick, where the kick is administered not with the raised leg, but rather the one touching the ground.

"Something like that." Laughter muffles my words.

We've captured the attention of several patrons, a few applauding Jack's performance.

"All kidding aside, Peter, I'm taking you to the emergency room to get you checked out. Your jaw could be dislocated and you probably have bruised ribs."

"Nah, I'll be fine by tomorrow. I'm just a little sore is all."

"All right, hero, I'll tell you what. I'll go along with you for now, but if you're not eating solid food by tomorrow, I'm calling your folks."

I promise to continue the ice treatment and provide a truthful report in the morning.

"Now we keep our fingers crossed Matthew recovers from the injuries you inflicted and he doesn't press charges against you. If you hear from or are paid a visit by the cops, call me right away."

Cheryl returns to our table, asking if we need anything else, and pushes aside the towel to examine my jaw. "I think you'll live," she declares, smirking.

I thank her for her concern and medical opinion, before addressing Jack.

"I think he's too embarrassed to bring the cops into this. He's gonna want to forget the incident, not retell it. Besides, I acted in self-defense. He was the instigator, the one who hunted me down. And if that woman was watching us from the start, I've got a witness. Even if she didn't see the whole thing, she would have seen the knife lying by Matthew's body. Maybe she kept it or turned it over to the authorities already. It will only have his prints on it, which won't be good for him."

"You may be right, but there's a lot of ifs and speculation in your assessment. Lie low tomorrow and hopefully the only calls you receive come from me. You should know the insurance my firm carries only covers trouble I get *myself* into."

"I'll keep that in mind, Jack," I say, acknowledging the message in his joking delivery.

Leaning forward, Jack turns serious. "I learned some things about Jason's past. Not that we need further evidence on this front, but Jason takes the role of protecting his family seriously."

Jack has my full attention. I'm captivated.

"Several years ago, a guy twenty years older than Jason's mom had the hots for her. She wasn't interested, but he wouldn't take *no* for an answer, and persistence turned to stalking. Armed with a BB gun, Jason, sixteen at the time, headed to the old geezer's house late one evening and fired multiple shots through his living room window. He then launched a boulder through the shattered glass. The large rock had a note attached: *leave my mother the fuck alone.*"

"Wow! How did you find this out?" I find myself in both shock, and in a strange way, admiration.

"The guy filed a police report. Nothing came of it. They called Jason's mom, who explained the situation, and promised to talk to her son. End of story."

I'm on the edge of my seat, awaiting the next tale. I don't need to prompt Jack.

"About six months later, Matthew played in an annual seventh-versus-eighth-graders football game. A kid named Billy Seaver made the mistake of sucker-punching Matthew during a break in the action. Jason met up with him after the game and Billy spent the next day in the east wing at Quincy Memorial. Luckily for Jason, Billy's parents didn't press charges."

"Jesus!" I'm not sure why this surprises me.

Jack doesn't need to spell out the relevance. Once Jason discovers I put his brother in the hospital, he won't care who started the fight. Amy enters my thoughts. Being around me could jeopardize her safety.

On that cheery note, we change gears, with Jack filling me in on Jason's current situation. Either he's holed up in a cave or has fled the Cayman Islands. He and the woman he was shacking up with have vacated their hotel. His whereabouts now is anyone's guess. This bafflement includes QPD. Jack's sources say Jason's picture will appear on WANTED signs all over Vermont, as well as in neighboring states. QPD intends to use the media to help track him down, so we can expect to see Jason's mug on national news broadcasts. Jack surmises unless he has friends high up in the Witness Protection Program, his days of freedom are numbered. The authorities have wire taps in place on his family home phone. They have also confiscated all the computers in the house.

The mystery waitress, it turns out, is even smarter than Jack thought. QPD detectives have located and interrogated all of the wait staff that were *officially* working the day of the murder, and they all have been cleared. During a second round of questioning, a couple of waitresses mentioned a new waitress—one they recall only being around a day or two—may have been working the day in question. The widowed Mrs. Chang has no records for this phantom worker. She wasn't on the payroll. More damaging to the investigation, she also never filled out an employment application. Meaning, she wasn't a restaurant employee. She must have observed the wait staff dress code—black slacks, a white button-down shirt, and black shoes—and purchased a matching outfit. From there, Jack figures she told other waitresses it was her first day, grabbed a serving tray, waltzed into the kitchen, piled plates of food from the pickup area onto her tray, and played the part, acting like she belonged. The restaurant being crowded, with lots of commotion, made it easier to blend in.

She just needed to fool one person—*me*. After handing off the murder weapon, the letter opener I presented to her, to Jason, she was out of there. Pretty clever. Genius, really.

Having parted ways with Jack, I'm back at my place, going

through in my head how I'm going to explain my disfigured appearance to Amy. I don't want her seeing me like this, nor does going out to the movies, amidst the public masses, sound appealing. I'll also need to put off my folks, who left a message inviting me to dinner.

Deciding to go with the truth, especially since we're in the early, delicate stages of our relationship, I fill Amy in on what I've been up to since leaving her place this morning. She understands me wanting to cancel our date, but has a compromise plan.

I take a long hot shower, hoping to wash away the pain. It doesn't work, but I'm the cleanest I've been in some time. Dressing is a deliberate activity. Any kind of movement involving bending is a reminder of my afternoon sparring. I've traded in the Linus look for an ice pack I keep in the freezer, which I'm applying with the palm of my hand. It might be my imagination, but the swelling seems to have gone down. I negotiate dinner with my mom for the day after tomorrow.

Before I know it, Amy appears at my door, take out Chinese food and a DVD in her arms.

"Oh my God, your face! How badly does it hurt?" She makes a scrunching expression.

"It's not as bad as it looks."

"You look awful." So much for sugarcoating it.

"Okay, then it feels exactly how it looks."

"You poor thing." Her concern touches me.

"I'm just joking. Really, it doesn't hurt much at all. I'll be fine by tomorrow. Besides, you should see the other guy."

I take the bags from her and place them on the kitchen table, happy to find a large container of Wonton soup.

"You didn't need to do all this, but thanks. I guess if my deformed face doesn't scare you off, you really do like me." Looking at the DVD—*Field of Dreams*—I add, "Good movie selection."

"Well, I know you're a sports nut, and I like Kevin Costner. I can't believe you don't have Netflix, or a way to get movies without leaving your home. It's a good thing I have a library card, although their movie selection isn't too great."

"Yeah, I'm old school that way. I still have a cassette tape player, too."

"You really need to embrace technology, you know."

I let her enjoy her ribbing, glad the conversation has shifted away from my face. She gently touches my cheek, making me wince, and plants a soft kiss on my lips, which feels nice. I extend the kiss, the beginnings of a make out session, but am quickly reminded of my limitations. Any jaw movement remains a risky proposition. Both of us famished, we bust open the cardboard containers. Moo goo gai pan, shrimp lo mein, and fried rice, along with the soup for me.

"Oh wait. I almost forgot. We have to start with a fortune cookie." Amy kicks off her shoes.

She tosses one my way as she opens hers, discarding the cookie and going right for the slip of paper. Before sharing, she asks what mine says.

"It says 'thank you for letting me out of this cookie'." I can't resist. It really says I will be getting some good advice soon. Sounds like a horoscope reading.

"What does yours say?" I'm hoping for words of encouragement concerning her love life.

"It says tell your boyfriend not to get into any more fights." She can't conceal a devilish smile. Her wittiness is undeniable. I can't help but laugh.

"I like the sound of that. Being your *boyfriend*."

I join her on the couch, where she's made herself comfortable. I lean in close and hug her, gently kissing her on the neck. She tells me to put in the movie, as she dives into the moo goo gai pan, impressing me with her skilled use of chopsticks. It turns out to be a nice evening. Amy succeeds in distracting me from my discomfort, while ensuring I ice my jaw at regular intervals. She makes several trips to the freezer, keeping the ice pack cold.

I don't remember falling asleep, but when I wake, it's early morning. Amy has gone, off to work, but she left a nice note. She reminds me I still owe her a movie night *out,* and recommends I spend the day *snailing around.* I love her expressions. She'll be calling to check in on me. Of course, Amy interjects some humor. The p.s. reads: "Don't play any football today."

⟞⟝

I test my jaw mobility, moving it up and down, side to side. While it still hurts, the pain level has subsided. I go to the bathroom and examine myself in the mirror. The swelling has gone down considerably. I speak a few long, rambling sentences—I'd be getting strange looks were I out in public—and am relieved the associated throbbing has lessened. My jaw is healing. I'll keep applying the ice, since it seems to be working. My ribs also feel better, as I can perform bending exercises without gritting my teeth. I still feel resistance, but can tolerate the discomfort.

At a little before nine a.m., I give Jack a call. He's skeptical, but pleased, with my medical report. He agrees to call off the dogs for now, until he has a chance to concur with my diagnosis, reserving the right to notify my folks and escort me to the hospital if I'm being deceitful. He has ascertained Matthew spent the night at Quincy Memorial Hospital and has yet to be released. Jack doesn't know the extent of his injuries. He plans to show up, posing as a family friend, to find out more information. Jack has scanned police reports filed since yesterday afternoon, and, thus far anyway, my fighting incident hasn't been reported. Likewise, no lawsuits have been filed against me.

"You've been busy, Jack."

"Well, the way I figure it, if you're sent to jail, or have to pay out on a lawsuit, I'm less likely to get paid by you. So, it's not that I care about you or anything. It's purely self-interest."

"Just the same, I appreciate it." I know he *does* care about me, but I'm not going to embarrass him.

"The good thing about Matthew being confined to a hospital bed is it makes it harder for him to hunt you down. You need to be prepared for this when he gets out. I'm not saying he will, but something tells me you haven't seen the last of him. You should consider getting protection. Your *Karate Kid* moves are great and all, but won't be of much use if he's packing."

"You're saying he'll come after me with a gun?"

I don't buy it. I know he has a knife and was prepared—hell, attempted—to use it on me, but a gun is another story.

"Like it or not, you've upped the ante. All I'm saying is to think about it. In the meantime, keep your doors locked and be careful."

"Okay, I'll be careful, and will give some thought to the whole protection thing." Switching gears… "I'm gonna call William to find out what he's hearing about Jason. Maybe the cops are watching Matthew, so I'll inquire about him as well. Although, they obviously weren't watching him yesterday."

"That's a good idea. Let me know if you're planning any more Lone Ranger escapades, so I can talk you out of it. Sitting tight is about all we can do right now. Oh, I almost forgot. I just came from the post office and guess whose picture is posted there?" He tells me it's Jason, before I can respond. "And I'm betting this isn't the only one in town."

"That's good news, Jack. Of course, he's probably nowhere near Quincy."

"Don't be such a pessimist. I've got to get going. Get some rest and keep your jaw iced."

"Thanks, Mom, I will."

He simply hangs up, paying no homage to my humor.

Sir William sounds happy to hear from me. Coming from him,

I don't take "Peter, my boy" as condescending. After some chitchat, I ask what he knows. Fortuitously, he had lunch yesterday with his pal on the force, and he inquired about Jason Felding. Internally, they are now referring to the Chang murder as the Felding case. There's no doubt within QPD that Jason is Chang's killer. The suspect list has been narrowed down to one. Kind of like when they *knew* it was me. Today is the day the manhunt for Jason goes national. The day Jason's picture hits the airwaves. William tells me to stay tuned to CNN to get the full story. He doesn't know any more about where Jason's hiding than Jack does.

With my TV tuned to CNN in the background, I plop down on my couch, ice pack pressed to my jaw. I've got the Linus toothache look going again to keep my hands free. I've got my laptop computer, well... on my lap.

Becoming a registered private investigator in Vermont requires both training and experience. I can't expedite the experience part, two years of full-time work under the supervision of a licensed Vermont private investigator. The training consists of forty hours in a board-approved program. I'm enrolled in the program, and, conveniently, am able to take the courses online. My first class is ethics and professional conduct. I jump right in.

I'm half way through a lesson outlining the consequences resulting from unethical behavior, when I hear "Quincy, Vermont" coming from the TV. Sure enough, the anchor talks about Jason, wanted for two murders, one committed in his hometown of Quincy, the other in the U.S. Virgin Islands. He makes a plea to the public to help locate this dangerous fugitive. Processing these words, I recognize *I'm the public*. My assistance is being requested.

My ringing phone halts my daydreaming.

"Turn on your TV! Your case is on CBS national news!" Amy says in a frenzy.

"Yeah, I know! I've got it on."

Her excitement is contagious. Of course, the newscast had me in pretty good spirits already. I ask her to come over, saying I have more good news to share.

———⊸◦⊂⬤⊃◦⊂———

I pour Amy and myself a celebratory glass of wine. Joining her on the couch, I *clink* my glass against hers.

"Now that the cops have things under control, you and Jack can call off your search, right?"

"Well, I wouldn't go that far. Jason hasn't been apprehended yet."

Amy raises her eyebrows, signaling her confusion.

I continue. "Jack will probably say our work is done, but my investment is more personal. Until Jason is either behind bars or dead, I need to do whatever I can."

Amy shakes her head in disbelief, withdrawing from me, scooting down the couch.

"You think, you, a lawyer, have a better chance of catching Jason than an entire trained police force? Isn't that a little egotistical?"

I ponder her assessment. "You're right. The cops are on top of this. And with the manhunt in place, it shouldn't be long now. Jack and I can back off." I move close to her again, placing a hand on her knee. I'm anxious to get to the reason I called her over. "I didn't mean to upset you. Anyway, I have something else to keep me occupied now. The exciting news I wanted to tell you about."

Feeling she has gotten through to me, she changes her tune. "Oh yeah. What is it?"

"I registered for a PI program. I started on my first course just before you arrived."

"Really? Shouldn't you be looking for a job now? I thought once this mess was over, you'd go back to being a lawyer."

"I did too. But I really like investigative work. I like what Jack does. I've enjoyed trying to track Jason down. In a way, my contempt for Jason has sparked this interest, this newfound passion."

"So, you're giving up on law altogether? After spending years studying it in school and getting a degree? You're a member of the bar association."

Amy inches away from me again, causing my hand to lose contact with her knee.

"I still like the law. And my training will serve me well as an investigator."

"You know, despite all the jokes, as an occupational group lawyers are respected. There's a sleaze factor associated with PIs. You know, taking pictures of cheating spouses and all. It's not all about tracking down murderers."

"I know this. And you're right that I don't know exactly what I'll be getting myself into. I figure if I don't like PI work, I could be an investigator for a law firm. They all employ investigators. For now, though, I like the idea of distancing myself from law firms."

I'm not convincing her. I mention a reality. "I may need to pick up some part-time work in the interim, until I secure full-time PI work."

This doesn't help. Amy stands now and paces.

"I thought you were just helping Jack out, since you hired him, but I didn't realize you wanted to *be* him. We're not married or anything, but I'm surprised you enrolled in PI classes without telling me. PI work can be dangerous, too."

She stops pacing and faces me. "The prospect of staying up all night worrying about you isn't something I'd relish."

She returns to the couch, albeit on the opposite end from where I'm seated. I don't bother closing the gap.

"All this happened quickly. I enrolled this morning. It's not like applying to an undergraduate university. You basically pay a fee, and you're in."

Shifting from explaining myself to a position of strength, I went on, "I thought you knew how much I've enjoyed investigating and would appreciate my initiative."

Amy rises again, unsure of what to say. She eventually finds the words. "I just thought we shared things, Peter. I don't like things sprung on me. I need a little time to process this."

It's my turn to be at a loss for words. Before I can come up with an appropriate response, she says she'll call me soon, and heads for the door.

CHAPTER 22
JASON

I'M APPLYING PRESSURE WITH A warm, wet washcloth to the top of my scalp, trying to stop the bleeding. I just shaved my head. Chopping off the bulk of my hair with scissors was easy, but once I got to the fine hairs, necessitating shaving cream and a razor, things got a little dicier. I did fine for a while, until impatience kicked in. Rushing led to nicks, which triggered the flow of blood I'm dealing with now.

The discovery of my picture hanging inside a local convenience store prompted this new look. The accompanying caption—me being wanted for serious criminal offenses—jolted me. I discreetly ripped down the flyer, but know there are plenty more where that came from. Fortunately, I've got a full beard now, a contrast to my clean-shaven look in the photograph.

I'm in Lake George, sixty miles north of Albany. I bought a canoe and spent a peaceful day on the lake, plotting my next move. I wanted only to rent a canoe or row boat, but that required leaving my driver's license as collateral. I need to get myself a fake ID. I checked into the Sundowner cabin complex last night, and have been keeping to myself since. It was my third stop, the only place I could get into without proof of identification. The clerk who checked me in was more than accommodating upon learning my cash payment included a hefty tip for himself.

Part of me wishes I'm capable of letting bygones be bygones.

The chances of getting caught increase greatly by returning to Quincy. I can't deny this. Yet, logic isn't driving this decision. Garrison needs to be punished. Fatally punished. If done right, I'll be in and out before anyone notices. My actions will be swift and calculated. Ideally, I'd be armed with a gun, the most reliable and efficient weapon. The odds of me purchasing a gun without supplying identification are nil, however, so my tried and true friend, the knife, must do. I'll execute the hit at night, when the probability of him being home is greatest. I'll try his apartment first, then the girl's place. I don't intend to harm the girl, but if she gets in the way, I'm prepared to do whatever the situation calls for.

I check in with Matthew. He's still in the hospital. They want to monitor him for another day and run more tests. He's suffering from headaches, par for the course when you've been concussed. He hits me with devastating news. I've amassed national notoriety. I'm being billed as an at-large murderer, considered armed and dangerous. A reward is being offered for information leading to my arrest. *Shit.*

This development, while disheartening, provides clarity on one front. If I'm going down, I'm gonna get my money's worth. I'm taking Garrison with me. I'm not crazy or insane or delusional. I'm perfectly capable of rational thought. I know the difference between right and wrong, good and bad. The line blurs when the only way to right a wrong is to break rules and be bad. I possess the ability to apply reason. To process factual information and draw logical conclusions. I can do all that.

Which explains why I'm coming to terms with the reality I'm going to get caught. I realize this will end badly. I understand probability and odds. I understand the insurmountable odds I must overcome to escape punishment. Sure, I'm clinging to that long shot. I'm not going to give up, to turn myself in. I won't make it easy for the pigs chasing me. But I'm grossly outnumbered.

Initially, nobody was looking for me. Then it became a few.

Now I'm up against an army. I'm an army of one, no match for my opposition.

———◦◦◦———

Anticipating there will soon be a greeting committee blanketing the New York to Vermont state line, I plan on hightailing it into Vermont. Unfolding the Northeastern map I removed from the glove box, I lay it out on the kitchen table in my cabin. Grabbing a pen from the bedroom nightstand, I circle my route, the quickest path to Vermont. My entry town will be Castleton, via Whitehall, New York. From my cabin to Castleton looks to be about an hour-and-a-half drive. Then another two hours to Quincy.

I find myself, again, wishing I had a gun for the upcoming ambush. How do you get ahold of a black market gun? I have the money to overpay for one. Should I scour the streets, seeking out the bad sections of town? I consider contacting a couple of my Quincy buddies. While a loyal friend, I can't say I'm a reliable one. I would often blow these guys off when they wanted to hang out. I haven't said dick to them since before the Chang stuff went down. Weighing the pros and cons of involving them in my caper, the scale tips heavily in favor of silence. Screwing me in return for reward money would be difficult for those losers to pass up.

Matthew went to battle with Garrison carrying only a knife and wound up getting his ass kicked. And that was with catching the skinny punk off guard. Who knows what weapons he may have at his disposal when I invade him on his home turf. I don't really want to hang around the seedy sections of towns in Vermont. Besides increasing the odds of running into lowlifes, who may or may not have guns for sale, I'll also be more likely to run into cops. Scavenging the underbelly of upstate New York will take time I don't have. I compromise, deciding to hit a local hardware store, to load up on weaponry, the most lethal they have. An axe comes to mind.

If I can't handle Garrison, I deserve to be locked up. Besides, nothing against Matthew, but I've always been the better fighter, stronger, scrappier. I'm street smart. A survivor.

Winging it, I throw my shit together and storm out of the cabin complex. A few miles away, I spot a Lowe's. Making my way to the hardware section, I find a long-handled axe, capable of inflicting serious damage, as well as extend my reach, neutralizing any incoming sissy kicks. I browse around and wind up buying a shovel, chain saw, and rope, in addition to the axe. The axe should be all I need, along with the knives I already have, which I'll conceal on my person. The other items could come in handy, depending on how the situation plays itself out.

On the road again, with only the radio serving as a distraction, my thoughts drift to Tess. Bitterness creeps into my psyche. Why did she leave me? It's a rhetorical question. Bitterness turns to jealousy and the thought *if I can't have her, I don't want anyone to* enters my crowded mind. I allow the acidity to linger, before snapping myself out of my misery. Rational thought prevails, and I'm back to feeling grateful for the time I had with her. For the loyalty she displayed during my darkest hours. I redirect my anger where it belongs: Peter Garrison.

I'm in Whitehall before long, just a few miles outside of Vermont. I brace for the unknown, for what lies ahead. I review my options. A U-turn at the first sight of trouble is the *chicken shit* move. The registration in the glove box names Emily Hughes as the vehicle's owner. A computer check would bring up a picture of a woman in her sixties or seventies, a tough resemblance for me to pull off. I could try going with *this is my mom's car and I don't have my license with me.* Of course, with suspicions raised, a close comparison between my wanted picture and the face they'd be staring into could very well register as a match. Assuming a scrutinized examination, I settle upon the chicken shit option, hoping I'll be able to either abruptly change directions without detection, or outrun them.

My worries are for naught, as I barrel into Vermont without incident, without slowing down. The only greeting I receive is in the form of a Welcome to Vermont roadside sign. I audibly exhale, wiping perspiration off my forehead. If a patrol had been set up and had I decided to chance it, dripping sweat would have been a pretty good giveaway of my nerves. I didn't realize how tightly I've been gripping the steering wheel as I let tension out of my arms, thus releasing pressure.

About twenty miles past the state line, I pull over and get out of the car. I stretch a little, walk around some, acutely aware of stress leaving my body. Of course, it will build back up in a couple of hours' time. For now, though, I enjoy the moment. It's a beautiful day, sun shining, a light breeze, not a cloud in the sky. Knowing my lifestyle may change dramatically in the near future, I drink in all nature has to offer.

Back in the car, I've been so consumed by making it to Vermont, I didn't notice how close to empty my tank is. I won't make it to Quincy without filling up. Getting gas will be a risky proposition, but I don't have much choice. Like ripping off a Band-Aid, I stop at the next station I come across and waltz into the convenience store, nonchalantly scanning the place for my picture. So far so good, without knowing what may be hanging behind the counter. My luck continues as I pay for my gas, bottled water, liter of Coke, and a candy bar, without raising an eyebrow. I pour the water over my head as the gas fills my tank.

On the road again, I maintain my speed at the posted limit. I don't want to get pulled over, but also am not in a particular hurry. Not yet anyway. Once the fun begins, there will be no time for deliberation.

I call Matthew and learn he was sent home this morning. He's still recovering, still having headaches, still nursing sore ribs. He hounds me, asking where I am, what I'm up to. As much as I'd like to clue him in, even recruit him for my attack on Garrison,

I can't involve him. I'm already a criminal, with nothing to lose. Matthew doesn't have a blemish on his record, other than the alcohol incident. He must be on pain meds since he seems sleepy and doesn't fight me too hard. I promise to call him tomorrow.

Before I can get off the phone, my mom jumps on the line. She tries to convince me to turn myself in. She'd rather see me in prison than living on the lam.

"Fugitives wind up dead, Jason."

"You've been watching too much TV, Mom. Sometimes the bad guys win."

Ignoring my comeback, she goes on, "I've got the money to get you a good lawyer. Good lawyers can do amazing things. There are always extenuating circumstances, special considerations. People get provoked, things get out of control. We live in a forgiving society. You need to keep the faith. I've been praying for you, Jason, and I know God is watching over you."

"So you've suddenly become religious? I thought we were atheists. You can't turn it on and off based on circumstance." That I'm even arguing this point angers me. "Besides, you're gonna need that money down the road for yourself. Giving it up to pay for some lawyer's kids' braces won't keep me out of jail. What I've done is bad, Mom. Not even God can save me."

"Don't say that. Please let me help you. I'm gonna talk to a lawyer. See what he has to say. You can't stop me from doing that." She can be as defiant as I can. "You did what you did out of love. For Matthew. You're not a cold-blooded murderer."

"Maybe I am. You do what you want." Acknowledging she's worried about me and has my best interests at heart, I soften. "Look, Mom. None of this is your fault. Whatever happens from here, please remember this: you've been a great mother. You had your hands full, having to play mom and dad to Matthew and me, but I wouldn't trade you in for anyone. I'm sorry for the snowball affect my decisions are having on your life. Please don't worry about me."

The tears she had held back now flow as she begins imparting more wisdom. I cut her off, saying I need to get going.

Clearing my mind, I try to enjoy the drive. I notice and appreciate the foliage. It's early autumn and many of the trees sport colorful leaves. People flock to Vermont to witness the brilliant yellow, red, and orange leaves on maple, beech, and yellow birch trees. The maples, sugar maples to be precise, are the most predominant. Probably because I grew up here, I never understood what the big deal was. It's like living in a beach house. Over time, I'd imagine, the ocean view gets taken for granted. For whatever reason—maybe because I've been away for a little while, or maybe due to my possible pending incarceration where my *view* would be cinderblock cell walls—I'm soaking up the landscape.

Okay, enough with the fucking trees. Enough with letting my mind drift. My mind needs to be sharp. I pass a Quincy city limits sign. *It's game time.*

CHAPTER 23
PETER

"**N**ice shot. That's what I'm talking about. You braced for the recoil and held steady. And look at the result. A target hit two rings from the bullseye." Jack's enthusiasm builds my confidence. We've been here, at Dead Eye Shooting Range, for an hour or two. Following a brief lesson with an unloaded gun, and watching Jack show off—I mean demonstrate—I fired a few rounds with his Smith and Wesson .38 Special. I now have a Colt 45 in my hands, Jack's weapon of choice, what he carries on the job. He insists I take one of his many guns home with me until this situation with Matthew subsides. About the only gun he doesn't have is a Clint-Eastwood-favorite 44 Magnum. I jokingly ask if he's got one of those at home.

The passage of time has allowed my injuries to heal to the point where I've stopped pampering myself. The swelling of my jaw is barely perceptible, and I devoured a hearty pancake, bacon, and egg breakfast without contorting my face. The pain has given way to merely a little soreness. I'm only nominally aware of the lingering aching in my midsection.

About a dozen folks, all armed, occupy range spaces. Most, like us, wear noise-canceling ear muffs.

"It's fun when you hit the target. Of course, I've missed a lot more than I've hit."

"Hey, we're standing twenty five yards away. When you need to fire for real, your target will be much closer. All you need to know at this point is how to load and unload, operate the safety switch, aim, and fire."

"I appreciate it, Jack. Everything. You know, taking me under your wing and all."

"Now don't go portraying me as a momma bird. I just don't want to see you get killed. My conscience couldn't handle that. It would disrupt my sleeping pattern."

He uses humor to obscure his sensitive side. He's from my parents' generation, where males were ingrained to be tough and unemotional. He was probably raised in a household lacking displays of affection.

"I still don't think I need a gun. Matthew may be a little misguided, but do you really think he'll come after me again?"

"Since your encounter with him happened under my watch, as a result of an assignment I gave you, I'll feel responsible if something happens to you. Considering I have no desire to babysit you twenty-four, seven, the least I can do is lend you a weapon to protect yourself, just in case. I'm a firm believer you shouldn't possess a gun unless you know how to use it. Thus our little outing today. Normally, I'm not an advocate for harboring an unregistered gun, but this instance warrants an exception."

While I wouldn't characterize Jack as warm, he is caring, loyal, and decent. Dressed down, in jeans and a T-shirt, he's tall and fit. He moves athletically, suggesting he could dash across the grass field separating us from the targets in record time.

"So you're saying I'll be arrested if I'm caught with your gun?"

The humiliation of being fingerprinted and booked at a police station isn't something I want to relive.

"Keep it hidden, but readily accessible. The only way it will be discovered by authorities is if you use it. Under such a scenario, the idea is you'll be alive to explain yourself. Between this and having *Peter was a law abiding citizen* engraved on your headstone..."

He doesn't need to finish the thought. I get the picture. He has more fatherly-like advice to disperse.

"If you're serious about being a PI, I'd go through the training to get licensed to carry a gun as soon as you can. The bad guys have guns, and PI's have this habit of running into bad guys, so we need to be armed to level the playing field."

"You've said you never had to shoot anyone, right? Have you ever been shot at?"

My research into the life of investigators didn't list shootouts in the job description.

"Nope. Never shot anyone or been shot. It's more of a Boy Scout thing. Be prepared. So far, I have only used my piece to intimidate, which works well, by the way. Guns provide a sense of security and should be used for defense only. Kind of like your karate stuff, right?"

"Yeah, the instructors drilled that into our heads."

"Good, then it won't be a foreign concept when you repeatedly hear it during firearms training."

"It was part of the mantra we'd repeat at the end of each class, before our final bow of respect. We must have bowed in respect fifty times a session. It's the one move all students master."

Jack ejects the clip from my 45, hands me an empty one, along with some bullets, and has me load the clip and slide it into the gun's chamber. With the .38, also called a 6-shooter, each of the six bullets load directly into their own chamber, an easier process. I learn the clip is also called a magazine, and while technically there's a slight difference between the terms, for the layman (me), the terms can be used interchangeably.

Jack puts a hand on my shoulder, diverting my attention from the targets. "Now before you get too infatuated with this PI business, you should know a lot of the work is more sedate. Stuff like infidelity cases and tracking down long-lost relatives."

"I know, Jack. I've done my research. I want this, and need the change. Being a lawyer has lost its luster."

I empty the clip, hitting the target four times, most along the outer edge. Still, I'm proving to be a quick study.

"Not bad." He sees from my grin that I'm impressed with myself, so tempers his praise.

"This is fun. I'm getting the hang of this. Can I try the .38 again?" I know I can do better than my earlier showing when I wasn't comfortable with my stance or with closing one eye for better aim.

He hands me his .38 Special and six bullets. I load the chambers, release the safety, and fire away. Four target hits, two within a couple of rings of the bullseye.

"Am I a natural or what?" I'm not cocky by nature, but feel at ease around Jack.

"We'll move the targets back next time and see how you do," he says with a laugh.

"I need to get back to work, Peter." Seeing my frown, he continues, "You aren't my only client, you know. And the others don't require interfering with an active murder investigation."

I grin, wishing I had a retort.

"We need to go over how to clean a gun, but that can wait." He's bent over, packing up his bag. "Okay, decision time. You want the .38 Special or the 45?"

"I'll go with the .38. It should be enough to thwart any intruders."

He reaches into his bag, hands me the gun and a box of ammo. I'm reminded to load the gun when I get home and turn on the safety. With that, we head out to the parking lot.

Back home, the rush from firing guns still lingers. Not sharing the experience with Amy, however, tempers my excitement. A couple of days removed from our spat, I miss her. A lot. Risking incurring her wrath, I decide to call her. I've rehearsed my opening line, and stick to the script.

"Hi Peter." A warm greeting, to my relief.

"I'm sorry, Amy. I didn't mean to exclude you. You're more important to me than anyone. Being apart has made this apparent." I'm trembling as I speak. I pick up a flashlight resting on my couch and squeeze it to stop my hand from shaking.

"I'm sorry, too. In hindsight, I overreacted. I was going to call you later. Why don't you come by in a little while so we can talk."

A shower, change of clothes, and some online classwork later, I'm back in my car, pulling into Amy's driveway. Once I'm inside, Amy surprises me by wrapping her arms tightly around me.

"I missed you too," I say, smiling.

She ushers me to the living room, and we plop down on her couch.

"I'll support your dream. If being a PI will make you happy, who am I to stand in your way?"

I like what she has to say and have no intention of interrupting.

"It still scares me that you'll be dealing with seedy characters, though."

I jump in, trying to quell her concerns. "As a lawyer, I dealt with unsavory clients all the time."

"Yeah, but your encounters took place in courthouses and law offices. As a PI, you'll run into undesirables on the streets and in back alleys."

A chuckle escapes my lips. "Back alleys? Didn't you say most of my detail would be taking pictures of cheating spouses?"

"Yes, I said *most*. All it takes is once."

Leaning back against the couch cushion, I can only respond with, "I'll be careful."

Holding my hand, she continues. "I'll get used to the idea. Your will and desire are traits I like about you. Most people lack passion."

I draw her close to me and kiss her. Falling back into relationship mode, Amy asks what I've been up to. I tell her about my morning at the shooting range and the weapon Jack has loaned me.

"So, you're no longer the only one in our relationship with a gun," I say smugly.

"I'm envious you have something that trumps my Taser."

I brag about the holes I put in the targets (hmm, maybe I'm not as humble as I'd like to think). She brings me down a notch, asking how far from the targets I stood. It dawns on me that she and Jack have some common personality traits.

Amy understanding my zest for PI work and encouraging me in said pursuit reinforces my love for her. She means everything to me. Which is why I can't put her in harm's way. I'd never forgive myself if she were to get hurt on my account.

Amy catches me in deep, pensive thought. My eye brows furrow as I slip into serious mode.

"What's up?" Amy asks, sensing my consternation.

"Something has been weighing on my mind. And since my feelings for you are stronger than ever, I can't delay this any longer."

Amy sits up straight, awaiting the unknown.

"I think we need to cool things off for a little while," I say.

"What?" Amy springs up off the couch in an instant. "Why? Are you breaking up with me?" She's towering over me, crowding me. I stand up, eliminating her height advantage, if not her intimidating presence.

"No, I'm not breaking up with you. No way!" I pause, searching for the words I rehearsed. "Being with me right now is dangerous. Matthew is out of the hospital and probably coming after me. Jason may be hunting me down as well. I can't put you at risk."

Amy's tone softens, but it doesn't mask her unhappiness. "Don't you think this is something I can decide for myself? Besides, Jason is far away from here, in hiding."

"His wanted poster is all over town. That means the police

think he's likely to return. They do profiling based on similar cases, you know."

She's not buying it.

"There's a better chance of him turning up in Alaska," she retorts. "Furthermore, I'm not some helpless female. I can take care of myself. I carry a Taser in my purse, in case you've forgotten." Her volume rises again.

"I know all that, Amy. And if we were talking about your run-of-the-mill muggers, I'd like your chances. You did nothing to warrant being pursued by madmen. I'm the one who beat up Matthew, not you. I need to protect you. As the man, it's my duty."

"Did you really just say that?" She's smiling as she speaks. A smile of disbelief, which, combined with her bulging eyes, form a crazed facial expression.

I've set her off. Before I can extricate myself from the situation, Amy launches into a lecture.

"Let me fill you in on something. My last boyfriend tried bossing me around. Treating me like I didn't have a brain. Making decisions for me. For my own good. I'm not gonna relive that experience."

She's pacing as she unloads. It's distracting, although her message is quite clear.

"So, I'll tell you what. I'll make it easy for you. I'm all for *cooling things off,* as you put it. Get out of my house!"

Fuming now, she turns away, pointing at the front door.

I didn't envisioned things playing out this way. Being told I'm brave, gallant, and honorable is the reaction I expected. My head spins, and I'm unsure of what to do or say. She's standing in place, statue-like, her arm still raised, signaling me to leave. I stifle a comment about knowing where her door is. I don't say anything more, considering how well I've done so far, not to mention her unreceptive current state of mind. I'm frozen in place, until jarred by a reminder.

"Get out now!"

I exit without further ado, feeling a breeze as the door slams behind me.

Back at my place, I'm moping and slumping around. I'm exhausted, and could use a nap, but my active mind won't allow for that. I consider calling Amy, to explain, to apologize, but decide waiting until tomorrow is the more prudent way to go.

I'm due at my folk's house for dinner, and despite not feeling up to doing anything, I'm starving. I haven't eaten since a banana this morning, before meeting Jack at the range. Plus, canceling on my mom on short notice will trigger an inquisition.

I arrive for dinner right at six p.m., wearing a turtleneck in an attempt to hide remnants of my injury. My mom has the front door open before I get to the doorknob.

"Hello, stranger. I'm glad you remembered how to get here. How…"

Her voice trails off as she stares at me before grabbing hold of my shirt. Pulling from the top downward, she reveals my touch of puffiness, my attempt at squirming away fruitless.

"My God, what happened to you, Peter?"

"It's nothing, Mom."

Hands on her hips, she awaits an explanation. I go with the truth—omitting the part about the knife—knowing I'm well past the age of parental punishment. She stares at me in disbelief in the doorway.

"Can I come inside now?"

"Yes, of course." She calls out for my dad, telling him the news from three rooms away.

The frantic tone gets my dad moving, the three of us nearly running into each other in the hallway, outside the kitchen. Hushing my mom, I calmly repeat the story as she tugs at my turtleneck, fully exposing the swelling. My dad has to put on his reading glasses to detect what all the fuss is about. Any concern he has is overridden by pride. He's thrilled by the way I defended myself, beating the crap out of Matthew. He's also elated the karate classes he sent me to was money well spent.

"You're missing the point, Doug. Which is, this nut coming after Peter in the first place."

She pauses, turns around to face me, still clearly distressed. "Are you hurt anywhere else? Did you see a doctor?"

"I'm fine, Mom. I don't need to see a doctor. I've been icing my jaw the past couple of days and it's almost completely healed."

I illustrate with exaggerated jaw movements. "See?"

Her expression tells me she doesn't. "What I *see* is your desire to be a PI will lead to more fights like this. I don't want to be getting calls from the emergency room." She's borderline seething.

"That won't happen because I won't list you as an emergency contact."

Bad timing for humor, as she doesn't crack a smile. I try another tact.

"Mom, Jack has been a PI for fifteen years and he's still in one piece. No visible scars, doesn't walk with a limp, his face intact. You've said yourself he's handsome."

My dad, the peacemaker, puts his arms around us, huddling us together.

"Let's not get carried away. Peter can take care of himself. He's an adult, capable of making his own decisions. He's passionate about this PI stuff, so let's support him and see how it works out. Now, Peter, you've got to understand your mom will always worry about you. It's comes with the territory. I worry about you, too. I just hide it a little better."

His speech works. My mom has stopped shaking, and she gives me an apologetic hug. I'm thinking how glad I am Amy isn't here to witness this madness.

I break the ensuing, awkward silence, asking if we'll be eating soon. "I'm kinda hungry, Mom. You invited me over for *dinner*, remember?" This time the humor is well received.

Conversation is minimal as we stuff ourselves, my folks apparently as hungry as I am. When we come up for air, my dad inquires about Amy. I explain we've only gone out a handful of times, but I like her a lot. I keep to myself that, in fact, I *love* her. I talk about her work, her sense of humor, her sassiness, the little I know about her family, and her caring nature. I don't mention this afternoon's blowout fight.

"So when do we get to meet her?" Asks my mom.

"Soon, Mom," I respond vaguely. I'm tired and not prepared to discuss my protection plan, a plan I've been second-guessing since getting tossed out of Amy's house.

———————⊸◦◔∅◦◦⊂———————

The sight of my repeated yawning prompts my folks to commence the goodbye ritual soon after we polish off the delicious wild salmon meal.

CHAPTER 24
JASON

THE COOL THING ABOUT STAKING out someone in an apartment complex is nobody knows who you're waiting for. Most don't even notice you, and the ones that do don't care. I'm in a strategic parking space, facing outward so incoming traffic has to first drive by me, and second, more importantly, walk past me to reach the locked gate granting access to the units. There's no neighborhood watch here. There are security vehicles at many complexes like this, but I've been here over two hours and haven't spotted any.

From my days shadowing Garrison, back when Chang still had a pulse, I know he drives a blue Volkswagen Jetta. Or at least used to. Matthew has seen his car more recently than I have, but he'll know what I'm up to if I ask him.

It's eight p.m. and my patience has run out. Time to try the girl's place. I'm guessing Garrison doesn't get laid much, so if he's found someone willing to put out for him, he's probably there every night. Matthew saw him at her doorstep with what looked like a bottle of wine, pretty much ruling out her being a hooker or one night stand.

Ten minutes later, I'm in a nicer section of town, her tree-lined street filled with big houses and manicured lawns. Peter nabbed himself a rich chick. The curtains are closed, but lights are on in several rooms of her place. The driveway is empty, but both their cars could be inside the two-car garage.

Camping out anywhere near her house will raise suspicion, so I loop around the block, finalizing my plan of attack. The lots are sufficiently large and staggered, so that there isn't a house directly across from hers. It must be my lucky day. The street dead-ends, nothing but woods beyond it. I park as close to the trees as possible, as far from the nearest house as I can. I'm just a guy going for a moonlight hike. I fish a sweatshirt out of my duffle bag, using it to camouflage my axe.

I cover the few hundred yards to the girl's house with fast, purposeful strides. Standing in her driveway, I ready myself for action, wrapping my sweatshirt around my waist. I make my way to the front door, confident I've avoided detection. Wanting the advantage of the element of surprise, I ring the bell, then crouch low, out of the line of peephole sight. My ear presses against the door, listening for the sound of approaching footsteps. Nothing. More silence.

Finally, after about a minute, I hear someone coming to the door. The footsteps halt and it's quiet for a moment, presumably as the peephole is checked. I'm willing the door to swing open so I can get on with my ambush. If it doesn't open soon, I'll need to set plan B into motion. A couple seconds of silence elapse, followed by the sound of steps walking away. Plan B time.

I race to the large window I passed on my way to the front door, jamming my axe through it, shattering it. Yeah, the axe is overkill, but it spares my body cuts from shards of glass. Using the tool in another non-traditional manner, I hurriedly clear away enough glass to allow me to jump through. Within seconds, I'm inside, pushing through the drapes. A scream pierces my eardrums. The high pitched *yelp* of a woman.

She's running away from me, halfway across the room now, heading for the kitchen. The glass breaking must have drawn her attention to the window, stalling her momentarily, or she'd be out of the room by now. Is she running to a back door? To a gun? Thinking quickly, I yell, "Stop or I'll shoot!"

This gets her to slow down and glance backwards, to see if there's really a gun pointed at her. Concluding I'm merely a madman wielding an axe, she resumes her dash, but the delay creates just enough time for me to catch up to her. As she reaches for her purse on the kitchen table, I clutch her by the shoulder, spinning her around so she's facing me, before she can get anything out of her purse. This elicits another scream, along with a two-handed shove into my chest.

Slight as she is, she barely budges me, but does succeed in bringing out my anger. Tossing the axe aside, I wrap my arms around her and throw her against the wall. She's stunned and has blood dripping from her leg. After picking up the axe, I dig inside her purse to see what she was after. There's a miniature gun in there. Some sort of Taser. I pull it out, and with it now pointed at her, I let her know how this will play out.

"Hey, I'm not going to hurt you. It's Garrison I have the beef with. Where is he?"

"I don't know what you're talking about. Who are you?" She's defiant, and doesn't seem to know who I am. If she does, she doesn't know what I'm capable of. Despite her boldness, she visibly shakes.

"I'm dangerous and crazy. That's all you need to know about me. Now I'm going to ask you one more time. Where's Peter Garrison? You know, the guy you've been *fucking*." She's caught off guard by this, my knowledge of her circumstance.

"Oh, *that* Peter Garrison. I have no clue where he is. We broke up."

She recovers quickly with a smart mouth, while confirming my belief I can use her to draw Garrison in. I curse myself for leaving the rope in my trunk. Being tied up would take the edge off her. Another idea comes to mind.

"Okay, here's what's gonna happen. You do everything I say and you'll remain in one piece. Like I said, I've got nothing against you. You defy me though, try to get away, or do something stupid, I won't hesitate to use this gun of yours or my axe."

While keeping the gun aimed at her, I seize her purse, then motion for her to get up. I escort her to a bedroom, grabbing a wooden dining room chair on the way. I spot the closet in the room and force her inside. She protests mildly before accepting her position of weakness, realizing she can't stop this from happening.

I lean the chair at an angle so its back wedges against the door knob, effectively locking her in. I saw this done in a movie—the knob turned, but the door wouldn't open—and hope it works.

She tries to get out, to no avail. She's feisty, and not very good at following orders.

"How long are you going to keep me in here?" she asks, with a hint of desperation.

"It depends on your behavior. I don't want to hear a fucking peep out of you or I might just try out this stun gun on you. I'm also getting kinda itchy to use my new axe. Did you know the pinky toe is considered an expendable appendage?"

No smart-ass comeback this time.

"I'll tell you what. To keep you from boredom, I'll let you know what I'm doing out here. Right now, I'm digging through your purse, searching for... ah, here it is... your cell phone. Much fancier than my disposables. Let's see if I can cut through the sophistication and find... yes... Contacts... scrolling... scrolling... what do you know—Peter, the first P name. You've got a lot of friends. Too bad none of them are here now. Now I'm gonna text your boyfriend and have him come over."

Her phone, a Samsung Galaxy S6, is loaded with apps. I fiddle with it, navigating through icons and menus.

"Let's see... Options... Send Message... I'm in. This isn't so hard. What should I say to get him here fast?"

"Like I said, we broke up. So he won't come."

"Have some faith. I'm a resourceful guy. How do you address him? *Darling? Sweetheart? Snookems?*" I get the silent treatment. "I'll just skip the greeting and get right to it."

I type in a message, satisfied it will do the trick. "Tell me what you think of this: 'Come over as soon as you can. I miss you.'" I interpret her lack of response as concurrence.

"I like it, too. Short and sweet."

I press a button and receive immediate confirmation via an accompanying *whoosh*.

"Now we wait. You know, I don't even know your name."

More of the silent treatment. I dig into her purse again, this time pulling out a wallet. Inside I find a driver's license.

"Amy. It's very nice to meet you, Amy. This picture doesn't do you justice. Now I'm peeking through your purse some more while we wait for your boyfriend to reply."

I begin humming the *Jeopardy* theme music. A few bars in, I'm interrupted by a *whoosh*, this time signaling an incoming message.

"It's Peter. He says he misses you, too, and will be over in twenty minutes. He just got back from his parents' house." A whimper comes from the closet.

"Why are you doing this? Please don't hurt Peter. He's a good guy. What did he do to you, anyway?"

Her brave front disintegrates. Does she really not recognize me? She must have seen my picture by now. Maybe my shaven head and beard are cutting it as a disguise. Maybe she thinks I'm Matthew. In any event, I'm not going to arm her with information concerning my identity or motivation.

I'm worried about my makeshift door lock holding up to the barrage which will ensue once I leave the room. Matthew never tried kicking the door down when we were kids. He knew he'd be in trouble with our mom had he damaged it. Amy will have no such concern.

I debate the prudence of surprising Garrison before he gets inside, versus forcing a confrontation upstairs where I can keep an eye on Amy, perhaps using her as a hostage. Once in the house, he'd call out for her, meaning I wouldn't catch him off guard, so I rule that out. It comes down to whether I bring her downstairs with me—I'd have to gag her if I did—or confront him solo, an easier scenario for my planned attack.

I conclude even if she gets out of the closet, I'm the one with the weapons, not to mention superior physical strength, and will have no problem handling her. I'll wait until I hear Garrison roll into the driveway, then take him out at the front door. If the girl becomes a problem, I'll kill her first, in front of Garrison, robbing him of any chance for departing peaceful thoughts in the ensuing moments before I chop him up.

CHAPTER 25
PETER

I'M DRIVING HOME FROM BOSTON Market, where I watched a video lecture for my evidence class, while devouring a chicken and mashed potatoes dinner.

"Hey, William. I hope you're not still at work."

It's almost nine p.m. and he usually calls me from his office.

"Oh, no. I'm too old to be working this late. Listen, Peter, my friend at the department called to say there has been a Jason sighting in Quincy. Some guy he went to school with swears he saw him driving around town a few hours ago. Undercover cops are watching his house. It could be a false alarm, but my buddy thought you should be warned. If it's really him, he's bald now, with a beard. The guy didn't get the make of the car, or the plate number, just that it's largish and white, which isn't much to go on. There aren't any unaccounted for incoming or outgoing calls to Jason's mother or brother."

"Thanks for the heads up, William. I appreciate it."

"You bet. I'll keep you posted if I hear anything more. Have a good evening, Peter."

"You too."

I pull off the road, allowing William's news to sink in. Only a mile or so from my place, I pull a U-turn, and head back home. Driving with a sense of urgency, I'm back in a flash, sprint to my apartment, and retrieve the revolver I hid in my room. I resist calling Amy, despite my instinct to make sure she's okay. I'm sure it's paranoia, but William's call, combined with the Boy Scout motto lodged in my mind (thanks, Jack), has me thinking worst-case scenario.

If Jason somehow found his way to Amy's house, calling now would tip my hand. My phone chimes, indicating an incoming text. It's Amy, asking me to come over. I'm suspicious, thinking it improbable she has reversed course so soon.

If Jason is indeed at her house, employing trickery to lure me there, I want him to think he's succeeding. I text back saying I'll be right over. I consider phoning Jack, but resolve to assess the situation first. No need to disrupt his evening. Besides, I'm armed.

Violating several traffic laws—speeding, failure to yield right of way, reckless driving, to name a few—en route to her place, I arrived in record time. There are no white cars in the driveway, or anywhere in sight. A good sign. I exit my car, gun in hand with the safety switch off, and walk towards the front door, keeping my eyes and ears peeled for movement in the darkness. I'm almost there when I hear a *crackling* noise and simultaneously feel like I've stuck my finger into a live electrical outlet.

A figure emerges from behind the bushes a few yards away, a gun in his hand. How did I not see him? As I'm trying to process what's happening, searching my body for evidence of bleeding (I see none), my muscles lock up and I involuntarily drop to the ground, unable to move. Reflexively, I check myself again for blood... still don't see any... the gun seemed small... maybe a BB gun or something... no, they are longer, like rifles... am I going to die? I'm feeling pain, but this immobilizing thing is my chief concern at the moment. Check that. It's the lunatic, now charging me... with an axe... shit... it's Jason.

"Peter Garrison. Peter fucking Garrison."

He stands over me, axe gripped tightly, mocking me.

"Where's Amy? What did you do to her?"

"She's fine. She's locked in her bedroom closet. I didn't lay a

197

hand on her. Of course, she won't be so fine once she discovers your dead body on her front lawn."

His tone is matter of fact. No hysterics. I believe him that he hasn't harmed Amy. I also believe he intends to chop me up.

I need to try reasoning with him. Beneath the tough exterior, he's really just a kid standing up for his brother.

"Jason, I'm sorry about what happened to Matthew. I did my best defending him. I wish it turned out differently. The outcome would have been the same with any defense attorney. It's another example of the imperfections in the legal system. He never should have been sent to jail."

I'm stalling, slowly regaining my facilities.

"You think?" His sarcasm projects his anger. "Matthew never hurt a fucking fly. And since you courtroom officials couldn't get it right, I'm forced into the fray. To correct injustice."

"You know, Jason, I'm as disillusioned with our legal system as you are. I left defense law because too many innocent people got put away. But that doesn't make it okay to kill people. That's warped justice."

"You think you're superior to me, Garrison, but we're the same person. Yeah, you got me on book smarts, but speaking eloquently doesn't define a person. I'm talking about the essence of who you are, who I am. When you found out your girl was in danger, you didn't call the cops. You didn't follow protocol, didn't go through the proper channels. You came here to handle things personally."

His grasp on the axe remains tight, his eyes still trained on me.

"I didn't come here to kill you," I say. "Only to free Amy and turn you over to the authorities." Big words from a guy in a defenseless position. Lucky for me, Jason has more wisdom to impart.

"Yeah, what if I raped your girlfriend? What if you had a kid and I molested him? How would you feel then?"

"Not good. Not good at all," I concede.

It hits me that I can't possibly imagine what he's going through.

The helpless feeling, the inability to alter the fate of his violated brother. I've been on a mission to exact retribution for being humiliated and inconvenienced. I survived my prison stint without lasting scars. I've been cleared of any wrongdoing. My life isn't ruined, my loved ones are fine.

"I underestimated you, Garrison. You've proven to be tough and resourceful. A worthy adversary. It's all over for you now, though. Beating my brother to a pulp was a mistake. A costly mistake that you must pay for."

He takes a big wind up, the axe high in the air. As he reaches the apex of the upswing, and commences the forceful descending motion, I will myself to move. There's a delay between my brain instructing me to get the hell out of the way of the impending downward strike, and my body actually nudging, but I'm able to roll from a flat-on-my-back position to my side, just as the axe makes contact with the ground, precisely where my chest was a split second ago.

Frustrated, and cursing me out, Jason tosses the axe aside, exchanging it for a knife, which he produces in a magician-like manner. Planting my palms on the dirt, I scoot myself forward as a lunging Jason grazes my calf. Now I see blood, though not nearly as much as had he hit his target—my heart.

My muscle control gradually returns. Whatever he shot me with begins to wear off. The pain dissipates, as well, except for the tightness and throbbing in my leg, that is.

My faculties functioning again, it strikes me that I'm no longer holding my gun. I must have dropped it when I was zapped. I haven't been shot for real yet, meaning Jason may not have noticed I was armed. I held the gun by my side, kind of hidden, so in the darkness, he must have missed it. I scan the ground near the front door and, after a moment, spot it a few feet in front of the bushes.

I turn my attention back in time to see Jason's foot about to connect with my head. Raising both arms to act as a shield,

I partially block the incoming blow. Although able to redirect the angle of the kick, he connects solidly with my neck, causing excruciating pain. I evade another stab attempt by leaping to my feet. The blade catches my shirt as I'm rising, ripping it to shreds. He's on top of me before I'm able to lunge for my gun. I'm wrestled back to the ground, my eyes focused on the knife still in his right hand. Grabbing his wrist in a bid to shake the knife free, he catches my forearm, drawing blood and a howl. I maintain my grip on his wrist until he lands a punch to my face with his left hand.

Damn that hurts. He must be ambidextrous. More blood. I see it on his fist, signifying my nose or lip as the source. My focus still squarely on his knife hand, I jerk my knees into my chest, waiting for him to create a little space between us, which he complies with, as he readies to thrust his knife into my stomach. I forcefully extend my legs upward into his rib cage. I don't hurt him, but gain a valuable second or two, allowing me to get onto my feet. He still has the knife and, unwittingly, blocks the path to my gun.

Keeping me at bay, he reaches into his pocket, revealing his gun. Shit. I forgot he still had it. He zaps me again before I can get out of harm's way. In my haze, I hear him cursing me as he heads for the bushes. To retrieve his axe? While I'm urging my body to snap out of it, a vision appears before me. It's Amy! She's barreling out the front door, yelling. The distraction buys me much needed time.

Jason turns to Amy to fend her off, but she surprises us both by revealing from behind her back some kind of aerosol—pepper spray! Holding the can head high, she presses down on the nozzle. In an athletic move, Jason somehow avoids the incoming stream and pounces on Amy, pinning her to the ground.

Fighting through lingering pain, in my face, calf, and arm, I navigate to their masses. Shaking off wooziness and stabilizing my limbs, I gather myself for a last stand.

"Don't be stupid, Garrison."

Jason has his knees pressed onto Amy's shoulders, his butt on her stomach. Despite a valiant attempt, she can't wrestle free. Reaching into his pocket, he pulls out a knife and positions it near Amy's throat, to keep me at bay. With a sense of urgency, I seize the moment.

Racing to Amy's feet, causing Jason to turn his attention away from her, I launch myself into the air and deliver a full-forced karate kick. Jason attempts to thwart the incoming blow with his left forearm, his knifed right hand poised to strike me. My foot shatters the impediment—his forearm—continuing on to connect with his head. The force of my attack lifts him off Amy, onto the ground beside her.

Before Jason can recover, I lunge on top of him, pummeling him with rapid-fire punches to the face. Amy, on her feet now, kicks him in the midsection several times for good measure.

Amy and I remain silent. I want to make sure the bastard is unconscious before embracing her. Confident Jason won't be moving anytime soon, I reach for my phone, which somehow managed to remain in my pocket throughout the fracas, and dial 911, requesting police assistance in the apprehension of Jason Felding. A pair of handcuffs and an escort to death row comprises the required *assistance*. I relay the need for medical attention as well.

"Peter!" I'm supplying my name and contact information as Amy shouts out, pointing at a car coming right at us.

Focused on beating Jason into oblivion, we didn't notice it sooner. A truck, approaching at about forty miles an hour, has traversed the driveway and climbs onto the lawn, quickly closing the distance between us. I break for my gun, yelling at Amy to get inside. She doesn't make it in time. Matthew—yes, it's him—out of his truck, has a gun pointed at her head, ordering her toward him. I've got my gun pointed at Matthew, but know I've missed my opportunity to seize control of the situation. Amy slowly backpedals, away from the house.

"NOW! And Garrison, stay right where you are and toss your weapon to me or I swear to fucking God, I'll shoot your whore." His instructions leave no room for interpretation.

He calls out to his brother, not getting a response. "Listen, Matthew. Jason will be okay. He's not shot or anything. Just has the wind knocked out of him. I only acted in self-defense. There's no need to do anything stupid. Let her go. She didn't do anything. Jason had her locked in a closet. She barged free and came outside."

I think she stopped kicking Jason before Matthew got close enough to make out what happened. While talking, I'm weighing the odds of hitting Matthew from where I'm standing, maybe fifteen yards away. I'd scream for Amy to hit the deck as I pull the trigger. It's risky, but probably not as risky as surrendering my gun. The question running through my mind is how close the nearest squad car was at the time of dispatch. The operator put out the call before asking me for details. Can I stall him until the cops show up? If Amy weren't in the equation, I'd take my chances in a shootout.

Dissatisfied with Amy's pace, Matthew moves to her, each step upping the endangerment factor. Should I pull a Clint Eastwood? I dismiss the idea, along with a passing thought to make a break for the side of the house, in the hope of drawing him away from Amy. I doubt his ability to hit a moving target, but he might combat my rebellious act by shooting Amy.

Ignoring Amy's courageous plea to take Matthew out, I succumb to his demands, throwing my gun at him, hoping like hell for the cops' imminent arrival. Worst case, I figure I can trade my life for Amy's. Let him kill me, if it comes to that. I'm the one he wants to destroy.

To my amazement, Jason's arm twitches and a muffled, low moan escapes his lips. He's not jumping to his feet or anything, but I underestimated his tolerance for taking a beating. To my horror, instead of running to Jason's side, Matthew maintains his gun leveled at Amy's head. And then the distinct sound of a gunshot.

"NOOOOOOO," I cry out. Amy drops into the bushes, adjacent to where she was standing a moment ago. This can't be happening. I've stopped breathing, frozen in disbelief. An instant later, Matthew hits the deck as well.

———◦◦✦◦◦———

Mid-fall, Matthew loses the grip on his gun, and it lands on the ground a few feet from where he lies. I'm not sure what's happened, but sprint towards his gun, scooping it up, along with my gun. Without breaking stride, I go to Amy, frantically screaming her name, asking if she's okay. She doesn't immediately respond, but the welcoming sight of Jack, and the sound of his voice, clear up my confusion.

Running from the direction of the road, he instructs me to stay with Amy, saying he has the brothers covered. Processing that only one gunshot was fired soothes me. Still, I'm relieved to find Amy blood free. She must have passed out from the trauma of thinking she was hit, death oncoming. A natural conclusion to draw, one I jumped to myself.

I help her come to then slowly get her to her feet. I wrap my arms around her, pulling her into me. I'm beyond grateful she isn't hurt. I feel her heart racing as she leans on me for support.

Matthew, still on the ground, writhes in pain from a shoulder wound, presumably from a .45 caliber bullet. He's losing a lot of blood, but he'll survive. None of us rush to his side to apply a tourniquet. Jack frisks him, ensuring he's not packing another weapon, then does the same to Jason, who carries a Taser and two knives. I cover Jason with my free arm. Jack disarms him, without resistance, as Jason remains fairly comatose.

I tell Jack I've already called 911, while he pokes at his phone.

"Jack, how did you —" He raises a hand, cutting me off, as the wail of approaching sirens fills the airwaves. He mouths the word "later". He has me take Amy inside, to fetch her some water. A long night of questioning lies ahead.

Amy and I are alone for the first time tonight. Leaning against the kitchen counter, she assures me Jason didn't hurt her.

"Did he really lock you in a closet?"

"Yeah. Well, he propped a chair under the door knob."

"How did you get out?"

"I rammed into the door with all my force a few times, and the chair legs must have slid, because the chair crashed to the floor."

I stare proudly at her, impressed by her strength and resourcefulness.

She continues. "Luckily, I have wooden floors. He was sloppy. If he had put rubber under the chair legs, it would have provided friction."

"Fortunately, he's not as smart as you are." We both smile.

Amy changes the subject. "I'm sorry. You're not a chauvinist. You're a good man. Better than anyone I know."

I try to speak, but she's speed-talking, so I let her finish.

"You were being chivalrous and I chastised you. I needed you to protect me after all. You saved my life."

She throws her arms around me, crying onto my shoulder, muffling a continued apology. I start to say I'm sorry too, to explain my behavior, but my speech yields way to a stronger, all-encompassing feeling.

"I love you." I string together the words representing my sentiment, my passion.

"Me too. I mean, I love you too."

We kiss, holding each other tightly. I don't want to let her go.

———————— ◦◦◦ ————————

Amy and I return outside as the cops arrive. The crime scene is littered with bodies—notably the two injured criminals on the lawn—and weapons. Amy feels better now, walking on her own volition. I filled in the blanks for her as to what transpired during her blackout. She's aware of Jack's courageous actions, bravery which makes him our savior. Time for only a condensed version of the misery she endured inside with Jason, she assured me he didn't hurt her.

We head over to where Jack stands, near the brothers, his gun now holstered. Matthew sits up, applying pressure with his palm to his injured shoulder. Jason squirms around, still sprawled on the ground.

Before we can express our gratitude, a pair of uniformed officers carrying flashlights penetrate our circle. A middle-aged guy with a goatee, who appears to be the lead detective, checks on the brothers. Paramedics arrive, and are directed by the detective to attend to Jason first, not yet coherent, and then Matthew. Amy has one of them to check me out. Since the cuts to my arm and calf aren't deep, and the bleeding has stopped, the paramedic cleans the wounds, applies ointment, and wraps them with bandages. He performs an abbreviated neurological exam, and though he clears me, I'm encouraged to get checked out for lingering effects from the Taser.

Detective Samuels supervises as the brothers receive medical attention, then are loaded into the ambulance. Samuels assigns both of the officers to ride along before joining Jack, Amy, and myself. As the paramedics exit the street, another squad car pulls up the driveway. Right behind follows yet another city vehicle, later identified as the crime scene unit, its members wearing surgical gloves and gathering evidence into plastic baggies. Mentioning Jason in my 911 call was the magic word.

After excusing himself to speak to the new arrivals, the detective returns to us, notepad and miniature tape recorder in hand. Having obtained our consent to be recorded, and getting our names stated for the record, he instructs us to fill him in. We all begin talking simultaneously, but as Samuels discerns we each were present at various stages throughout the ordeal, he has us report things chronologically.

Amy begins with her account of Jason breaking into her home, taking her Taser, trapping her in her closet, and texting me on her phone.

I pick up the story from there, recounting the events leading up to the situation at hand. For good measure, I summarize my encounter with Matthew a few days ago. Samuels jots notes, periodically interjecting questions. He plays a little devil's advocate, challenging parts of my tale. I detect a satisfied smirk as I'm able to repeatedly substantiate.

Jack wraps things up nicely, answering questions I myself wondered about. After Sir William called me, he had called Jack, who swung by my place. Seeing I wasn't home, and unable to reach me on the phone, he contacted my folks to get Amy's last name. Armed with a high-powered, long-range flashlight and a Colt 45, he parked in front of Amy's house, exited his vehicle, and inched forward to about fifty yards from the action. His arrival on the scene was undetected and timely.

The moment he shone his light, he saw me tossing my gun, and Matthew aiming his gun at Amy. Quickly assessing the predicament, he acted. Of course, being the marksman I know him to be, he could have killed Matthew, instead doing only what was necessary to defuse the situation. Jack goes on to say he was prepared to fire a second bullet if the first didn't do the trick.

Our stories come across as believable and unrehearsed. Detective Samuels thanks us for our patience, and more importantly, for apprehending a wanted murderer. He commends Jack for reacting in a responsible manner, subduing Matthew without taking his life. In compliance with due process, he informs us he'll need to verify our version of what went down, including checking text messages from Amy's phone and calls made by Sir William. The crime scene unit will dust the weapons gathered for prints, as well as objects in Amy's house, including her bedroom closet door.

All this comes across as formality. Samuels, ecstatic over finally putting this case to rest, essentially let us tell our story in unison, as opposed to what transpires on television, where suspects get sequestered in separate rooms. We don't even have to *come down to the station.* We're to remain in Quincy for the next few days, making ourselves available if needed.

⸺◦◦◦⸺

It's approaching midnight as Jack, Amy, and myself sip coffee in the kitchen.

"Jack, I haven't had a chance to thank you for saving my life. Thank you. Very much. It's good to be alive." I shake his hand, patting his back with my free hand—a man hug.

"You saved my life, too, Jack. I'll be forever beholden to you. I can see why Peter speaks so highly of you. You put your life on the line for us." She embraces him—a real hug.

"Your appreciation is touching, both of you, but it's not a huge deal. Lots of people in my situation would have done the same."

"Are you kidding me? Nobody would have done the same." Amy is drawn to Jack even more, a witness to his modest nature.

"Amy's right, Jack. Besides, you're in the vast minority of those who could have hit Matthew from where you were standing, let alone hit his right shoulder, as you were aiming for."

He cuts off further singing of his praises, redirecting the focus on us. "You know, considering that Jason ambushed you both, pitting you against a murderer with a weapons advantage on you, you guys more than held your own. If Matthew hadn't crashed the party, you wouldn't have needed my assistance. I mean, I'll have to work with you, Peter, on hanging onto your gun. It works a lot better when in your possession. But considering you were zapped by a Taser, and unarmed, for having to wrestle a guy with an axe, knives, and a Taser in his arsenal, you did a good job keeping him at bay."

I allow myself to grin, as he continues. "And Amy. You exhibited incredible bravery, charging an armed lunatic with pepper spray as your only defense. I see a bright future as a PI if you're interested in a career change."

She laughs before responding, "Yeah, I was so brave that I fainted."

"You were in complete control of your wits during your pepper spray attack, saving me from decapitation," I point out.

"I don't think you could pull off the headless look, Peter. You don't have the body for it." Jack seizes the opportunity to interject humor.

We all laugh, longer than the comment warrants. We're releasing tension. Considering how the night began, things turned out pretty well. It will take a while for our nerves to settle, but we're grateful to have *a while* in our futures.

"Well, guys, I need to get home and have a real drink. I've got a bottle of whiskey waiting to be tapped. You're welcome to join me if you like."

"Thanks, Jack, but I think we've intruded on you enough for one day," I say.

We say our goodbyes, promising to check in with him soon.

Amy doesn't want to spend the night here, so she packs a small bag, and we get the hell out, headed for my place. On the ride home, I relay the curious interaction between Jason and myself.

"Then why did he fight you? It sounds like he understood you. Like you guys were on the verge of friendship."

I arch my eyebrows, letting her know she's stretching it, before responding. "He doesn't want to go to jail," I say simply.

"You mean he doesn't think he can cut it there?"

"I mean if he's imprisoned, he can't watch out for his family."

The radio station we're tuned into interrupts its programming to broadcast a statement from the Quincy police department. Jason Felding has been captured and is in custody. His case will be fast-tracked with an indictment expected to be handed down by a grand jury set to convene in the coming days.

Two pit stops—bottle of wine, fast-food-joint burgers—later, we're in my living room, stretched out on the couch, numbing our minds and filling our bellies. We're too exhausted for words. There'll be plenty of time for rehashing the night's events. Amy leans into me, her head resting on my shoulder. In no time she dozes off. I look at her admiringly. I'm a lucky guy.

It all comes back to justice. Retribution. Settling a score. Being wronged, or even the perception of such, is quite a motivator. An unparalleled motivator. Rarely are there instances in any facet of life where one garners such inner strength, resolve, passion, single-mindedness, a stop at no cost determination. If such purpose and focus could be summoned and channeled towards things like school work, occupational performance, relationships, and helping our fellow man, the world would be a better place.

Sure, on a small scale, this happens. A minority of the population pull this off. Conversely, the majority of the population seem to have the retribution gene. Something inside us demands being treated fairly, with respect. Speaking in slang, nobody wants to be *dissed*. When stripped of basic decencies, we feel violated, unable to let bygones be bygones, to let it pass, to turn the other cheek, to be the better man. Sure, there are degrees of violation, and yes, there are plenty of instances where people tolerate repeated abuse—it's especially sickening when said abuse is directed towards women or children, at the hands of physically stronger men. Not all vengeance is carried out to the extent Jason took things. But even for those who don't act out, I imagine a desire exists within to do so. Most of us have thought or said *how dare he treat me like that?*

209

Maybe how we deal with being with dissed speaks to our level of self-control. Maybe we don't know what we're capable of until the occasion presents itself. I, for one, never considered myself the vengeful type. While I'm not in Jason's league on this front, I've surprised myself with the passion with which I pursued my manner of retribution.

EPILOGUE
JASON

Three months later...

I'M RUSTLED AWAY FROM A game of Texas Hold 'Em by a hack informing me I have a visitor. My mom is the only one who comes to see me, practically daily. I told her to skip today, but figure she baked me something that couldn't wait.

I didn't fight the murder charges against me. When the DA himself approached me, requesting "how about you save the good citizens of Quincy some money and plead guilty," I replied "Okay, I will. On one condition." The condition was to drop pursuit of the waitress. They had nothing on her, anyway. I signed my life away. *Without the possibility of parole* was the verbiage included in my life sentence reading from the judge.

I haven't seen Matthew since he packed his bags and left Quincy, a week or two into my incarceration. The bullet in his shoulder was successfully removed arthroscopically, though he battles persisting pain. He attended the first of his scheduled physical therapy sessions, blowing off the rest. For his part in the melee, he managed to escape with just community work, a restraining order to stay away from Garrison, the girl, and the PI, as well as losing the privilege to own a gun. The presiding judge strongly recommended psychiatric treatment. He was charged with assault and a few weapons offenses, but his lawyer orchestrated a sweetheart plea bargain.

He ran far away, to Florida, never being a fan of cold weather. He needed to put all of this behind him, and while acknowledging the impossibility of removing from his memory all that has happened since the night he sipped booze outside Chang's restaurant, remaining in Quincy would be too much of a constant, painful reminder. I encouraged him to go and never look back.

As much as it hurt my mom, she knew it was best for him. My mom also knew she couldn't leave her home. The place she was born. The only home she has ever known. Nor could she leave me. I tried persuading her to go with Matthew, arguing life would be simpler, more fun, and less agonizing. That spending her days driving back and forth to prison, going through metal detectors, getting frisked, is no way to live. She believes Matthew will return to Quincy someday, once he puts the demons to rest. I don't think he'll ever come back, but don't tell her this.

Matthew calls occasionally. I hear the pain in his voice. It's as if he's the one whose life has been stripped away. He harbors guilt, knowing I wound up where I am defending his honor. I tell him none of this is on him. I made my own choices. My brain doesn't function like most. I've got some screws loose, always have. If not now, I would have gotten myself into trouble down the road.

It kills me knowing the bitterness he carries with him. He used to be a happy kid. He had a naïveté about him that allowed him to enjoy the goodness in life, while discarding the unpleasant. It could be argued my actions are responsible for his current state of affairs. I blame Chang. His phone call was the snowball which morphed into the avalanche responsible for hijacking Matthew's existence. If I had it to do over, I'd kill the bastard again.

I've gotten to know the guys in my poker group pretty well. It's one thing to want to keep to yourself, keeping your head down and doing your time. Pulling it off is an entirely different matter. I broke after a few weeks. I've learned not all the guys in here are out to take your head off. Most of them only want to do their time and get the hell out. I was starting to go insane as a hermit. I wasn't going to make it for *the rest of my natural life.*

Turning the corner, bringing the visitor room into view, I abruptly stop in my tracks, causing the hack escorting me to trip up. I'm led to a table with two chairs, one already occupied by my awaiting visitor. Seated, I just stare, stunned into a trance.

"Hi, Jason. How are you?"

"Hi, Tess." I can't get out any more words. I have so much to say. So much I've wanted to say if given the opportunity. Questions. But seeing her, here, now, those thoughts are pushed away. As if willing myself into the past, to a simpler time, I merely respond: "You look beautiful, babe."

———————

PETER

We're gathered at my parents' house. My mom has prepared one of her infamous feasts. We've already polished off the main course— pot roast, mashed potatoes, and green bean almondine—and now sip coffee, allowing the food to digest, before busting into the array of awaiting desserts.

The occasion is me getting a job. Jack hired me into his firm. In more than ten years of existence, this marks the first time he isn't flying solo. He has always had a comfortable business, never hurting for clients. Following his role in bringing Jason to justice, the media portrayed him as a hero. Headlines referred to him as lionhearted, a warrior, a conqueror, a champion. QPD and local politicians heaped praised upon him. In short, Jack is a local celebrity.

Endearing him even more to the public, he shies away from the attention, turning down public appearances and deflecting praise. Subsequently, business has never been better. His clientele now extends well beyond Quincy. He has to turn away work. So, bringing me on board isn't a completely altruistic gesture.

For my part, I received some press as well. The stories about me were of the *human interest* nature. Patsy comes full circle, exorcising his demons. Like Jack, I'm more comfortable out of the spotlight than in it.

Amy, portrayed as little more than a footnote in the ordeal—suiting her just fine—despite saving my life, amazed me with her bravery. Words can't express how much her display of support, love, and commitment means to me.

Along with being my boss, Jack has become a close friend. He's shown me the ropes, divulged secrets of the trade, encouraging me every step of the way. The last few months I've been working as his apprentice. He promised if I completed my training program, got my firearms permit (he wants me to be able cover him with more than karate moves), and demonstrated the competence he knew I was capable of, he'd hire me as a salaried employee, full benefit package and all. I upheld my part of the bargain, and Jack kept his word.

He's starting me at fifty thousand, about what I was bringing home as a probate lawyer. Should our company exceed expectations, I'll partake in profit sharing as well. In two years, when I'm eligible to become licensed, I can expect a sizable pay boost. The PI trade is exploding. Industry wide, over the past few years salaries have risen by more than forty percent. As Jack explains, there are a lot of dirty people in this world, creating the need for dirty work, work not many are willing, or desire, to perform. Those able to satisfy this need, often a desperate need, are duly compensated.

My passion for investigative work is rooted in retribution. I wanted Jason to suffer. Like I had during my stint behind bars. The cops have procedures to follow, and the rights of all, good or bad, to protect. Jack and I, while small, have no such limitations or rules hindering us.

My dad is proud of me. He thinks I've found my niche in life. My mom and Amy, while also proud, pepper Jack with questions, looking for reassurance I'll be safe, won't be thrust into dangerous situations. The only guarantee Jack furnishes is I'll be happy. He says I have an aptitude for this work, and when you're good at something, it's more enjoyable. We toast my good fortune. We toast the new partnership Jack and I are forming. We toast the new home Amy and I purchased together—we moved in last week.

Once the chatter settles down, I clink my coffee mug with my spoon to get everyone's attention. There's another cause for celebration, one more toast to be made. Actually, it's more of an announcement.

"Mom, Dad, Jack. Amy and I are having a baby. Amy is two months along and we couldn't be happier."

I omit mentioning the obvious, that this wasn't planned, that while we're in love and committed to one another, we'd prefer to have more time to enjoy life as a couple, to travel to Hawaii, to save up money.

Congratulatory hugs and kisses follow. My parents have gotten to know Amy over the past three months, having become quite fond of her. She has endeared herself to Jack as well, with him especially appreciating her quick wit.

"I hate to break this news to you, Peter, but our firm doesn't grant time off for paternity leave. You'll be expected in the office the day after delivery."

I've come to relish Jack's dry sense of humor. It took me a little while to be able to distinguish his ribbing from his seriousness. He follows up his banter with a hearty congratulatory man hug. My mom addresses the elephant in the room.

"So, when are you kids getting married?"

"We're going to take this one new adventure at a time," Amy answers more eloquently than I could have. "New job, new baby, new house. We're going to let all that settle in before we tackle the wedding planning thing."

My mom isn't convinced, but my dad eases the tension.

"That's sound reasoning. Besides, between having to buy you housewarming and baby shower gifts, we'll need time to save up for a wedding present."

This evokes laughter all around. I put my arm around Amy, the two of us cuddled on the couch, soaking in this joyous occasion. A few months ago life threw me a curve ball, playing havoc with my simple, predictable existence. Life is messier now, less calculable, but for the first time, the future excites me. I intend to embrace each day.

ACKNOWLEDGEMENTS

Thank you, Stacy Juba, my editor extraordinaire. Thanks, Aaron, for guiding me through all the phases to authorship. Doug, Carley, and David, thanks for reading early drafts and providing insightful feedback and encouragement. Nate, RCS, Josh, Mom, and Barrie, thanks for your excitement, encouragement, and support. Karen, thanks for the great cover. Thanks, Robin, for the outstanding proofreading. And Faith, for enduring countless "what sounds better" questions, thanks for your contributions.

(handwritten note)
Doug
David } 3 bros,

Carley
Nate } children
Josh

CPSIA information can be obtained at www.ICGtesting.com
Printed in the USA
LVOW08s1840180416

484151LV00002B/255/P